REGENT

Regent

Book One of The Balance of Power trilogy

ISBN-10: 0-9818714-8-8

ISBN-13: 978-0-9818714-8-6

White Wolf Press, LLC

Rutherfordton, NC 28139

THE WORLD OF GODSLAND

THE DAWNING OF POWER TRILOGY

Call of the Herald

Inherited Danger

Dragon Ore

THE BALANCE OF POWER TRILOGY

Regent

Feral (forthcoming)

Regal (forthcoming)

DEDICATION

For Tracey

TABLE OF CNTENTS

CHAPTER ONE

Wisdom is the reward for surviving our own stupidity.
— Wendel Volker

R*un!*

Instinct and compulsion drove Sinjin's lean, teenage body to greater speed, his shoulder-length, auburn hair streaming behind him. Running was the one thing he did well, and the landscape slid by in a blur punctuated by moments of perfect focus. Leaping over a protruding tree root, his eyes locked on another dark-robed figure moving within the trees. Startled, Sinjin lost his step and nearly went down, but through strength of will, he heeded his father's command and ran.

Faster. Run, Sinjin, run!

Ahead the trail turned sharply upward on a direct course to the top of a steep incline. An unfamiliar pain stabbed Sinjin's side, and he placed a hand over it, hoping it would make the cramp go away. It didn't. The Wood Run was designed to challenge even the best runners, and it succeeded in that, but Sinjin gritted his teeth and persevered. Sweat stung his eyes by the time he crested the steep hill. He wanted to stop and rest, to slow his labored breathing, but knew he could not; something was wrong. There should be no one in these woods, especially not shadowy figures in black hooded robes, and his father's mental commands reinforced his fears. It was unusual for Prios to speak with Sinjin over such distance, and Sinjin knew it must have required a great deal of energy and effort. It was equally unusual for Sinjin to be competing in the Spring Challenges, something that had been expressly forbidden.

Stop!

It took a moment for Sinjin to react to the abrupt command, and his momentum carried him forward. The air sang a sharp note, and a dark flash crossed the trail only a hand's width in front of Sinjin's unprotected abdomen. Thrown from his balance, he lost control of his limbs, and a loose rock turned his ankle. Using his next off-kilter step to hurl himself upward, he tucked and rolled, just as Uncle Chase had taught him. The air sang once again, and a slender bolt struck a nearby tree, giving Sinjin a clear view of the deadly implement. It was not like the thick, stubby bolts used to hunt game; this was delicate and precise and seemed a much more frightening weapon.

Cut the course! Turn left ahead!

More shadowy figures moved within the trees. Sinjin started to turn but caught sight of the next ribbon on his right. Tied around the trunk of an elm, it was the last of seven ribbons he needed to collect. Each was signed by Master Edling, and all were required as proof of staying on the Wood Run course. The thought of facing Master Edling and his father made Sinjin want to quit the race and get home, but he could win this race; he knew it. He'd allowed Durin to talk him into it because he'd secretly desired it. Things were not going to go well for him when he got home—if he got home—and he knew this might be his only chance to win. It wasn't the prize he sought; it was the chance to prove that he was good at something—the best, even. Youthful desire overwhelmed sense and his father's command, and Sinjin turned sharply to the right.

Barely slowing, he grabbed the long end of the slipknot and charged toward the clearing, but just as the lush grasses of the Challenge fields came into view, a dark-robed figure stepped onto the trail and raised his arms before him. Sinjin could not see what weapons threatened from within the folds of the overlong sleeves, but he felt the danger.

His blood froze and he nearly ran headlong into death's embrace, but his training was not so far from his mind. Without slowing, he ran up the trunk of a nearby oak and flipped himself backward over the stunned assassin. Using the longest stride he'd ever attempted, Sinjin propelled himself into the clearing. A roar erupted from the gathered crowd, and Sinjin knew he must be running a faster time than Hester had. All he had to do was finish the race to defeat a living legend. Bolstered by this thought and the sight of the exuberant crowd, Sinjin ran. His shoulders itched, almost expecting a bolt to strike and demanding he at least turn his head and look back, but the pain never came.

Durin stood at the head of the crowd, jumping, shouting, and pointing at the sand clocks.

Sinjin suppressed a smile. Then he lowered his head and poured all the energy he had left into a final sprint. At the finish line, he stuffed his seven ribbons into Master Edling's hands. The crowd erupted. Edling, who normally wore a haughty and sour look, could not keep the surprise from his face.

Get home. Now!

Sinjin barely heard his father's voice in his mind, and that worried him more than anything else. Durin's dumbstruck gaze followed Sinjin as he ran past, not even bothering to accept his prize. Sinjin just placed a hand on his aching side and kept moving.

Durin ran up alongside. "What are you doing? You won! You beat Hester's record! You have to stop and accept your prize. You're supposed to get a wreath of vespa and a kiss from Alissa. I can't wait until Kendra hears about this."

"My dad already knows," Sinjin said between sucking in breaths. He couldn't even think about Kendra; she was an unsolvable problem.

Durin's look was apologetic, as it often was, his expressive face and liquid-brown eyes almost comical. "I didn't think he would find out—at least not this soon. Sorry."

"And there are people trying to kill me."

"What? Really?" Durin asked, stumbling as he tried to keep up.

Sinjin just grunted and jogged north toward his home, and for once, Durin matched his pace.

By the varying light of five herald globes, Catrin hunched over a crumbling scroll, trying to unlock its secrets before time rendered it back into dust. Her translucent hair fell to one side, a constant reminder of the consequences of power. Four more herald globes rested in small iron pedestals, which currently held down the corners of the ancient vellum. Each globe cast its unique glow over the surface of the scroll accompanied by muted reflections from the polished stone table on which they rested. Catrin didn't notice the white and blue filaments that arched from her delicate fingers to the table.

She sighed and closed her eyes. Vast amounts of knowledge had been uncovered in the past decade, much as a result of the ancient cache Catrin herself had found at Ohmahold, but little had been deciphered and even less truly understood. So many of the things they found seemed meaningless and out of context. Each discovery brought more mystery than certainty. The scroll that currently held Catrin's interest discussed the principles and behaviors of energy. It had been found deep within Dragonhold.

That name still made Catrin shiver. She had proposed Volkerhold as the name of her keep, but the instant Chase had suggested Dragonhold, people latched on to it. Leave it to her cousin to come up with a name irresistible to most yet made Catrin very uncomfortable. She'd seen the true majesty of dragons, and it seemed an impossible name to live up to, especially since her relationship with Kyrien was in question. He was a free beast, and nothing bound him to her. After the war with the Zjhon, he had come to her once every year for eight years straight. For the past two years, though, he'd been absent.

For months Catrin had been trying to make contact with him, but he was distant, and what little communication they managed was garbled and only served to worry and confuse her. It disgusted her that deep down she also wanted more dragon ore. Kyrien was far more to her than just a source of the precious stone, but she was suffering without it. Working the stone into herald globes, though tedious, calmed her nerves and filled the hold's coffers. Truly, a visit from her dragon would do her good. With another sigh, she pushed the scroll aside, unable to achieve the level of focus needed for translation, and a sloppy translation would do her no good at all.

Other papers and scrolls awaited her attention, but she returned to one she'd read a dozen times before. It was from her cousin's husband—a man she had nearly married, a man who might have wished he'd married her instead of her acerbic cousin Lissa. While the letter was polite enough and the words themselves gave no real reason for alarm, the letter's presence alone was cause for concern, and Catrin couldn't help feeling that there was a cry for help hidden beneath the bare words. The messenger had refused to tell exactly how he had come into possession of the letter, but he had said that it hadn't come directly from Wolfhold or Ravenhold, and he had no way to guarantee its providence.

Once again, Catrin's thoughts wandered to Thorakis the Builder, the man said to have saved the Greatland from starvation by building massive fisheries. Much of Jharmin's letter told of Thorakis's achievements, including a huge network of man-made rivers within walls of stone. It was almost too much to believe, and though Jharmin spoke well of Thorakis, there was something else, but Millie's sudden arrival and the worried look on her face brought Catrin to her feet.

"Come quick," Millie said as she pulled Catrin from the room, her breathing heavy. "It's Prios, m'lady, he's taken ill."

"Where?"

"In the viewing chamber, m'lady."

Catrin charged ahead, her lithe form moving easily, leaving Millie to shuffle along behind her, the older and heavier woman's joints allowing for only so much speed.

Though Prios was Catrin's first concern, she also worried that this would cause undo anxiety over the safety of the as of yet untested viewing chambers. Catrin knew the perils of improper astral travel, but she also knew the chambers would be safe. Still, she felt like less of a person for having those thoughts. Any right-minded person would be thinking of her spouse.

When Catrin turned the corner, she found Prios supine on the rough stone floor of the first viewing chamber, his head in Brother Vaughn's lap. Though he was breathing, his pale complexion and trembling hands troubled Catrin. Even in his current state, he looked beautiful to her. The kindness in his eyes offset the hard lines of his regal visage. Even staring into empty air, his expression was locked into a look of compassion.

Seeing her dragon ore carving, Koe, lying beside him, chalky and depleted, Catrin was shocked. Even in its most inert state, the carving had an imposing feline form. Koe had been fully charged, glossy and slick, and had been resting in their bedchamber. Prios would not have taken the carving without very good reason; he knew how important it was to her. She'd never been able to carve another like piece; no other dragon ore had ever revealed its true form to her. A sick feeling clutched Catrin's gut, and she asked, "Where's Sinjin?"

Brother Vaughn, his long gray hair pulled back into a braid, looked up with an apology in his eyes. "Prios charged in here, saying he had a bad feeling about Sinjin and that he needed to use the viewing chamber. I tried to stop him, but he just stared out the opening and fell to the floor. He'll be back. I just know it. He's strong."

Catrin slapped Prios hard across the face. Millie sucked air through her teeth, but Catrin knew he would feel only the most intense sensations while out of his body. Shouting in his ear, just as Mother Gwendolin had once done for her, Catrin told him he was going to die. She scanned the painful memories, hoping to recall something that would help save Prios. Without the grounding effect provided by the chairs of stone and metal, he would have nothing to guide him back to his body. He would be lost.

Lost.

Whether the thought came from Prios or from Catrin's subconscious, the effect was the same, and it drove Catrin to reckless action. Without the aid of the stone chairs to anchor her or the monks' chanting to shake loose her spirit, Catrin gazed out of the viewing portal, pulled deeply on the energy around her, and wrenched her soul free from its mortal trappings. Though she left most of her physical senses behind, she did not miss Millie gasping, "By the Gods! She's gone too. It's like they're trying to kill me!"

Unlike Catrin's previous experiences with astral travel, movement was anything but effortless. Just staying whole required most of her concentration. The world seemed to pull at her spirit from a thousand directions, slowly tearing her apart. What movement she did manage was clumsy and out of control, but her son's life and that of her husband were at stake, and nothing would deter her. Driven by a mother's instinct, her spirit flowed down the Pinook Valley, over Edling's Wall, and into the lands that had once been her home. An almost irresistible urge to visit what had been her family's farm tugged at her. Painful memories rose unbidden, the dull ache of loss all too familiar. With extreme mental effort, she focused her energy and thrust those feelings aside. Nothing mattered more than finding Sinjin and Prios.

The world moved wildly beneath her, bucking and lurching as she cast out her senses, searching for familiar patterns of energy.

Go back.

Catrin barely heard Prios in her mind, but his words struck like thunder. She could feel his pain and the effort it had taken to communicate with her. His essence was nearly depleted, and someone interfered with his attempts to return to his body. Feeling helpless, Catrin reeled with fury. Never before had she tried to influence the world around her when traveling outside her body; always before she had been but an observer. Now though, she sensed an enemy approaching her son and another slowly killing her husband.

Dark energies swirled around her as Sinjin and Durin half limped and half jogged into view. The pain in Sinjin's eyes made it clear that he was in no condition to outrun anyone. The darkness coalesced into two figures that materialized as if made from nothing but shadow.

Durin saw them first and shouted, "Run!"

"I can't," Sinjin said, but he picked up his pace as much as he could. It would do no good. Both assassins raised their arms and aimed at Sinjin.

Though they could not hear her, Catrin screamed and thrust herself into the face of one of the men, feeling for his eyes with her energy. A sound like a sizzling pop split the air, and the assassin fell to the ground, screaming and clutching his still-hooded face. The second assassin seemed frozen in time, yet Catrin watched in silent horror as a slender bolt sliced the air on its way to Sinjin's heart. Leaves rustled as what felt like a tornadic wind rushed past Catrin, and she recognized Prios's spirit. Emotion overwhelmed her as she watched him alter the flight path of the bolt so it soared harmlessly over Sinjin's shoulder. A moment later a wall of malicious intent slammed into her like a wave of fire and nausea. Catrin struggled to hold herself together as her unidentified adversary tried to help the world tear her spirit apart. Everything turned a shade darker, and Catrin knew she would soon succumb. As the assassin aimed once again, she made one last desperate attempt to communicate with Sinjin: *"Run!"*

Never before had Sinjin heard his mother's voice in his mind, and the sound of it terrified him. It felt as if those words might be her last. Screaming, he ducked under the next bolt loosed by the assassin. Behind him he heard a wet *thunk* and a grunt. Turning to look, he saw Durin drop to one knee, his face pale and drawn. Anger welled up in Sinjin and would not be denied. Howling, he turned and ran toward the assassin, who seemed surprised and momentarily stunned. Using what Uncle Chase had taught him, Sinjin coiled his muscles and focused his core strength to launch his attack. He struck with more force than he could naturally muster, and he felt tingling hands assisting him and reinforcing his strike. The assassin went down and did not rise.

With a lump in his throat, Sinjin turned to Durin, who was now on his side, one leg trapped beneath his body at an awkward angle. It looked to Sinjin as if he were already dead. Tears filled his eyes, but he forced them back. When he pulled Durin from the ground and wrestled his limp body over one shoulder, the boy moaned and Sinjin risked a moment of hope—it was a brief moment. The assassin, too, moaned, and Sinjin moved off as fast as he could while carrying Durin. Once again his shoulders itched, waiting for the next deadly bolt to strike. He nearly dropped Durin at the sound of a snapping branch, but it was Uncle Chase and five of his best men who approached.

Chase rushed forward when he saw the boys and charged past them, looking for their assailants, his soldier's body rippling with intent. Sinjin turned to watch his uncle go, terrified by Chase's deadly charge but also by the thought of losing him. The valley behind was now empty, though, and nothing of the two assassins remained. It was as if they had been taken by the wind. Only the still form of Durin and the deadly bolt protruding from his shoulder gave evidence that they had ever existed.

"What happened?" Chase asked. "Never mind. It doesn't matter. We need to get you back to Dragonhold. Bradley, Simms, you carry Durin. Jorge and Morif, grab Sinjin." Words of protest were cut short as Sinjin suddenly found himself slung over the shoulders of two men who immediately began to run. The desire to run on his own two legs was nearly overwhelming, despite knowing his energy was already spent.

CHAPTER TWO

The power of words, used with artfulness and skill, can be immeasurable.
— Surry the Minstrel

ou should all be ashamed of yourselves," Millie said as she walked among the beds in the now overfull infirmary. The tears that gathered in her eyes seemed to anger her further. "When you are all well enough to hear me, you can be certain I'll tell you what I *really* think. I most certainly will. Selfish and thoughtless, not to mention plain stupid. Did I mention stupid? No respect for a fragile, old heart such as mine."

Her footsteps echoed off the cold stone walls.

Sinjin waited until Millie thundered from the room before raising his head. He alone was unscathed after the events of the previous day. Fault was his alone to bear, yet those he loved had paid the price for his impetuous and selfish decisions. Millie was right; he truly was detestable. Tears threatened to fall from his eyes as well, and his chin quivered. Durin groaned, causing Sinjin to leap; it was the first Durin had stirred since Brother Vaughn had administered a series of poultices. Each one had seemed to pull some of the poison from the boy's body, but no one knew if it would be enough.

"Durin," Sinjin whispered. "Can you hear me? Wake up. Don't make me beat you into consciousness."

Durin's eyes did not open, but one side of his mouth twitched and turned upward. It lasted only a moment; then he was gone again. Sinjin's parents were faring no better, and the room began to close in on him, forcing him to accept the guilt and responsibility. Part of him wanted to run until he could run no more, to escape from the horror of having killed his parents and his best friend. What kind of monster would do such a thing? He'd risked everything on a silly race. He'd won the race and lost everything else.

Returning in a rustle of skirts, Millie entered the room looking pale, and she leaned on the rough-hewn walls. "Master Edling is within Dragonhold," she gasped between breaths.

Sinjin's head snapped up. Master Edling had never entered Dragonhold, and not since the erection of the wall bearing his name had he come north of it. It wasn't until recently that anyone could cross the wall. As a result of the Pinook Treaty, a gate had been built and limited trade established. Looking at the still forms of his parents, a chill clutched his bowels. This was no time to show weakness. Sinjin was not weak minded or completely unprepared. "Tell him my parents are involved in matters that cannot wait and will occupy them until after nightfall."

"Edling and his gaggle of fools are not here to see your parents," Millie said with a look that Sinjin knew all too well. "They're here looking for another fool, one that seems to have won a race, I believe."

Standing as rigid as stone, Sinjin allowed Millie to dab powder around his eyes.

"We can't have them thinking you've been crying," she said. "Now look at me. Your eyes are as red as roses. But I can't fix that."

That did little to bolster Sinjin's failing confidence as he walked to Dragonhold's main entrance. What had once been a jagged gash in the stone wall had been carved into a broad entranceway. The inner gates, which had been constructed using whole tree trunks, stood open, showing the cloudless sky beyond. Within stood Master Edling and his party, which was dwarfed by the massive scale of the ancient hall. Delicately curved pillars the size of greatoaks extended high into the darkness, leaving the ceiling of the chamber hidden from view. Some said the place was named Dragonhold because dragons could fly within the hold; others said an ancient dragon lived in the darkest depths of the mountain fortress. Sinjin knew he could use the majesty of his home to his advantage.

"Master Edling," he said with a bow that was little more than a nod. He could almost feel Millie's pride as he had shown just enough respect to offset the insult. Again, he could sense Millie's approval as he let the silence hang between them. Someone less trained might have launched into apologies or explanations or excuses, but Sinjin knew better; Millie and Uncle Chase had seen to that.

"Lord Volker," Master Edling said after an uncomfortable silence. "I had hoped your parents would accompany you. I was so looking forward to congratulating them on raising such a fine and strong young man—not to mention fast. Hester was none too pleased that you broke his record, I can assure you that! I don't believe I'd buy any butter or cheese from Hester if I were you," Edling finished with a condescending smile and a too-deep bow.

Sinjin, again, said nothing. Those behind Master Edling shuffled their feet and fidgeted, perhaps uncomfortable on Edling's behalf.

Master Edling coughed. "Yes . . . as I was saying . . . you left without claiming your prize. The Spring Challenges and Summer Games are based on tradition, and some traditions simply must not be broken, for the sake of continuity. It is for that reason that we have come to you. I present you this wreath as a sign of your victory. Let your countrymen know that your right to the title Champion has been duly earned and cannot be taken away."

Sinjin accepted the wreath, knowing Edling had other, less honorable reasons for coming to Dragonhold, such as assessing his enemies' hold in person.

Alissa stepped forward and Sinjin was utterly unprepared for her kiss. He had expected a quick peck, but she grabbed the back of his neck and kissed him deeply. Sinjin took a step back, and she moved with him, as if she'd forgotten anyone else was present. When finally she allowed Sinjin to pull free, there was a look in her eyes that made Sinjin feel like a doe before a mountain cat. His skin flushed and his face reddened nearly as deeply as Alissa's father's as the man ushered her to the back of Edling's party.

Sinjin flushed even further when he looked into the gathered crowd to see Kendra Ironfist looking like a storm cloud—her face flushed, her eyes afire. Despite it all, Sinjin had to admit that she was beautiful, though he'd never admit it to her. Too many times she'd caused him trouble. Still, her long brown hair softened the scowl on her face, and there was a certain twinkle in her glare. Sinjin's current circumstances once again demanded his attention as another strained silence hung over the hall.

"Thank you all for coming here to present me with this prize," Sinjin finally said. His face still burned and a tremble crept into his voice, but he kept from showing his fear. "If you will excuse me, there are matters that require my attention."

"I had hoped for at least a brief tour," Master Edling said. His eyes took in the details as he scanned the great hall. The tile mosaic floor had been returned to its original glory, and the ancient suits of armor that lined the walls gleamed under a patina ages in the making. Ornate entranceways led to halls shrouded in shadow, and Sinjin guessed that Master Edling must dearly wish to know what lay beyond.

"Perhaps another time, Master Edling."

A long silence allowed the tension to rise as Master Edling attempted to silently compel Sinjin.

"Perhaps you could have your steward contact me, and we can arrange for a proper tour," Millie said from behind Sinjin, who gave no indication that he would speak again.

"Uh, yes. I suppose that would be best."

Sinjin knew it would be a long climb back down the wooden stairs that led to the valley floor below and that it would most likely be dark by the time Master Edling's party reached the bottom. Insulting Master Edling was a risky thing to do, and Sinjin was in no mood for taking more risks, but he definitely didn't want Master Edling to know that his parents were incapacitated. If Edling wanted to launch an attack on Dragonhold, this would certainly be the time to do it.

Edling left without another word, his party hurrying in his wake.

"If I weren't so angry with you, I do believe I'd be right proud about now," Millie said.

Sinjin turned to see her smiling, and the weight on his soul was just a little lighter. "Thanks, Millie. I'm sorry about all the trouble I caused."

"I don't suppose you'll be making that mistake again, now will you?"

"No, ma'am."

"It wasn't all your fault, now. There're darker forces at work here, and you've just got to be more careful. If they were to have killed you . . . why, I don't know what I'd have done." There was a catch in her voice.

"Yes, ma'am."

"Now you run to the kitchens and get something in your belly. Can't have you falling over too."

Sinjin's stomach agreed with Millie, and he jogged toward the kitchens. Leaving the cool air behind, he descended to the great forge. Rhythmic ringing echoed through the tunnels of stone, and the heat of the central fire radiated from the heart of Dragonhold. Here, all those who needed fire could do their work. Sinjin glanced into the smithy on his way by and could see Strom's muscular form glistening in the orange glow of hot metal. He was not a lumbering brute of a man, but he was lean and powerful, the cut of his muscles making him look like a living sculpture. His hammer blows set the cadence for the chorus of the forge. In the adjacent chamber, Osbourne and Milo worked glass into wondrous forms. As he peered in, he could see them putting the final touches on a glass dragon made in Kyrien's image, an image that was becoming ever more popular despite his long absence—or perhaps because of it. Sinjin pulled his gaze away as thoughts of Kyrien led to thoughts of his mother and father.

The smell of baking bread overtook the earthy fragrance of the smithy and smelting room, and more savory aromas drifted in from the kitchens. Sinjin charged past the bakery and slowed to a respectful speed when he reached the main kitchen. He couldn't count the number of times Miss Mariss had told him to slow down in her kitchens, and as he'd gotten older, he'd begun listening to her—most of the time. Several smacks on the back of the head with a wooden spoon had helped motivate him.

When he entered, an unnatural silence greeted him. The kitchens were a place of noise and constant activity, but everyone in the keep knew what had happened the day before, and the cooks silently waited to see what he would say.

Miss Mariss had been fanning herself near one of the precious few ventilation shafts, seeming reluctant to come talk to Sinjin. "I'll never get used to this heat," she complained, as she had many times before. "The kitchen in my inn is always hot, but you can walk outside and escape it for a bit. Here you just cook along with the meat! Do those men really need that much heat to forge metal and make glass?"

Sinjin walked alongside Miss Mariss as she talked. Absently she grabbed a wooden bowl and a slate. Into the bowl went red sausage, smoked bacon, salt-cured ham, eggs, and walnuts, Sinjin's and Prios's favorite breakfast. Onto the slate went a small loaf of dark bread that had been cut open and stuffed with soft cheese and honey.

"Go," Miss Mariss said, not giving herself or anyone else the chance to ask him questions she knew he did not want to answer.

Sinjin left without looking anyone else in the eye, but when he turned the corner, he literally ran into the last person in the world he wanted to see. Kendra looked down at the honey that now stained her smock, which was snug and seemed to demand that Sinjin stare at it, and she cast Sinjin one of her least pleasant looks. "You oaf!"

"Kendra! You apologize this instant!" ordered Kendra's mother, Khenna.

"It was my fault. I wasn't looking," Sinjin said, and he tried to slide by both of them, but Khenna blocked his path.

"This won't do. Kendra, say you're sorry."

"I won't because I'm not sorry. He thinks he's better than everyone else and he's not!"

"Forgive her, Lord Volker," Khenna said, causing a flush of a different sort to run over Sinjin's face. He hated to be called "Lord Volker," especially now. And Kendra was the last person he wanted to hear someone call him that.

"If he's a lord, then I'm a horse's—"

Kendra's words were cut short, and Sinjin did not look back. The less he did to provoke Kendra, the better. It was not that he feared her, but a battle with her was one he could not win; this he knew from experience. Khenna was a trained fighter, and Kendra had proven a quick study. She challenged his authority at every opportunity, and one time he let his temper get the better of him. "Go back to your momma's skirts," he'd told her. It was a stupid thing to say. She hadn't even waited for him to finish the sentence before spinning on one leg and landing a kick on his jaw. That was all it had taken. After he'd regained consciousness, his mother had scolded him for fighting with girls. Confrontation with Kendra was best avoided.

"Some champion," Kendra said as Sinjin retreated.

Watching his food grow colder, Sinjin quickened his step. It was then that he realized there was nowhere he wanted to eat. Normally he would eat with Durin's family since his mother usually ate in her workroom and his father often ate by walking through the kitchens and grabbing whatever attracted him—a habit that drove Miss Mariss to distraction. Sinjin remembered the pain in Durin's parents' eyes when the news of his friend's condition had been delivered, and he could not face that pain again, especially not when it was his fault. As he neared the barracks, he considered eating with the guards, but the heated shouts from within the barracks caused him to keep going. It seemed the entire hold was in turmoil as a result of his thoughtlessness. As he neared the halls where he and Durin had played as children, he remembered a nearly dark alcove where they used to hide; perhaps he'd not completely outgrown the spot.

Behind the statue of some ancient king, Sinjin crouched. Beside him a glowing rune chased the darkness. Carved into the stone were delicate yet cavernous sigils. The narrow, fine lines cut deep enough to allow light from the central fire to shine through. The sigils had caused quite a stir after the lighting of the great hearth. When they began to glow, people feared some ancient magic had awakened. Sinjin thought that perhaps it had.

Putting his slate over the rune, Sinjin let the warm air reheat his now cold food. Most now agreed that the runes were the ancients' way of distributing warmth to the entire hold from the central fire, but some still held on to the belief that the runes were magical.

"Haven't seen him," a voice said in the distance, and Sinjin heard footsteps approaching. He pulled his knees to his chest and waited for them to pass. The pain in his chest had become unbearable, and he did not want to be found. He was afraid he would be unable to find his voice.

"How are they?"

"Not good," Sinjin's uncle Chase said, and Sinjin pulled his knees tighter, trying to will himself out of existence. It was all his fault.

"Do you know what happened?" the voice Sinjin could not quite place asked quietly.

"No, not really." Chase hesitated. "Our best guess is that someone is interfering with their return. They've both traveled before, and I think they would have found their way back unless someone hampered them, as Prios once did to Catrin."

Sinjin's heart beat fast. He was sure they would hear his quickened breathing. How would he explain his eavesdropping, especially now that they were discussing things that were normally kept hidden from him?

Their family history was not entirely unknown to him, but certain details were never discussed in his presence.

"What can we do to help?"

"Keep your eyes open for Sinjin and hope for the best, I suppose," Chase said. The pain in his voice brought Sinjin to tears. Guilt stabbed at him, but he remained silent.

"Our prayers are with you."

The footsteps faded into the distance, and Sinjin knew he needed to get back to the infirmary. A whiff of his now warm food made his stomach growl, but he froze in fear as a shadow detached itself from a nearby alcove and moved along the hallway slowly as if afraid to be seen. Sinjin willed his stomach to silence as the figure melted back into the shadows. Afraid to move, Sinjin waited in terrified silence.

Chase paced the polished granite floors of the war room, waiting for the rest to arrive. With consensus unachievable, the tension at these meetings had been growing for months, and the present crisis stood only to exacerbate the situation. With a deep sigh, he looked up. Around a table hewn from the very rock that surrounded him, oppressing him, sat three of the five people he expected. Two chairs would remain empty, a fact that haunted all of them. The chairs had been a gift from Jharmin Kyte, the husband of Catrin's cousin. It was said that Lady Lissa broke every vase within Wolfhold when she found out. The chairs themselves were a marvel. Carvings of dragons wrapped around the arms and legs. Gilded threads woven by the hands of a master graced stiff cushions, which Chase thought were far nicer to look at than to sit upon.

Strom sat, tracing the designs on the outer edge of the table with his fingertips. The construction of this place had baffled him from the first time he'd entered it, and Chase could see his mind working, trying to figure out just how the ancients had done it.

Brother Vaughn and his wife, Mirta, huddled in quiet conversation, discussing the condition of Catrin and Prios. Chase couldn't keep from listening, and he did his best not to despair. When Martik and Miss Mariss arrived, he nearly snapped at them, but the platters of food they carried greatly improved his mood.

"If Catrin were here," Miss Mariss said, "she'd grumble that none of this food was grown within Dragonhold, so I'll do it for her. 'We need to grow more food within the hold. We must be self-sufficient, or all we've done will be for naught.' Now eat up." There was a catch in her voice, and the food was consumed in relative silence.

When the trays were empty, the silence remained. Finally, Chase cleared his throat. "I know we all wish Catrin and Prios were here, so let's just get on with the usual business, and then we can talk about what, if anything, can be done to help them. Agreed?"

All those assembled nodded.

"The guards are in order and are on high alert. I have men looking for Sinjin, and once we find him, we'll be keeping a closer watch on him. I shouldn't have let him out of my sight, and I won't make that mistake again. As for the finances, things are as grim as ever. I'm not sure how much longer we can keep paying the number of men required to protect us. That's my report."

"The smithy is fully operational, but we need more ore. As I've said before, we either need to start new mines or reopen some of the old mines. All the good mines are south of the wall, and Edling will just raise the prices and drain our coffers. If we create new mines as extensions of the keep, then we might be able to create additional open areas for some sort of agriculture."

"With the number of herald globes it would take to provide enough light to grow anything," Brother Vaughn said, "we could sell the globes and import our food supplies."

"There's still the possibility of growing mushrooms in the dark," Miss Mariss interrupted. "Then we only need light to harvest them."

"Even if we can grow enough mushrooms to feed the hold, we can't live off mushrooms alone," Martik added.

"Can we at least agree that we should invest more time working on mushroom farming methods?" Chase asked with an edge to his voice.

The others nodded.

"On a positive note," Mirta interjected, "our herb- and flower-drying efforts have provided enough medicinal herbs and spices to last at least three winters. Our stockpiles of nuts and dried fruits are also enough to last several seasons with proper rationing."

Chase tried not to frown, knowing even that success would not satisfy Catrin. If the hold were ever to be truly self-sufficient, they would need to find ways to satisfy all of their needs from within the hold. While Chase understood her motivations, every passing day made it more difficult to convince people that the hold needed to be self-sufficient. A warming weather trend had brought bountiful harvests, and the populations north and south of the wall were growing rapidly. The darkness of Catrin's visions seemed worlds away, and there were few people who believed they would ever need the protection Catrin so desperately sought to prepare. These thoughts weren't new, and he'd yet to find a solution, so Chase set his jaw and committed himself to simply making forward progress.

"The fishery remains healthy, and we've found a kind of pond moss that grows well in low light. Berman Ross found it in a cave down south, and since we've introduced it to the waters, it has flourished. We may be able to create a sustainable fishery yet."

This effort at least was one that everyone was behind. If the subterranean lake now known as the God's Eye could prove a reliable source for food and fresh water, then it truly would be a gift from the gods.

"How about your efforts, Brother Vaughn?" Chase asked. "Have you found anything new?"

"Not much, I'm afraid. I've found more references that confirm the keep once had fresh water running throughout, but I can find nothing to indicate the source. The basins and channels throughout the hold make it obvious that water once flowed, but what needs to be done to make it flow once again is a complete mystery. This whole keep is enough to relieve a man of his wits. Hidden chambers, hallways that go nowhere, strange runes that seem impossible to re-create—truly the ancients knew a great many things we do not."

"Perhaps we should consider sending another envoy to meet with Thorakis," Miss Mariss said.

"We've already sent two envoys, and neither has returned. I think we've already received our answer," Chase said then took a deep breath, preparing himself for Miss Mariss's reaction to that statement.

"I wish I knew what happened to those men!" she blurted, surprising Chase, who suddenly found himself coughing. "If they're on the Greatland getting fat and leaving us to our fate, why I'll . . ." Miss Mariss continued under her breath, but her words were not meant or fit for the ears of others.

Chase shared her frustration. Since the end of what was now called the Herald War, it seemed every bit of news from the Greatland was tied in some way to a man most called Thorakis the Builder. Some called him Thorakis the Savior, but that name was less popular here on the Godfist. Regardless, the man's accomplishments were undeniable, and already people around the world, including present company, were trying to figure out how to duplicate some of his feats. The establishment of an enormous fishery had been his initial achievement. Feeding the masses gave him the ability to effect great change. Every achievement brought more people to his cause, and those people further increased his ability to achieve the otherwise unachievable.

"Whatever the cause," Brother Vaughn finally said. "I don't think we can expect any help from the Greatland any time soon. I suggest we continue as we have been, and we are bound to discover new things over time."

His statement was greeted by silence. It sounded all too familiar, and since most of their meetings ended on a similar note, it did not inspire confidence.

"On Catrin's behalf," Chase said, "I'll note that we still have approximately a thousand herald globes. With no sign of Kyrien, we don't expect to have more any time soon. I suggest we hold on to them. If we can't produce more, then we'll need to get more for the ones we have. We've orders for ten times the amount we have, so it won't take long before the offering prices start to go up. I also know that Catrin wants several hundred to remain within the hold at all times, so there really are very few that remain to be sold."

"We'll have to keep an even closer watch on those we have," Brother Vaughn said. "I know those within the hold are trustworthy, but greed can make people do things they normally would not."

"Agreed," Chase said. "Based on Prios's last report, there are no places available within the academy, but people continue to arrive on every ship in from the Greatland and the Falcon Isles. Now we even have ships coming from Garaway and Foss. We need to figure out what to do with these people."

It was an increasingly troubling problem. Most of those who came seeking entrance to the Herald's Academy were turned away, and the majority had no way to return home. The fact was that most of them were misfits and outcasts, sent to the Godfist by their families with the anticipation that they would not return. In the absence of any quantifiable method of judging each person's potential, the academy had simply accepted all those who came until there were more than Prios and his staff could handle. After that, everyone was turned away with few exceptions. Generally only those who had manifested powerful abilities on their own were admitted. In some cases students of less potential had to be excused. It was a difficult and disconcerting process.

"We also need to figure out who will maintain order until Prios can return to his duties," Chase added, and again silence filled the hall. "And most importantly, we need to figure out a way to help Catrin and Prios. There must be something we can do, and Brother Vaughn, I think you are the man to figure out exactly what that is. Unfortunately I also think you are the man to run the academy in Prios's absence."

"I'll do everything I can to achieve both, but I'm going to need some help."

"We'll do what we can to get you what you need," Chase said.

"I've an idea," Mirta said. "I know I'm no expert, but I remember the tale of Catrin's astral travel to find the Firstland. She had no stone and metal throne, as she had at Ohmahold, and she became lost. Was it not the dragons who assisted her return? Did she not say that they aided her?"

The rest of the group seemed dubious, but it was Brother Vaughn who gave their concerns a voice. "While our memories agree, I don't see how that will help us at this particular time. Catrin has been calling out to Kyrien for years, and he has not returned."

"But we could try," Mirta interrupted. "Perhaps this is something the academy could help with. Maybe they can call out to the dragons and ask for help. What harm can it cause?"

Brother Vaughn nodded slowly, his deep brown eyes thoughtful. "I don't suppose I see any harm in it, and it might help the people to feel they are doing something productive. We must, of course, continue to keep Catrin and Prios's actual condition secret. Perhaps we could just tell everyone that we need them to call the dragons here so we can obtain more dragon ore."

"Maybe you should just throw the dragons a party," Martik added with a smirk.

"I hadn't thought of that!" Mirta exclaimed.

Martik rolled his eyes.

CHAPTER THREE

Light blinds as readily as shadow.
— Hurakin the Assassin

Black sails crowded the horizon beneath a roiling mass of darkness. Unlike any storm clouds Pelivor had ever seen, towering formations curled in on themselves and emanated malevolence, as if the clouds themselves wished to destroy him and everyone else aboard the *Slippery Eel*. Even if the storm were simply a storm, the fleet of black ships drew ever closer, and Pelivor could feel their intent. It made his knees tremble.

"You just need to believe you can do it," Kenward repeated, as if those words could somehow convince Pelivor that he could do something that only the most powerful person on all of Godsland could do. Though he considered Catrin a friend, she was the Herald of Istra, and he was nothing compared to her. Though he'd shown the slightest spark of talent with Istra's powers, it had been only that, literally, a spark.

"I'm trying," Pelivor said, doing his best not to let his annoyance put an edge on his voice. Though Kenward was the captain of the *Slippery Eel,* he was also a friend. Cold air pressed his loose-fitting silks to him, and his normally tight and deeply tanned skin drew even tighter, making him look as if he were carved from stone.

"I know, but—"

He didn't have to finish the statement; both could see the darkness closing in on them. The towering clouds looked as if they would swallow the world, and sudden bursts of lightning illuminated them from within, dark silhouettes standing out against the temporarily lit backdrop. Pelivor took a deep breath and tried to calm himself with no success. Lives depended on him, and he had no reason to believe he would succeed. All he had to go by were Kenward's descriptions of what Catrin had done, and those were decidedly vague. Perhaps if she were here, she could teach him, but she wasn't here. He also didn't have her dragon ore figurine or staff to draw energy from; the only power within his grasp was what he could draw from the air around him. He could feel it, smell it, and even taste it, but he had no idea how to gather it or focus it. He might as well try to gather fog with a bucket.

Walking back to the bow, Pelivor couldn't help feeling like a charlatan as he spread his arms wide. The crew remained silent, watching him, willing him to succeed, knowing another failure would likely mean death for them all. That thought made Pelivor ill. When Grubb approached with a mug of aromatic broth, it was all Pelivor could do to force it down.

"It'll cure what ails ya," the ship's cook said, his voice steady and a half smile on his face. Pelivor wished he shared the man's confidence, and it must have shown. "Don't worry. That man's been trying to kill me for years, and he ain't succeeded yet," he said, jerking a thumb in Kenward's direction.

Handing the empty mug back to Grubb, Pelivor hoped this day would not change that. Ever since they'd left the Greatland bound for the Godfist, loaded with precious cargo, he'd had a bad feeling in his gut, and since the appearance of the black fleet, his fears had only grown.

Kenward paced from bow to stern and tried to avoid making eye contact with Pelivor, knowing the man was near his breaking point and there was nothing he could say to ease the burden. For years the *Slippery Eel* had been among the fastest ships on the water and had evaded even the most determined pursuers, but she was weighed down, and the ships behind them moved faster than any he'd seen before. He wondered again if the unnatural storm drove them to such great speed or if some new design allowed them to cut the waves faster than ships that had come before. Using his looking glass, he could see nothing that distinguished those ships from any other, and he came, once again, to the conclusion that some malevolent force drove them forward. The sense of impending evil was the most telling factor, and Kenward felt a rare wave of fear overtake him. Despite his efforts to hide the fear from his crew, he knew they could sense it, and that alone was enough to put them all on edge.

Watching Pelivor from behind, he prayed the gods had not lost patience with him, and after tossing another gold coin into the waves, he hoped it was enough. A dim glow pulsed around Pelivor's hands, and Kenward dared to hope, but nothing happened. Soon after, the glow faltered and the sailor lowered his hands, his frustration clear in his posture. Again Kenward ran through his options, and again he came to the conclusion that nothing he could do would save them. Catrin's stonework thrones, cut from the mines deep below Ohmahold, were too heavy for his men to move without rope, pulleys, and substantial frameworks—none of which would be available until they reached the Godfist. He'd known the risk and accepted it, but now their precious cargo became their biggest liability, and jettisoning the other heavy cargo would destabilize the ship, only making the problem worse. Pelivor was their only hope, and that hope was as thin as gossamer.

"They're gonna catch us soon," came the voice of Bryn, the bosun, and Kenward turned to him with an annoyed glare for stating the obvious. "I know we can't unload the thrones, but if we just keep going as we are, we'll have to fight them on their terms."

"What are you suggesting?"

"Do something they won't be expecting," Bryn said with a wink, the freckles standing out on his reddened skin, which never seemed to tan, and his blue eyes twinkled.

Kenward grinned, a plan forming in his mind.

Pelivor watched in horror as the darkness swallowed the blue skies above them. Soon the black ships would overtake them, and all of them would die because he had failed them. His friends would die because he was feeble and weak minded. *No.* He would not give up. Catrin would not have given up, and he let the memory of her drive him. He remembered how she had fought to make him think more of himself and how he had grown to love her. Even if he could never have her, he would always have her in his heart.

With a shuddering breath, he set his jaw and let his fears melt away. Catrin had believed in him, and he let that belief become his own. Opening himself to the energy around him, he pulled it to him as best he could and let it fill him, slowly and steadily. Before he had let his impatience and fear drive him, but now he tried something different, filling himself with more energy than he'd ever held before. It felt as if he would catch fire or simply explode, but he continued to gather energy and hold it within him. It was like holding his breath, and his body began to burn with need, every instinct telling him to release it before it was too late, but still he held on, knowing that failure meant death.

The world around him ceased to exist, and he felt as if he might pass out, but he held the image of Catrin in his mind. She became his focal point, and by concentrating on her, his body's urgings became more distant and less poignant, as if he were but an observer of his own form. With her translucent hair blown back by the wind in his mind, Catrin's face held the strength of nations; her eyes, the fire of the sun; and her body, the might of the world. Though she was slender and slight, she looked as if she could pull the moon from the sky and cast it into the seas. When she looked at him, he felt her warmth wash over him, and he smelled her fragrance. In that moment he remembered their kiss, knowing it would be the only one they would ever share, yet it was enough to sustain him and hold him in thrall. Always before he'd let the guilt prevent him from reliving the memory, knowing that she'd given her heart to Prios, but this time was different. She loved him too—he knew it—and something told him that just this once, Prios would not object. Pelivor did not wish to steal her; he only wished to take strength and solace from her love and friendship. She had urged him to believe in himself, and for once he allowed himself to do just that.

In the next moment, though, everything changed. The deck beneath his feet lurched, pulling Pelivor from his meditation as the *Slippery Eel* executed a sharp turn. Crewmembers armed themselves and prepared for battle. To his surprise, Farsy and Nimsy held one of the light anchors they used in rocky areas where they were likely to lose the anchor. Angular and pointed, this anchor was nothing like the heavy, rounded anchor used in deep water with sandy or muddy bottom.

Now charging straight toward the approaching fleet, the *Slippery Eel* cut through the waves, seemingly pulled closer by a strange inflow, as if the storm itself were sucking them in. Pelivor despaired, his chance lost, and now all he could do was arm himself for the inevitable battle. No more could he hope to save his shipmates or himself; all he could do was hope to die fighting. It was a sickening feeling, yet there was a release in it. A strange and unfamiliar calm came over him as he watched his death approach. Those around him stood silent and stoic as they, too, accepted their fates with honor and grace.

The ships before them began to separate and turn, only two holding their course. As they drew closer, Pelivor expected to see men on those greasy black decks, but what he saw caused his fear to return. There were men but beside them were reptilian creatures in crude armor covering skin that looked nearly as tough as the armor. These demons watched with cold eyes as the *Slippery Eel* approached, and when the two ships flanked the *Eel,* they began leaping across the distance that separated the ships. Their strength and speed far exceeded that of their human counterparts, who could never have made such a leap.

Given no more time to contemplate this new enemy, Pelivor found himself facing a towering demon with golden eyes and elongated pupils like those of a snake; the pupils narrowed as the monster eyed its prey. Opening its mouth in what Pelivor could only guess was the equivalent of a smile, it bared its black gums and curved, yellow teeth. The stench of death reached out first, followed by a whistling mace that nearly took Pelivor's head from his shoulders. Taking a step backward, Pelivor wanted to run and hide, his courage fleeing in the face of such evil, but there was nowhere to run. Even jumping overboard would only lead to his death, and he did what he would not have thought himself capable of: he planted his feet and faced the demon.

Drawing energy as quickly as he could, having lost hold of his previous store, he extended his hand and lashed out with all the power he could muster, hoping it would be enough. A thread-thin line of blue light reached between his outstretched hand and the chest of the hulking demon, and a loud crack split the air, but the attack had no other effect. The demon tilted its head back and issued a barking laugh before raising its mace. Pelivor waited for the killing blow, but the demon suddenly stiffened and dropped to the deck, accompanied by a loud clang and a sinister sizzle. Behind where the beast had stood was Grubb, smoking skillet in hand. He offered Pelivor the briefest smile before both braced themselves.

"Hold on!" Kenward shouted. "Now!"

Pelivor watched as Farsy threw the anchor at one of the passing ships. It landed on the deck and skidded across the oily planks, looking as if it would simply slide back into the sea, but the sharp tips caught on something and bit deeply. Nimsy released the coiled rope as it raced away from him.

"Brace!" Kenward shouted.

A moment later the *Slippery Eel* slowed sharply, and water rushed over the rails as it spun around. Timbers groaned as the cleat holding the anchor rope strained against the tremendous force. The black ship also turned, and its stern dipped low in the waves, sending water rushing along its deck, causing it to dip even lower in the water.

The creaking of timbers accompanied the sounds of battle as the demons tried to bring down Kenward's crew. The sight of their ship rapidly sinking beneath the waves drove them to reckless action. As the ship sank, though, it threatened to take the *Slippery Eel* with it, and Kenward ordered the rope cut, but the demons charged in and protected the straining rope, seemingly intent on making sure the *Slippery Eel* joined their ship on the ocean floor. Splinters of wood filled the air as the rope cut through the railing, and the ship began to list badly, its prow pointing toward the depths. Just before it seemed they would be pulled under, the rope caught on a sharp edge and snapped, recoiling with massive force and taking pieces out of the demons that had been guarding it. As they reeled from the stinging lashes, Kenward's crew forced them through the gap in the railing to join their sunken ship.

The other ship they had passed was now executing a full turn, and the *Slippery Eel* headed straight for it. Howling in what sounded like maddened glee, Kenward ordered all sails unfurled, and the *Slippery Eel* reached ramming speed, its secret weapon hiding just below the surface.

"What've you got?" demanded the gate guard, whose dour face presided over the Kraken crest emblazoned on his armor.

"Vinegar," Kevlin Weil responded, thinking the man looked as if he'd never smiled.

"Who wants a whole wagon load of vinegar?"

"Grimwell," Kevlin replied, knowing that uttering the name of Thorakis's wizard was considered taboo. The people feared he would hear them and visit his dark powers on them. Kevlin didn't believe in wizards, but the people saw more of Grimwell these days than they did of Thorakis. It was difficult not to smile when the guard took an involuntary step back. Kevlin had apprehensions of his own about meeting Grimwell, but the wizard had sent out a request for all of the vinegar and spoiled wine that could be had. He didn't even want the spoiled wine cultured; it was ludicrous. But times such as these didn't afford a man the luxury of picking and choosing his customers, and Thorakis's coffers seemed almost bottomless. With more people flocking to his protection every day, Kevlin knew whom he would serve for at least a time, and this was an opportunity to distinguish himself and establish a more regular trade relationship. Kevlin would wager that Thorakis was ill and that Grimwell was planning to succeed him. Given the way most people felt about Grimwell, Kevlin didn't think it likely the wizard would rule for long. Being a realist, Kevlin thought it best to earn whatever coin he could now before the hard times returned. He'd heard others come to similar conclusions, and it seemed the tide was turning. The wise prepared for such things.

"Get this stinking mess away from my gate," the guard said after a brief inspection.

Kevlin chirruped and smacked his mare, Hera, on the rump with the lines, and his wagon slowly rolled a wobbling track toward the gates of Riverhold, the largest construction project in known history. The keep was a marvel, and Kevlin was approaching one of the first magics, as the people had come to call them. Before him waited a wall of granite, unadorned and seemingly singular and whole, but as Hera stepped onto what seemed like a loose bit of cobblestone, she snorted and sidestepped. Kevlin held on as a hissing sound echoed around him. Hera turned her head, and he could see the white in her eyes; he was beginning to have serious thoughts of turning around and abandoning the idea of selling to Thorakis.

Beneath the hissing sound came a low, deep rumble that had Hera backing up as fast as she could. Kevlin jumped from the wagon and grabbed her by the bridle before she turned the wagon over. Before them, the granite wall split not cleanly down the center, but in a complex geometric pattern that allowed the two stones to come together as a mesh. The massive gates rumbled open. Though Kevlin was uncertain how much actual 'magic' was involved, he could not argue that the term was fitting. Never before had he seen such power and majesty. Knowing Hera would not walk through those gates willingly, he calmed her enough that he could retrieve a cloth sack from under the seat of his wagon. Using the sack, he blindfolded Hera and walked her slowly through what now looked to Kevlin like the jaws of a monster. Beyond lay the second magics.

Riverhold was unlike any other hold. It straddled the mighty Yan River as part bridge, part keep, and part dam. From a distance, the spans looked delicate and too thin to support the weight of the keep, like the legs of an overly fat spider. Up close, the spans looked much more substantial, but the white and swirling water that flowed underneath, just before plunging over a thousand-foot waterfall, made it seem as if every step might be his last. While leading Hera over the span, he almost envied her. Traders made this journey every day, but that did not stop his mind from replaying the image of his and Hera's plunging into the water and over the falls.

At the foot of the span waited a pair of guardhouses that sat before what appeared to be another wall of solid stone. The guards waved him past, and he walked Hera forward. The stone beneath him gave under his weight and sank lower and lower. It was a sickening feeling, and Hera began to tremble. He put his hand on her neck and spoke soothingly, but she broke into a sweat and refused to stand still. The stone walkway before them continued to sink until it became a downhill entrance that ran under the massive walls of the keep proper. The moment they were within the awaiting courtyard, the stone moved back up without a sound and seemingly unbidden. It made the hair on Kevlin's neck stand on end, and all he wanted was to make his trade and get out of this place. Even the most practical man could see that there were unnatural forces at work here.

Other traders waited in the courtyard, and Kevlin removed the blindfold from Hera. The sight of other horses relaxing nearby helped to calm her, but she was still skittish.

"Kevlin Weil!" shouted a young and shrill voice. "Kevlin Weil!"

"Over here!" Kevlin said, waving.

"You're t'come with me right away, sir. You're late, sir, and hisself is proper angry, he is."

Kevlin didn't bother to explain why he was late, as the young man turned and trotted back toward the inner keep, which towered above him.

"Are you coming?"

"C'mon, Hera old girl," Kevlin said. "Just a bit farther, and we'll be there."

Hera moved forward but it was obviously not fast enough for the young man's liking based on the looks he shot over his shoulder.

Kevlin cast his gaze left and right, trying to take it all in. To his left, the roar of rushing water was accompanied by a low, grinding sound, and enormous pillars rotated as if turned by the arms of some lumbering hulk. To his right were the now legendary hammers of Riverhold. These stone hammers, big enough to crush a house, beat relentlessly on softer rocks to grind them into powder. Kevlin assumed the rotating columns were part of the mill. Though he knew the river provided the power to run these massive machines, it still seemed as if it were more than any man should be able to accomplish. Thorakis had mastered the Yan River, and Kevlin was humbled.

The keep proper moved like the inner workings of the most elaborate wooden toy, and it was difficult to conceive that this was worked in stone. Shafts of light poured through the room at strategic angles so that even the shadows seemed alive. Ahead waited a pair of immense stone soldiers, looking ready to strike.

As if this place needed to be more frightening, Kevlin thought.

When Hera passed through one of the light beams, she jumped at the sound of stone moving. Had he not heard stories, Kevlin would have turned and run; instead he stood on trembling knees and watched the mighty statues bend down and look at him, their stone blades poised to run him through. In truth, the swords were so large that they would more likely crush him and Hera than pierce them. As he led Hera between the statues, both heads turned smoothly and almost silently to follow Kevlin's every movement. They were so detailed, even their expressions changed as they moved. Their cold and baleful glares held him in thrall. For the briefest moment, Kevlin considered stopping and backing up to see if the statues would notice, but he thought better of it. Ahead, his guide stopped, put his hands on his hips, and let out an annoyed sigh.

Kevlin kept Hera moving as quickly as he could, more to get away from the scrutiny of the stone guards than to appease his guide. Wondering if he would see the leaping elk or the stone eagle or any of the other wonders he'd heard about, Kevlin prayed he wouldn't encounter Thorakis's dragon. It was said that no one had ever seen it and lived to tell the tale. He was relieved and just a little disappointed when his guide led him to a nondescript hall.

"Wait here."

A moment later, Kevlin held his breath.

"If you can't get me what I need on time," the unmistakable voice of Grimwell echoed in the halls, "I might as well toss you into the hammer mill."

Dressed in a heavy, wool jacket so black, it seemed to suck in the light, Grimwell looked every bit the part of a wizard. Silver tipped the corners of his lapels and the tassels that hung down on the sides. Spiderwebs of lightning stood out on the black sleeves in glossy black thread; the subtlety of it drew the eye. The man's black hair was cut short and formed jagged peaks that framed his face. He wore no mustache, but his beard was trimmed into thin lines that ran alongside his mouth and into a point on his chin. All that dark coloring made the wizard's pale skin look almost translucent in comparison. There was no warmth in his black eyes and no trace of humor. Kevlin prayed this encounter would be over quickly.

"Open them, you fool," Grimwell said, and Kevlin started to move, but a look from the page stilled him. Grimwell had not even looked at Kevlin, and it was not Kevlin he addressed. The page moved to open the earthenware jugs resting on a bed of straw in the wagon. Grimwell inspected them and merely grunted, "Unload them."

Kevlin watched as the page made a number of trips to unload the wagon. He would have offered to help, but it was clear his aid was neither required nor wanted. When the last of the jugs were gone, Kevlin waited. Time slipped past, how much Kevlin could not guess. The place had a timelessness that could not be denied, but Hera's fidgeting agreed with Kevlin's feeling that it had been too long. Just as he began to wonder if the page would return, the sound of boots coming from the direction Grimwell and the page had gone made him straighten.

When Grimwell appeared, he made eye contact with Kevlin for the first time, and Kevlin wished he hadn't. Being the target of the wizard's icy stare made Kevlin wish he could become invisible. Perhaps he should just leave without getting paid. The coin no longer seemed worth it.

"Why are you still here?" Grimwell demanded.

Kevlin flushed and could not seem to find his tongue.

"Are you deaf or mute?"

Still Kevlin remained frozen.

"I suppose you wish payment for your insignificant contribution to the betterment of man?"

Kevlin tried to shake his head no, but even that ability seemed to have left him.

Grimwell sneered at him. "Here, take this, then."

Kevlin suddenly found himself able to move once again, and he caught the two silver coins Grimwell tossed to him. The wizard moved past and never looked back. Kevlin was left to find his own way out of the keep.

The coins clinked in his palm, and he retreated as fast as he could lead a blindfolded Hera.

Thorakis the Builder waited near the fire, resting in his wheeled chair. Pages waited behind him, on either side, ready to satisfy any need their patron might have. Thorakis looked older than his years would warrant, and his hands trembled when he pointed. His voice, though, remained strong and clear. "Take me to Grimwell."

The pages moved quickly but smoothly, certain not to jar the ailing genius. They had come to him with their families after the Herald War, seeking food, shelter, and protection from bandits and raiders. Though the Zjhon had ruled the Greatland in an unforgiving manner, they had at least ruled. Their downfall had left the Greatland in chaos. Some of the old families had regained their power, but most had been lost. The once safe countryside had become a place of smoke and death. Either page would give his life for Thorakis and do so knowing his family would remain safe.

When they reached Grimwell's study, which more resembled a laboratory, the right-hand page, Yoric, shouldered the heavy wooden door open. He knew better than to knock or announce himself. As the arm of Thorakis, to do so would belittle his patron. Grimwell bent over a basin filled with a murky yet glittering solution. The acrid smell of vinegar charged the air along with a coppery tang. A fortune in the orange metal had been worked into heavy wire. The copper reached from the basin to each of the earthenware jars, making the basin look like the body of a giant spider.

"Wait outside," Grimwell said. Thorakis's eyes narrowed.

The pages moved without a sound and closed the door as they left.

They would wait just far enough away so as not to hear the conversation inside. They knew their place. Others before them hadn't been so wise.

"You'd best be able to explain yourself, *wizard.*"

Grimwell finally looked up and acknowledged Thorakis. "Yes, m'lord. Of course."

"We've precious little gold left, and I'm told you've taken it along with most of the silver and copper. Where is it? You're not drinking again, are you? I heard you were buying large quantities of wine."

"Spoiled wine, m'lord."

Thorakis harrumphed. "I see what you've done with my copper. Where's my coin?"

Grimwell flushed. "The silver coin is here, sir." After ducking beneath the web of copper wire, he opened his strong box and showed Thorakis the silver coins, knowing his lord was very proud of the casting that bore his likeness. Destroying or defacing his likeness was listed among the highest crimes and was enough to land a person in the hammer mill.

"Where is my gold?" Thorakis asked, leaning forward with an unpleasant gleam in his eye.

"It's not . . . I mean, I don't have—" The look on Thorakis's face made him reconsider his words. "I've had our most trusted men grind the gold coins to powder."

Thorakis went rigid and his face flushed.

"Please, m'lord—" Grimwell stopped when his door rang with a loud knock, which could only be his men. The wizard breathed a mighty sigh of relief when the men carried in the sacks of gold powder. "You asked me to find a way to bring in more gold, m'lord. Please allow me to demonstrate." Grimwell knew the next few moments would bring him either glory or death; there would be no in between. Holding his breath, he carefully poured gold powder into the basin, trying not to react to Thorakis's sharp hiss. After agitating the solution, he pulled a silver coin from his pocket and connected it to a length of copper that had a notch in its end specifically designed to hold a coin by its edge. With trembling hands, he lowered the coin into the solution and prayed Istra and Vestra would not let him down.

Thorakis leaned forward, almost sitting on the edge of his rolling throne, and his eyes went wide as the silver coin began to gradually change from silver to gold. Thorakis did something he rarely did: he smiled. "You continue to impress me, Grimwell. I fear I may one day have to have you pulped for your insolence, but for today, you are forgiven."

Grimwell smiled but held his silence, savoring his victory for what it was, despite the threat.

"What of our ambassadors? Have they properly greeted the old families?"

Grimwell winced. "Some have, m'lord. Others may have as well, but I am awaiting word of their success. I assure you, m'lord, we'll achieve your will. The extra gold will ensure our success as I can now send additional ambassadors."

"Do not gloat, *wizard*."

"Forgive me, m'lord."

"Yoric!" Thorakis barked, and his pages soon wheeled him from the room.

Grimwell smiled.

CHAPTER FOUR

Fate is most unkind to those who fail to prepare for the worst of circumstances.

— Edmoor Reese, scribe

Anxious tension polluted the air around Brother Vaughn. His ability to sense what others were feeling was normally something he considered a gift, but when in a crowd, it could become overwhelming. Without the ability to filter out the feelings of others, he often found himself taking on the emotions projected at him. Thus, he found himself excited yet skeptical and cautious. The people would not turn down an opportunity for revelry, but no one seemed convinced that an impromptu party for the dragons could be as simple and innocent as Mirta and the others portrayed. The people of Upperton and Lowerton and those who lived in the keep all knew that dragon ore provided most of Catrin's wealth, and the thought of Kyrien bringing her more dragon ore seemed to supply enough motivation to stifle any uncomfortable lines of questioning.

Catrin's absence from the festivities was certainly not easily explained, yet no one asked. Most were content to let the Herald of Istra do whatever it was she did without the need for details. She was an enigma and probably best left that way.

The sound of a man clearing his throat brought Brother Vaughn out of his contemplation. "I'm sorry to disturb you, Brother Vaughn, but I've come to ask something of you," Cattleman Gerard said.

The timbre of his voice made Brother Vaughn look up. The man's anxiety drowned out that of the crowd. Brother Vaughn's eyes drifted lower, and his breath caught in his throat. Staring up at him was a girl as slight as the wind, pale and thin, with piercing, black eyes that spoke of more wisdom that her wispy form would belie.

"Does her father know she's here?" Brother Vaughn asked, already knowing the answer was no. This girl was Trinda Hollis, daughter of the man who'd murdered Catrin's mother and aunt and who had tried to kill Catrin and her father. She was a puzzle, to be sure. Though she was not responsible for any of it, her safety had been the motivating factor behind the crimes. The Kytes, the age-old enemy of Catrin's mother's family, had tortured Trinda to coerce Baker Hollis to poison the Volkers. The Volkers had somehow made peace with the Kytes and found forgiveness for Baker Hollis, but his name was never spoken within Dragonhold, and the sight of Trinda could bring only pain. "This could start a war," Brother Vaughn whispered. "You know that, don't you?"

"I do," Cattleman Gerard replied, his eyes downcast. "But I cannot turn away a child who's come to me for help. I just can't." Tears ran down the big man's cheeks, and Brother Vaughn could not help but respect the man's heart, even if he seriously questioned his judgment.

Though of an age with Catrin, Trinda was tiny and her manner childlike. Perhaps the trauma of her childhood had stunted her development, he thought. Trinda waited patiently, but when Brother Vaughn met her eyes, he was captivated. She radiated calm, yet there was a desperate plea in her eyes, one that pulled at every thread of his humanity. In her hands she gripped a folded parchment. She held it out to him.

My little girl needs help. Do not blame her for my crimes. Be kind to her, please.

No name, no seal, nothing that could directly link the note to Baker Hollis. Brother Vaughn refolded the parchment and handed it back, trying not to meet Trinda's eyes. "For now, take her to the Watering Hole. I'll see what I can do," his lips said, but his eyes told Cattleman Gerard that he was not at all optimistic.

At that moment, Mirta climbed atop a makeshift stage. The crowd grew quiet.

"Thank you to all of you for coming to honor our friend Kyrien, dragon to the Lady Catrin, he who has provided for all of us. Tonight we thank him or his service and we call for him to come back to us—with dragon ore or without. He is what is most precious to us, and I'm hoping you will help me express that to him through our thoughts and songs."

The crowd responded with what seemed almost genuine enthusiasm, though Brother Vaughn still sensed an undercurrent of trepidation. Yet when he looked down at Trinda, he felt a sudden and overwhelming sense of hope. Her eyes glistened and she looked as if she might actually smile.

"You want to help thank Kyrien?" Brother Vaughn asked, but Trinda just shook her head. Brother Vaughn thought for a moment. "You want to help ask Kyrien to come here?" This brought the most enthusiasm from Trinda that either man had ever seen. She nodded briskly, tears streaming down her face. Her little hands trembled, and Brother Vaughn could now better understand Cattleman Gerard's dilemma. He took her tiny hand in his and walked her over to where Mirta stood.

Mirta saw him coming and cast him a quizzical glance but continued as she had been. "I know we don't have any songs to sing specifically for Kyrien, but harvest songs are full of gratitude, so I thought we could start out by singing "The Piemaker's Dirge." Do you all know that one?" Enough people in the crowd clapped their hands that Mirta began to sing. Her voice shook with emotion, very clear as she started the song alone. Then slowly the crowd began to join in. Brother Vaughn cringed at the sound and thought the song might better serve to chase things away. He instantly thought less of himself for even thinking it and added his steady baritone to the mix.

Trinda pulled free from his grip and ran to Mirta, pulling on her skirts and shaking her head. Mirta looked down in surprise and stopped singing. The crowd trailed off, all eyes resting on Trinda. She took Mirta's hand and quite simply began to sing. Her voice was truly magical; it cast even the birds into silence and held those who heard it within her spell. Mirta, joined in, somehow knowing where the simple tune would go next, playing near-perfect harmony to Trinda. A woman in the crowd stepped forward and began to sing along, as the melody repeated and became recognizable.

Brother Vaughn held his breath as Trinda demonstrated more ability and control than any student of the academy had shown since its inception. A dim light shone around her and Mirta, and the crowd swayed in unison, following her movements like a field of grain blown by the wind. Time seemed to shift and move. Brother Vaughn didn't know how long they had been singing, though it seemed longer than he could reconcile. When he spotted something unbelievable soaring through the valley, his heart nearly stopped.

Frozen in place, Brother Vaughn was entranced by the gorgeous beast that winged its way through the valley toward the awaiting crowd, yet it filled him with fear. This beast looked nothing like Kyrien, and its gaze made Brother Vaughn feel more like prey than an ally.

Trinda seemed lost in a trance, and her voice alone continued to sing. The rest were trying to decide if they were excited or terrified; soon most opted for the latter. The glistening black dragon shone blue for an instant as it turned into the sun, but then it trimmed its wings and dived straight for Trinda. Like an arrow, it sliced the air.

Movement surged through the crowd as one person leaped, flipped, and twisted her way to where Trinda sang. In the instant before the dragon would take her, Kendra shoved Trinda to the side. Brother Vaughn's heart jumped into his throat as the fearsome dragon grabbed Kendra in its claws. With three flaps of its mighty wings, it sent everyone below sprawling and thrust itself higher into the air. Kendra appeared to be trying to wriggle free, but the great beast soared up to the top of the ridgeline. Once over the ridge, it could disappear into the Chinawpa Valley or even into the Arghast Desert. Brother Vaughn knew the girl would be lost.

The crowd regained its feet and froze, watching the dragon fly away. Then the people gave a collective gasp as another, larger dragon slammed into the first, sending Kendra tumbling out onto the rocky ridgeline. She landed hard and began to roll, loose bits of rock sliding around her. It looked as if she would be tossed over a steep cliff, but she slammed into a scraggly tree that held her fast.

Dark shadows raced along the valley, and those brave enough to look up became awash in primal fear. At least a dozen feral dragons had heard Trinda's call, and now they seemed to be looking for a free meal. Screams filled the air as people tried to find shelter, but the valley floor was all too vulnerable. The wooden buildings there were no match for the might of a full-grown dragon, and the steep climb to the main entrance of Dragonhold would leave them exposed for far too long.

Swallowing hard, Brother Vaughn realized there was no place safe to hide. Once again, he looked up and saw something his mind had difficulty grasping. From the top of the ridgeline, men were jumping onto the backs of dragons as they passed. Convinced he was losing his mind, Brother Vaughn did what he could to shepherd people into what little shelter could be found. The modest protection of the buildings was far better than standing on open ground, waiting to be eaten.

With Trinda over his shoulder, Brother Vaughn ran as fast as he could, the dragon's breath, hot, moist, and smelling of death, buffeted him from behind. Ahead the doors of the Watering Hole stood open. Miss Helen stood within, ready to pull the heavy doors shut, for all the good it would do them. He could see her screaming but heard no words. He could feel Trinda shifting and stretching, as if she were reaching out to the dragon instead of fleeing from it. It was the girl the dragon wanted, this Brother Vaughn knew, but he would not allow her to be sacrificed. Thus, he risked himself and everyone within the Watering Hole in an attempt to save her. The waiting inn seemed impossibly far away, and dust and debris flew around them. Brother Vaughn could feel the changes in air pressure as the leviathan approached, and he knew he was not going to be fast enough.

After a life of dreaming about giant, flying creatures, Brother Vaughn now knew just how terrifying such creatures could be. The deadly strike did not come, and Brother Vaughn fell into the Watering Hole, into waiting arms that supported and somehow turned him around just in time to see the door shut. Through the ever-narrowing gap, he saw that the dragon, which had been pursuing him, was also busy contending with one of the Arghast. The man stood atop the root of the beast's neck, which seemed to be the one spot where neither claws nor fangs could reach. In the last instant before the door closed, the dragon slammed itself against the canyon wall, trying to crush its unwanted rider.

Miss Helen pulled Trinda away from him and tended to her scrapes and bruises. Brother Vaughn and everyone else in the inn did their best to keep quiet. Constructed from multiple sections of a greatoak, the Watering Hole could withstand high winds and tremors, but a hungry flight of dragons might be too much for it. Cries rang out as the common room suddenly lurched sideways. Driven to his knees by the impact, Brother Vaughn noted that the dragons did not need to get them out to kill them; just turning the building upside down and giving it a shake would do the job just fine. Bowls, mugs, and even knives flew from shelves and cupboards as the Watering Hole shook. The highly polished bar cracked with an ear-crushing snap. It seemed the end was near.

Within the humble hall he called home, Chase paced the floor, biting his lip and trying to come up with a plan. Without a plan, his efforts felt fragmented and ineffectual. If he could only set his mind on some obtainable goal, he would be free to commit himself to that effort, but in the challenges they currently faced, he was powerless. He could do nothing to bring Catrin and Prios back, and it seemed he could not even find his own nephew within the hold. If anything happened to Sinjin . . .

"Sir!" came a shout in the hall, and Chase turned sharply, recognizing the voice of his second in command, Morif. The old veteran could address Chase on equal terms, but he seemed to pride himself on knowing his place in the chain of command. What worried Chase was a hint of panic in Morif's voice, which Chase had never heard before. "We found him, sir. Come quick. It's not good sir. Not good."

"Where?" Chase barked as he rushed from the room.

"Infirmary," Morif replied, and Chase took off at a run. This couldn't be happening.

Chase charged through the halls, a pain in his chest making it difficult to breathe. He stood to lose almost everything that was important to him. Catrin and Prios lay helpless, slowly dying, and now Sinjin. Suppressed rage made his face twitch, and he silently vowed to find whoever was responsible and wring the life from him or her with his bare hands. As he approached the infirmary, he heard a haunting melody echoing through the hold, distant yet clear. It pulled at him, but he shrugged it off and ran. Morif matched his pace; his one eye focused on the sloping hall ahead. Nothing was certain these days, and the seasoned warrior seemed ready to face anything, even the wrath of Millie. Though he was no longer charged with guarding her, everyone knew it was a position he could not fully relinquish.

"All of you, get out of here this instant!" came Millie's voice from within, and Chase had to wait for a line of people to stream out before he could force his way in. Millie cast him a glaring look that softened when she saw who it was. "It's not as bad as it looks. He's got a gash on his head, and it's a bleeder. I'll get him cleaned up and some fluids in him, and he'll be good as new."

Sinjin lay still on the feather-stuffed mattress, his eyes open just slightly. The bluish pallor to his skin made him look already dead. Only the steady rise and fall of his chest gave Chase any reassurance.

"General Chase, sir!" came a shout in the hall. "I must find General Chase. It's urgent!"

"Easy there, young man, breathe," Chase called into the hall. "It's all right. I'm here and I know Sinjin has been found. You may return to your duties." Chase turned back to watch Sinjin breathe.

"I'm sorry, sir," the young guard said, still breathing heavily and clearly uncomfortable with the position in which he found himself. "There is another problem, sir. The tribes of Arghast have gathered near the entrance to the God's Eye and they want to speak to Lady Catrin."

"What?"

The young guard looked as if he might faint. Chase stood silently for a moment, trying to decide what to do. The Arghast were renowned for their horsemanship and their fiercely insular culture. Relations between Catrin and the Arghast were generally good, despite the fact that their very nature made the tribes volatile and unpredictable.

Morif spoke softly, "Catrin generally offers them water, wine, and meat, sir."

"Get someone working on it."

"Yes, sir," Morif said, offering the wink of a one-eyed man that unnerved most but assured Chase that the job would be done properly.

With a last glance at those who meant the most to him, Chase wondered if any of them would ever be returned to him. With nothing more he could do, he left them in Millie's capable hands. For a moment he wondered where Mirta was since she was almost always near the infirmary, but then he heard the melody from outside again, and he recalled the party she was holding for the dragons. As insane as it seemed, he wished her luck. Maybe Kyrien really could help Catrin and Prios. That thought froze in his blood as the haunting melody shifted and was suddenly drowned out by cheers, which almost instantly turned to screams.

Chase ran.

When he reached the front entrance of Dragonhold, he gazed into the valley below, horrified by what he saw. Dragons. Not the color-changing regent dragons that had befriended Catrin, but those that seemed carved from pure darkness. Feral dragons, Chase realized, having heard the ancient descriptions. Verdant dragons had been said to be the largest and most plentiful during the last age of power; feral dragons, the most dangerous; and regent dragons, the most rare. As Chase watched, a man dressed in Arghast garb soared through the air and landed on top of a dragon that was swooping down on the still milling crowd. To his amazement, the man held on and even managed to secure a leather line around the beast's head. Soon, though, that dragon flew beyond Chase's view. Another took its place and soared straight for Chase, who took a few steps back then turned and ran. "We're under attack!" he yelled as the hold's wooden fortifications exploded.

Halmsa of the Wind clan clenched his teeth and held on as best he could, his clan's namesake buffeting him. The dragon beneath him certainly knew he was there and had been trying to dislodge him for some time, but Halmsa was strong and fast and clever. Even when the beast had slammed itself into the canyon wall, he'd been quick enough to slide around to the underside of the dragon's neck, just barely avoiding being crushed. Other dragons had nearly knocked him free as well. It didn't seem as if they were trying to protect their brethren. The beasts were just adept at flying within very close proximity to one another, at times glancing off each other or rubbing together in midair, yet they managed to do it without knocking themselves from the sky.

The sensation of flying overwhelmed Halmsa's senses for a time, and he simply enjoyed it. An instant later, the dragon dived steeply and aimed for a patch of tall trees. Branches rushed toward Halmsa at impossible speed, the first struck him like thunder. His world nearly went black, but he willed himself to stay conscious. The dragon, now desperate to be rid of him, had taken too great a risk and misjudged the trees. Halmsa held on to his leather lines alone, having lost his footing, and he was tossed wildly as the mighty feral dragon slammed into the treetops.

Despite the intense desire to fly once again, Halmsa climbed down, knowing this dragon would fly no more. Blood warmed his scalp and caked around his ear, but Halmsa's grin was huge. He'd flown a dragon!

His people had waited many lifetimes for this day, and he was among the first. Pride filled his chest and motivated Halmsa more than ever. There was much work to be done, but the first step had been taken. Riding a dragon was not at all like riding a horse, and they all had quite a lot to learn.

Limping and bleeding, he climbed along the ridge, watching the skies. The dying dragon thrashed in the trees, crying out its anguish. Halmsa fled but stopped as the skies above him filled with writhing black shapes dancing through the clouds. Like a practiced dance, they dived in near unison. Halmsa felt his courage tested as the dragons fell on their own, ending the dragon's suffering. Feeling exposed and vulnerable, he limped along the crest of the ridgeline toward the remains of Dragonhold's front entrance. He could see the wooden stairs swinging away from their moorings; the mass of people seeking refuge within the hold had no choice but to climb through the shattered timbers to reach the safety of solid stone.

Flames and dark smoke leaped from makeshift torches attached to metal-tipped spears. Guards stood at intervals on the stairs, guarding the line of refugees from the dragons, which patrolled the skies, waiting for a chance to grab an easy meal. Chase watched as Martik and his crew worked to repair the fortifications and entryway that had been reduced to splinters in a single devastating strike. In one day, the world had changed, and Chase knew they were not ready. *Boil Nat Dersinger and his visions.* Chase knew that Nat's visions couldn't have actually caused these events, but he needed to aim his anger and frustration somewhere. The dragons were wild creatures, and he could not expect them to show kindness or listen to reason. How could he fight such an enemy when so grossly overmatched? *Hide.* The thought made him sick, but the process was already under way.

He also knew that he could not blame Trinda for calling the dragons to them, though that hadn't stopped others in the hold from casting curses at the girl. How could he blame them; the girl's father had tried to kill Catrin when she was but a babe and had succeeded in killing Catrin's mother and Chase's mother. Chase was somewhat surprised that when he saw her, he'd felt no malice or revulsion. She still looked like a child, and her deep-set eyes contained the sadness of ages. Truly this girl deserved respite.

"She'll stay with us," Mirta had insisted, and Chase was grateful for it. Mirta had a heart full of kindness, and not for the first time, Chase congratulated Brother Vaughn on landing the ideal wife for him.

The great hall now looked more like a shantytown as people did what they could to claim their own space. The disorder seemed out of place amid the towering grace of the pillars and the worn but nonetheless mighty bas-reliefs.

"Out of my way, fool!" came Miss Mariss's voice across the great hall, cutting through the rising din.

Chase turned to see her marching directly toward him. He sighed.

"This whelp is trying to tell me that I can't take the grain and salt I'll need to feed all these people. It's going to take a mountain of food and an army in the kitchens to keep up with so many. The Herald was right all along, may her name be blessed! Now you listen to me—"

Chase raised a hand to stave off the rest of the tongue-lashing. "I hear you, Miss Mariss. I do. My men have standing orders, and you're going to have to work with them on this. I haven't yet had the chance to brief everyone on these new circumstances, and they are just trying to do their jobs."

"Do I look like I would steal all of our grain?"

"I know, I know." He turned to a soldier standing off to his right. "Jerrick, please allow Miss Mariss access to any supplies she needs. Get me an inventory of all our stores, and start working on a rationing plan that will stretch what we have for at least a year."

The young man looked up with fear and anxiety in his eyes.

"It's just a precaution. Don't panic and don't get everyone else any more wound up than they already are. Everything is going to be fine."

As if to disprove his words, shouts and screams rose outside, and Chase turned in time to see a huge black shape blot out the entranceway. The guards' battle cry filled the air, followed by cries of pure anguish.

"Go!" Chase said as the entering mass of refugees surged ahead, driven by fear. It was everything Chase's men could do to keep anyone from being trampled. Miss Mariss and Jerrick retreated, now fully aware that their squabble was the least of Chase's concerns. It was impossible for him to cut through the throng, and all he could do was listen to the cries of men and dragon.

"They got one!" a woman shouted as she entered. "The guards stuck one of them demons, and they brought it down, they did!"

"How many are there?" someone asked.

"Too many," the woman said. "Too boilin' many."

Chase gathered all the guards nearby and sent runners to get more. The men donned leather armor and readied every spear and pole in the hold. Most dipped the tips of their weapons in pitch and lit them from nearby fire pots.

"To one side!" Chase barked as he led his men out onto the wooden bridge and stairs, which swayed under the weight, the damage from the first attack still nowhere near fixed. The makeshift repairs that still held were strained, and it seemed that the entire staircase could collapse at any moment. Below, dozens of people still climbed, desperately trying to reach the safety of stone. Only two guards could be seen, and those were unable to prevent the dragons from plucking people from the stairs before turning on a wingtip and soaring away. The cries of the dying now echoed through the valley.

Abandoning caution, Chase charged down the stairs and was almost immediately engaged by a swooping dragon. Claws extended, it dived in close, reaching for a young man who was helping an old woman climb. Chase nearly went over the railing as he lashed out with his spear, which now seemed far too heavy and short. Still, the dragon shied away from the flames and turned his attention to Chase. When it struck, Chase was ready and jabbed the point of his spear at the beast's eye. Though he didn't manage to blind it, he did smear pitch around the dragon's eye, and it screamed as it flew back toward the coast.

Two more dragons were wounded, and too many people were lost before darkness obscured the battlefield. With the setting of the sun, the dragons retreated, and Chase watched them go, trying to figure out where they were going, but the beasts scattered, melting into the darkening skies. He and his men retreated, helping the wounded and the elderly finish the climb.

When everyone was finally inside, Chase ordered the shattered fortifications rebuilt. "Don't bother trying to repair the gates. Just fill that hole as best you can. For now, we just need to keep everything out."

Exhausted, Chase dropped to the floor. His arms ached from hours of overextended spear thrusts, and his stomach muscles felt as if they were all torn. Even breathing had become difficult, and he allowed himself to rest. Where were Catrin and Prios when he needed them most? he asked himself. Many of those Chase turned to for advice were gone. Benjin and Fasha had sailed with his father and uncle some six years back, their only guide a madman's map, and no one knew when or if they would return.

Just as the largest timbers were being rolled into place, there came shouts from outside. Chase turned to look as Mirta charged forward. A man in bloodied desert garb stumbled into the great hall, in his arms, Kendra. Men stepped forward to aid him, but he shouldered away their efforts. Mirta spoke to him in soothing tones, and when he reached a place where some blankets had been stacked, he laid her down.

"Help her," he said, his accent thick.

Mirta looked Kendra over, and her apprentice Loriana approached the Arghast, a damp cloth in her hand. He stepped back at first, but Loriana grabbed him by the arm and looked him in the eye. She guided him to the floor and tended his wounds. Slowly he relaxed.

"Catrin," he said with fervor.

"First we must get your wounds clean," Loriana said in a calm and even tone.

"Need Catrin," he urged, but as Loriana tended his wounds, he slowly eased back and fell to sleep. Loriana tensed when she heard him mutter in his sleep, "She will teach us to fly."

CHAPTER FIVE

Even the most supple rose must sometimes face the frost.
— Hadda Mick, farmer

Sinjin had never realized that light could hurt so badly; it felt as if it were trying to burrow its way into his brain. His vision swam until he took a deep breath, then he slowly began to see. His ears, however, worked just fine.

"You tell me this instant what happened to you!"

Millie's voice cut into Sinjin's consciousness like an axe, and it took him a moment before he could respond. "I don't know. I don't remember."

"What's the last thing you remember?" she asked, no less intent on getting an answer.

"Um . . . I . . . uh . . ." Sinjin stammered, ashamed that the last thing he remembered was hiding in an alcove and eavesdropping. "I don't know."

"How can you not know?" Millie asked, her glare suspicious. "What's your name?"

"Sinjin Volker," he responded, and he heard someone snort in derision.

"And what's my name, then?"

"Why, you're Millicent, former maid to the Lady Mangst and current keeper of the aforementioned Sinjin Volker."

"Your memory and attitude appear whole. If only you could tell me what you were doing when you sustained this injury!" Not waiting to see if he would say any more, Millie walked away, seemingly having trouble keeping from throttling Sinjin.

"This is all your fault," he heard Kendra say, and he almost had the sense to duck before her fist landed on his cheekbone.

"Kendra! Never hit anyone in the infirmary! How could you?" Khenna said, her mouth agape.

"It's all his fault."

"Are you all right, Sinjin?" Khenna asked.

Sinjin just moaned and levered himself out of the cot.

"Look at that eye!" came another familiar voice, and Sinjin's heart felt a bit lighter as he turned to see Durin grinning back at him.

"It sure is good to see you," Sinjin said.

"You look worse than I do now but not as bad as Kendra; she looks *terrible*. I'm betting most of those cuts and scrapes are going to leave scars. Hideous."

"If you two boys feel well enough to pick on this poor girl while she's a-healin'," Mirta quipped, "then you just get your butts out of here. There are more sick and wounded in this place than we have beds for. And go easy for once, the both of you! I don't want to see you back here 'cept for visitin'. Now git!"

Sinjin narrowly avoided Kendra as he stood to leave, his legs only vaguely responding to his commands, which he supposed were now more like requests. Durin was not so lucky or so quick, and the remainder of her salted fish slapped him in the side of the head.

"You just wait . . ." they heard Kendra say as they left.

"Things are a mess," Sinjin said once they were out of the infirmary and out of Kendra's range.

"You don't know the half of it. The dragons attacked while you were out."

Sinjin nearly choked and could find no words to respond.

"The Arghast showed up just before the dragons attacked, and now we know that they came looking for your mom because the dragons had been tormenting them."

"Why are the dragons attacking? Is it Kyrien?"

"No, no," Durin said. "It's not Kyrien. These dragons are nothing like him. They're as black as night and shiny, like a snake, and they're meaner than a cornered bear."

"And the Arghast want my mom to make the dragons go away?"

"Nope. Guess again. Get this: they want your mom to teach them how to catch and tame the dragons so they can fly."

"Now you're just telling tales," Sinjin said. He turned his head as he noticed a low din slowly growing louder.

"Am not. You'll see. Oh, and those people who shot me weren't assassins. Morif told Millie that if they had been trying to kill you, I'd be dead. What do you think of that?"

Just then they walked into the great hall, and Sinjin stopped, dumbfounded by what he saw and heard. A tent village had sprung up in the hall, and it seemed everyone had something to say at the same time. The noise was difficult to describe, and the great hall's acoustics only added to the effect.

"Told you."

Sinjin grew more anxious with every step, suddenly feeling cramped and crowded, wondering if anyone among the gathered masses wanted him dead. For once, seeing Morif shadowing him and Durin did not anger him. He felt safer knowing Morif was about. He'd taught Sinjin much of what he knew about fighting and about defending himself.

Fighting was not one of Sinjin's strong points, which had been proven on just about every one of his encounters with Kendra.

"No one goes out in the daylight now," Durin added as if it were exciting news. "We have to harvest at night. Brother Vaughn says that given ample food supply, the dragons will multiply. He said something about their gentryfication period being short, and that meant there could be a lot more dragons by spring."

"Gestation period," Sinjin said.

"Whatever. The point is that what your mom said was gonna happen actually happened, and now all these people are stuck in here. And let me tell you, stay away from the kitchens if you can. Sheesh, you'd think the world had already come to its end. It's like a kicked anthill down there, and Miss Mariss is in rare form. Last time I went down there for a snack, I came back soaked and covered in flour, and I can't do as much as I used to. That nearly dying stuff takes it out of you."

"I suppose that rules out some food, then," Sinjin said, his hand on his aching stomach.

"Are you kidding? Sometimes you just have to take your chances, and I need food," Durin said. Besides, with the old man following us, it's not like we can hide."

Sinjin noticed a tremble in his friend's hands that had never been there before. Guilt stabbed at him. *"All this is your fault,"* echoed in his mind. "Do you think my parents will live? I mean, do you think they will come back?" Sinjin tried to keep the hitch from his voice, but it betrayed him, as did the tears that gathered in his eyes.

"Of course they'll come back. Soon. I promise."

Sinjin wished Durin wouldn't make promises he couldn't keep.

"This is not a good place for you boys to be spendin' time. How 'bout we head to the kitchens and get some food? I'll keep Miss Mariss occupied while you make your escape." Sinjin looked up at Morif in surprise.

The weathered warrior smiled back. "I may be missing one eye, but my ears work just fine for an old man."

Durin winced. "Uh. Sorry."

Morif gave him a light smack on the back of the head. "Let's go."

What Durin had said about the kitchens was not as much of an exaggeration as Sinjin had thought, and the two ducked into the guard hall while Morif shouldered his way into the kitchens. The guard hall was eerily quiet; normally one of the more boisterous rooms in the hold, it stood nearly empty. Never before had so many guards been needed on duty at one time.

Durin and Sinjin sat at one of the long tables, feeling silly with so much table all to themselves. Morif returned sooner than either of them would have thought possible given the mass of people around the kitchens, but Sinjin supposed if there was anyone who could command the attention of so many, it was Morif. The man seemed to be afraid of nothing, and Sinjin had always looked up to him. He'd also gotten to see the other side of Morif—the side that loved to play pranks and to make Millie's face turn red.

"This is the best I could do at the moment," Morif said as he sat down across from them. Before him was a pile of food that would have lasted Sinjin three days. "Too bad there wasn't enough for you two."

Durin and Sinjin both laughed and grabbed some food. It was good to have his friend back, and Sinjin drew strength from that, but chilling fears still haunted him.

"There are a whole lot of people trying to figure out how to best help your mom and dad," Morif said, perhaps reading Sinjin's mind or perhaps he'd simply overheard the question earlier. "I think they'll be all right. When your mom traveled astrally from Ohmahold, she was gone for at least twice as long as your parents have been gone for. Worrying won't do you or them any good, so try to stay positive. A little work always helps keep my mind from worry, and Miss Mariss did say something about needing more flour."

Durin rolled his eyes.

Catrin's spirit floated in the half light, drifting on the breeze, feeling so weary. All she wanted to do was rest. Nearby, Prios lacked substance, becoming diffuse and wavering like smoke in the wind. Only the idea of losing him kept Catrin from giving up and letting herself become part of the oneness once again. She knew that, while she may have been created, she could not be destroyed; she could only change form. The need to protect Prios became impossible to ignore, and she called out for him. He did not respond immediately, and she willed herself closer, yelling his name. His form wavered and looked as if he would be whisked away and dissolved until that which was Prios was no longer whole.

"Prios! Wait! Don't go!" Catrin willed the words to him.

Slowly he gathered himself. Then he turned to her and smiled. "Oh. There you are. I've been looking for you."

If Catrin could have cried, she would have, but in this formless state, all she could do was hurt with no tears to release the pain. Both knew they were dying, yet neither of them could do anything to prevent it. Barred from returning to their bodies by what seemed a sea of dark shadows, Catrin and Prios had retreated to a place that was, for her, familiar. The place had once been her home before she and her family had been driven north. It was not to the hearth she went but instead to the place where she had spent most of her time: the barn. This place constantly reminded her of who and what she was, and this was perhaps the only thing that had saved them thus far. Prios seemed unable to anchor himself as firmly, and Catrin exhausted herself watching over him, protecting him, and finding him when he searched for her.

"I think we should go back," Prios said, and Catrin noticed once again that his energetic form was whole and his spirit spoke to her with its lips and mouth. It had been disconcerting at first since her husband normally spoke only in her mind. The loss of his tongue at the hands of Archmaster Belegra had prevented normal speech. "We'll die if we stay here."

"We've tried," Catrin said. "They are out there, waiting to tear us apart. I can feel them. I've nothing left to fight them with. If we leave, we die." Though the air reeked of power, her spirit was weak and insubstantial. Outside waited darkness that seemed to feed on the light of the many comets that now crowded the skies. It frightened her how quickly her world had changed.

"I could go out alone and lead them away," Prios said. "Maybe then you could get back. The world needs you. Sinjin needs you."

"The world and Sinjin need us both."

Weariness once again set in, just the act of talking depleting what little willpower Catrin still possessed. She turned back to Prios, expecting him to say something, but his form was fading, his eyes fixed on a point far away, and Catrin once again doubted either of them would survive.

Clouds hung low in the sky, and the light of a dozen herald globes lit the way as Chase and his men escorted farmers to their lands. The livestock were gone, much of Lowerton destroyed, but Chase was determined to get all the food, oil, salt, spices, and other goods they could into the hold. In the fortnight since the dragons had arrived, the hold's stores dwindled far too rapidly. Crops continued to ripen under the eyes of the dragons during the day, and it seemed one male in particular had claimed this area as his territory. The people called him Reaver. Venturing out in the daylight meant risking being eaten.

Bats flew overhead, attracted by the moths that gathered around the herald globes. Chase and his men were armed with spears, but it was truly little defense against a dragon attack. Only the darkness kept the monsters at bay. Many within Dragonhold would no longer use the hold's name, and Chase felt guilty for having come up with the name in the first place, as it now seemed grossly inappropriate. He couldn't have known things would work out this way, but that didn't stop him from tormenting himself about it.

Climbing along the terraces that lined the valley was treacherous in daylight, and the group moved slowly. A yawn slipped past Chase's defenses; the guards on duty pretended not to notice. Double shifts had become the norm, and the number of people caught sleeping on duty was embarrassing, but they were all overtaxed and trying to adjust. This new life they lived was far less forgiving than what they had known for most of their lives, and the people of the Godfist were a hearty folk who knew their share of hard times. What lay ahead looked grim, and everyone knew it. Even Master Edling seemed to see the need for unity, in his own haughty way. Messengers had been arriving nightly since the dragons first arrived, requesting refuge for a large number of citizens from south of the Wall. Chase knew it was a game of resources; that much he had learned from the Zjhon invasion, if nothing else. Every additional body in the hold was an additional body to feed.

"Knowing Edling," Morif had said to Chase, "he'll send us every person with a sniffle, cough, or rash in hopes that disease will wipe us out for him. Then he can just take Dragonhold for himself. He seems already to think it belongs to him." All his talk about Dragonhold belonging to the people of the Godfist sickened him.

Such cold realizations made Chase feel ill. These were his countrymen, in many cases people he grew up with or attended lessons with, and he felt as if he were abandoning them. In truth, he knew the Masterhouse could hold a large number of people, as could the cold caves. What he didn't know was how well or poorly the Masterhouse and cold caves had been restocked with supplies after the siege. If Master Edling and the council had been lax in their planning, then turning people away could be sentencing them to starvation. Of course, accepting too many could assign the same fate. Chase sighed.

The group had moved on, and he was no longer at his post. He hurried to catch up, and again the other guards pretended not to notice. Chase was their leader, their strength, and they all knew that double shifts for them meant triple shifts for him. Sleep had become something grabbed in the moments between crises, and tonight was little more than shepherding farmers with no signs of any threat. For Chase, it was an opportunity to survey the land and crops for himself, and if nothing else, escape from within that oppressive rock for a time. He'd never known himself to fear confinement, but living beneath a mountain of rock weighed upon his soul, and he longed for the freedom he'd once had.

Ahead, the terrace walls had been damaged, and great care was required to climb past the broken section. The earthen works looked as if they might slide into the valley under the group's weight, but they held. Beyond lay a section of ripe corn, essentially cut off by the damage on one end and a sheer face on the other. Chase felt trapped with the treacherous section as their only means of escape. He cursed himself for a coward, and when the clouds parted, he felt a bit better. At least with the light of the near-full moon and the comets, the trek back would be less of an issue. The herald globes provided consistent light, but they cast shadows, making climbing dangerous.

As a strong wind drifted down from the north, Chase looked to the skies. Dozens of comets cast their twinkling light across the sky, blotting out the stars so only the moon and comets could be seen. It was a strange sight to behold. For most of his life, in fact for thousands of years, there had been no comets in the skies. The prophecies had said they would come, and so they had. They also said Catrin would destroy the Zjhon and, in a way, she had, but what the prophecies said would come next made Chase quail. He had hoped it all to be fantasy, but the situation just kept getting worse with no signs things would improve any time soon. Perhaps he needed to accept the fact that it would get far worse before it got better—far worse indeed.

The farmers had gotten ahead of him again, and Chase was about to close the distance when he noticed something strange in the corner of his vision: light, then darkness, then light. As he looked back to the sky, he saw a pattern as something large blotted out the comets, and whatever it was grew larger with every passing moment.

"Get down," Chase said in a half whisper, half shout. A brief moment of pride filled him as the entire crew ducked down without another word. Many met his eyes, and he motioned to the sky, making his hands into the shape of flapping wings, now known as the sign for dragons above. When he turned his attention back to the sky, it was nearly too late. A blast of air pelted them as the massive wingtips came close to taking Chase's head off. He fell to his stomach and waited for the debris-filled wind to pass. When he stood, he braced himself and readied his spear. His men did the same without the need for command, and they waited for the attack to come. Instead what they heard was the snapping of trees and timbers followed by a mighty exhale.

"The beast has gone down on his own, sir. Should we move in and finish it off?"

"Bradley and Simms, with me. The rest of you, wait here."

The sound of labored breathing echoed on the wind, and Chase knew the beast still had the potential to be very dangerous. A wounded dragon could be worlds more deadly than a hungry dragon. More cracks and snaps echoed through the valley as the beast thrashed, accompanied by mighty roars that ended as grunts.

"We might be best off letting this one die on its own, sir. I'm no coward but I can't see risking lives if the beast truly is mortally wounded, sir," Bradley said.

"I agree," Chase said, "but I want to get a closer look at what we're facing."

Shouts from above rang out, and Chase looked up to see Morif leading a group of men down the stairs. There was no mistaking the towering presence that was Morif, and it brought a smile to Chase's face. There might be a bit of gray in the old soldier's beard, but he'd certainly lost none of his warrior spirit. As he rounded a bend and got his first glimpse of the downed dragon, he got an impression of size but little else, as most of the creature was engulfed in shadow. It was the size of a large male, and Chase's knew that even a swipe of its tail could be an end to anyone caught in its path. The valley was still, and the wounded dragon had gone quiet.

"Stay where you are!" Chase shouted across the valley to Morif and his men. "I'm going in for a look. You stay here," he told Bradley and Simms. The men seemed uneasy about his order but didn't argue with him. Descending into the darkness, Chase tried not to think about what it would feel like to be crushed to death. When he reached an area where the terraces ran near a rooftop, he leaped across and shimmied down the side of the building, which had been constructed of whole tree trunks and offered a variety of hand- and footholds. When he peeked around the corner, he found himself face-to-face with a very alive dragon. His heart nearly stopped.

It took his brain a moment to register that this was no feral dragon. The head was wider, and the eyes were more on the sides of the head. Color was hard to guess, but this dragon was clearly not the shiny black of a feral. Those huge eyes, flecked with green and gold, held Chase in thrall, and he knew. It was not like what Catrin had described when Kyrien showed pictures in her mind. Chase simply knew: this was no ordinary dragon; this was Kyrien, Catrin's dragon.

Catrin sat up so suddenly that Millie fell out of the chair she'd been leaning back in.

"By god and goddess!" Millie shouted while gathering her skirts. "Lady Catrin!"

That brought new shouts from down the hall, and Mirta soon charged through the door. Millie poured a mug of water and handed it to Catrin, who had yet to speak or acknowledge anyone else. Her hands trembled but managed to grasp the mug, and after a few moments, Catrin drank. When she looked around, she had eyes for only one: Prios. His still body was the color of ash.

"Back to the viewing chamber," Catrin said in a raw voice that left her coughing.

"You're in no condition to be up and walking," Mirta insisted, but Catrin would not be deterred.

"I'll carry him there myself if I have to," Catrin said as she stood on unsteady feet.

Millie wrapped an arm around her. "Do as she says! Guards! Help Mirta carry Prios back to the viewing chamber."

Men rushed into the chamber and carried both Prios and Catrin down the hall. Another man helped Millie, who was breathing heavily enough that she was having trouble complaining that she didn't need help.

"Get Brother Vaughn," Catrin gasped. "Tell him we need the chanting. He will understand."

"He tried for a time, m'lady, but when it had no effect after days, he finally gave it up," Millie said. "I'm sorry, m'lady."

Weariness washed over Catrin, and she hadn't the energy to respond. Instead, she just concentrated on breathing. Her body felt weak and disconnected, which was not unexpected. She'd been through this before, but this felt worse, as if troughs had been carved deep in her mind, and she doubted she would ever be whole again. For the moment only Prios mattered. Every second increased the chances he would simply fade away.

"Hold him in front of the left portal. I'll stand in front of the right," Catrin said. In truth, she leaned on the two young men flanking her only slightly less than Prios's unconscious form did. This was not entirely a bad thing as she uttered, "Hold on to me tight."

"Don't you dare leave me again!" Millie shouted, but it was too late, Catrin was already gone. Soon the air was filled with rhythmic chanting as Millie wept.

CHAPTER SIX

Faith is belief in the absence of reason.
— Barabas the druid

Demons held the darkness, which surrounded Catrin's spirit and tried to smother her, but she conjured a herald globe that shone brightly, like those that lived only short lives. It was something she had learned while her spirit had been trapped at the farm. The things she was adept at creating in the physical world she could conjure on the astral plane. She used the globe to pierce the darkness and find Prios. She found him cowering in the corner of the barn; somehow he'd made it back. Memories of their battle would forever haunt her. Kyrien had spoken to her, and he had seemed so close, but the darkness was too strong. Weakened by prolonged separation from their bodies, the two had been in no shape for a fight.

Again, the demons closed in around the farm, leaving them to rot inside. Catrin often wondered why they didn't attack, but she supposed it didn't matter; death would come either way.

Prios whimpered and pulled his knees to his chin.

"I'm here. I came back for you," Catrin said, but he did not seem to hear. Rocking back and forth, he seemed to have left this reality for another, and Catrin shouted for him to wake. Still he didn't respond. Movement caught Catrin's attention, and her spirit froze. Slipping in from the blackness came the demons, seemingly no longer willing to wait. The sound of movement behind her alerted her to more danger, and Catrin prepared herself for one final effort. She would carry Prios and simply make a run for it. It seemed like suicide since they would both be defenseless, but Catrin could find no other solution. At least they would die *doing* something.

Reaching down, she gathered Prios's energy, which had weight and mass and was more difficult for her to carry than she had imagined; she would not give up, though. Pulling energy from the night air, she conjured four herald globes, each taxing her but intended to drive the demons back. It didn't work.

Pain seared her soul as Catrin moved past the first of the demons. She spun slowly, awkwardly, and half fell out of the barn and into the night. Demons poured down the valley walls like a flood of evil. Shadow dragons flew overhead, ridden by men with twisted faces. Only Catrin's conjured herald globes cast any light, and she moved like a candle afloat on a raging river. Roiling clouds of deep black obscured the night skies. Her beams of light illuminated the fog, casting rays of color around her and Prios, but the darkness pressed in close, causing the sphere of color to shrink. Claws and slavering jaws broke through the light. Gibbering madness drove searing knives through Catrin's mind and she screamed.

Prios flung his limbs outward, seemingly awakened by Catrin's anguish, and he sent balls of lightning into the demons. Catrin screamed as burning embers branded her soul. With a cry of rage, she rose up and cast flames in a wide arc, knowing it was the last of her reserves. Any more and she would simply dry up and blow away.

Light parted the darkness. Like a knife of fire it raced from the skies and cast demons spinning as it came. Awestruck, Catrin saw Kyrien in the form of flame and lightning. He was even more beautiful than in the physical world, and he proved as deadly as well.

We have done this before.

Catrin wondered if she heard a bit of sarcasm or perhaps even a bit of reprimand in Kyrien's thoughts, which came to her in images and impressions. The fire dragon swooped down low and grabbed Catrin in his mighty claws. Demons leaped and snapped at them, but Catrin cast beams of light, scorching them with their brilliance. She gave herself to the effort, unconsciously drawing energy from Kyrien, and only his urgings moved her toward restraint. In a moment of exhilaration and fear, Kyrien caught the wind and soared higher, aiming at two holes in a rock face. An instant later, he slammed into it with a force that should have left a crater in its wake. Instead, it left Catrin's spirit once again in her body, gasping for air and waiting for the feeling to return to her limbs. Beside her, Prios lay nearly as still as death, his breathing slow and shallow. With the world spinning before her, she said, "Take me to Kyrien."

"But, Catrin," Millie said, so beside herself that she slipped; she almost never used Catrin's name in public. "You must rest and drink and eat and recuperate yourself. You're in no condition to go anywhere. And I'm sorry but Kyrien hasn't been here in years."

"He's here," Catrin said.

"Get more men down here!" Chase shouted as he watched his nightmares spring to life around him. Dark beasts loped down the ridgeline while others howled their way down the center of the valley. These creatures were different from anything he'd ever seen, but when one turned and howled, Chase saw traces of Gholgi, the fabled enemies of mankind he and Catrin had faced on the Firstland. These monsters were even more terrifying. There was intelligence in their piercing eyes accompanied by chilling savagery. They wore crude armor and wielded jagged weapons. Sounds barked among them sounded like a canine language. When a dark shape soared over them, the demons moved almost as one. In tight formation, demons created a mesh with their crude and varying shields. They approached Kyrien, who lay thrashing on the valley floor, his eyes focused on something no one else there could see. Behind the shield bearers came hulking beasts. Chase knew he was helpless, and the numbers he saw coming were more than his men could fend off, but Kyrien had saved Catrin's life more than once, and Chase would not let him die if he could help it.

"Find a good place to brace your spears," Morif shouted. "When they come, let them fight the Godfist itself instead of the strength of your arms. Let them impale themselves!"

Chase appreciated Morif's enthusiasm, knowing his men would need every boost in morale they could get just to keep them from turning and running. It was all Chase could do to face this new enemy—such malice!

Dust and dirt leaped from the ground, blinding and scouring, as the first of the dragons attacked. Morif stood facing the beast, watching it come, his spear lying on the ground before him. Just before the dragon reached him, he knelt down and raised the tip of his spear. The butt he jammed into a saddle of rock. The dragon was ready, though, and managed to make it only a glancing blow. Before it passed over, however, it knocked Morif and a dozen other men from their feet with a lash of its tail. Some did not rise again. More dragons circled and Chase knew it was only a matter of time.

Demons slipped past the downed guards and hacked at Kyrien's sides, trying to get to his soft underbelly but so far were stymied by his thick scales. One grabbed the spear from a downed guard and ran at Kyrien's eye.

Chase cried out, willing his body to move faster than he knew was possible. He was supposed to protect Kyrien. How would he ever tell Catrin that he'd let them kill her dragon? "No!" he shouted just before the demon was engulfed in liquid fire. It pulsed like lightning and blasted the air, sending Chase and others sprawling. Landing on his back, the breath knocked from him, Chase nonetheless found his soul lightened; Catrin stood atop the stair with lightning pulsing around her outstretched hands, lashing out at feral dragons and demons simultaneously.

"For Catrin!" Chase roared, and those around him rallied, many smoking and limping as they pulled themselves from the ground. The darkness was undeterred, and a flood of demons clogged the valley, the dragons protecting their flanks. More people streamed down the stairs with Catrin among them, warding off attacks from the air. She could not guard the people and Kyrien at the same time, which left Chase and his men vulnerable. The sight of Morif leaning on Kyrien with a spear in his hand did much to bolster Chase's morale; at least his old friend was not dead.

Thunder rolled through the valley, though no rain fell, and the skies were now clear. Webs of light arced overhead, and Chase could not look up for fear of losing what night vision he possessed. If he had looked up, he would have seen the massive black dragon bearing down on him. Instead, he was caught completely by surprise when what looked like a tree trunk slammed into him. The air rushed from his chest in a whoosh, and he flew backward. For a time he watched the battle rush away from him, but then his feet struck something.

The world spun wildly.

Darkness.

Catrin watched a dragon tuck its wings and dive, aiming for Chase, and she screamed, lashing out with more energy than she could control. Lightning struck the dragon and caused it to veer and land only a glancing blow on Chase. Still, her cousin's body tumbled through the air. The out-of-control blast also struck people around her, and just as Catrin hastily released the energy, it recoiled. The concussion sent those around her sprawling, and she fell to her knees, no longer in full control of her limbs. Before her was the most frightening thing she'd ever seen: the eyes of a feral dragon rising over a ledge. The beast clung to the rock and seemed to sense an opportunity. Gathering herself and trying to stand, Catrin prepared for the strike. One snap of its massive jaws, and she would be dead. At least it would be fast, she thought.

A high-pitched battle cry echoed sharply, and Khenna leaped across the gap. The fighter landed between the beast's eyes and sent a kick at one eye. The dragon blinked just in time, and its thick skin rendered the attack ineffectual, but then Khenna did something that stole Catrin's breath. Before the dragon could spring into the air, the woman took a coil of leather from her belt, held one end in each hand, and looped it over the dragon's snout. Had it made it under the lower jaw, Khenna might have been saved, but instead the leather strap only cleared the top jaw. The dragon bit down hard and leaped into the air. It turned and dived toward the valley floor. For a moment, Khenna stood tall, the wind whipping her hair and clothes. Catrin thought she might be able to stay upright, but then the dragon bit down again, and the strap snapped, one side breaking free and the other wedged between massive incisors. Khenna tried to catch her balance atop the head of a flying dragon, and for a moment she did, but in the next breath, she was tossed in the wind, still tethered to the dragon by the strap that was now twisted around her ankle. As Catrin watched in horror, they disappeared into the darkness.

There was no time to mourn Khenna as more dragons entered the fray. Far too many landed blows on Kyrien's still form. Catrin reached out to him, lending him energy she did not possess. Guilt washed over her as she pulled energy from those around her, making her nothing more than a leech. Disgusted, she nearly vomited, but then Kyrien flooded her mind.

They give their energy freely. They try in vain to aid me. You are simply focusing what they are unable to give. Do not run them dry, and you will have done no harm. Do what you must; just do not do too much. This is more important than you know.

At that moment she could not imagine anything more important than saving Kyrien and her people, but his thoughts left her weighted with responsibility. Though she knew not exactly what hung in the balance, she knew that it was partly hers to protect. Breathing deeply, she drew the energy and lashed out. Demon and dragon alike felt the fury of her wrath, and the darkness receded like twilight chased by the dawn. Slowly, gradually, they faded until only the cries of the dying filled the air.

When Catrin finally made it to the bottom of the stair, she fell to one side, unable to stand on her own without the aid of the railing. A man she didn't recognize caught her.

His eyes went wide, and she thought he might faint, but he stammered, "Are you . . . I mean . . . are you all right, Lady Catrin?"

"Almost," she said as another wave of dizziness overwhelmed her.

The man tightened his grip and kept her upright. "I need some help here! Need help for the Herald," he called out, and even in the chaos, people rushed to her aid.

From above came Millie's voice. "You're not going to die on me today, no you're not! Get some blankets around her before she freezes t'death."

Men scrambled to find something, and finally a man wrapped Catrin in a warm coat. In truth the cool air felt refreshing, but Catrin could not seem to find her voice. Her body trembled and her legs refused to support her. She continued to lean on the man whose name she did not know.

"You there," Millie instructed, "get some men and prepare a litter for Lady Catrin."

"That won't be necessary, Millie," Catrin said. "I'll be staying here with Kyrien."

Millie looked as if she would balk. A moment later she sighed. "Get up there and bring back blankets, tents, cots, everything we'll need for an infirmary. Tell Mirta we need all the bandages, stitching thread, and needles."

Wobbling, Catrin was grateful for Millie's efforts. She needed a place to sit down, but there were far more important tasks at hand, not the least of which was tending to the wounded. From the southern part of the valley, the silhouette of a man shambled toward them. A shout arose from men closer to that area, and Catrin felt an incredible sense of relief when someone said it was Chase. It was clear that he was injured, but she knew he was strong.

As the sun rose, the carnage became apparent, and guards were assigned the grisly duty of burying the dead and burning the bodies of the demons. When Catrin looked upon the demons, she found herself reminded of the Gholgi, yet these creatures were very different from what she remembered. Instead of lumbering brutes, these demons possessed delicate fingers and crude armor. The beasts she had encountered years before had seemed much more like wild animals. Bile rose in her throat as the wind shifted and the smell of death drifted around her.

Though her body screamed out for rest, she made herself stay awake.

"Take me closer to Kyrien," she said.

"Are you certain that's wise, m'lady?"

"Wise or not, please do as I say," Catrin said, driven by need; everything she loved was at stake.

"Yes, m'lady."

"What's your name?"

"I'm Zander, m'lady."

"You may call me Catrin, Zander, and I'm sorry I didn't recognize you."

"Yes, m— uh, Catrin."

"You make toys, do you not?"

"I do."

"Sinjin loves your puzzles. Thank you, Zander," she said, laying her hand on his shoulder.

The man looked thunderstruck and did not respond. Catrin urged him toward Kyrien. With the exception of his breathing, which was short and shallow, the dragon appeared to be dead, and Catrin worried about him and Prios. When she placed her hands on him, she was transported to the astral plane, assisted by some natural ability inherent in regent dragons. She rode a dragon of flame and lightning, gouts of fire ready to be hurled at their enemies. While the battle in the physical plane had ended, there was still fighting on the astral plane, and it was worse than what Catrin had left behind.

Prios stood within a ring of the Gholgi-like creatures, defending himself with a sword of fire. He looked so handsome yet so very much in danger. Her heart leaped and longed for him. Kyrien roared and dived, dipping to fly directly over Prios, then went sideways. Pure darkness slammed into them, liquid eyes focused for a deadly strike. In a single heartbeat, it drew back and struck at Kyrien's flaming throat. Monstrous spherical sparks leaped into the air and scorched whatever they touched.

Something akin to pain cut deep into Catrin's soul, and Kyrien reeled from the massive strike, but he flapped his mighty wings, turned, and dived. In the next moment he climbed sharply, and Catrin looked up to see the pale gray underbelly of the hulking wyrm.

Striking as quickly as she could, she sent only a small burst of fire, but it struck just under the beast's right wing. To Catrin's astonishment, the shadow dragon rolled over and crashed to the ground, crushing demons beneath. A writhing mass seethed around the spirit of Prios, and black blades with gleaming edges leaped from the battle seemingly at random. She could not imagine how he had found such strength, but then she considered the possibility that it was the same place she found her own strength: the love of her spouse and son. This brought a battle cry to Catrin's lips, and she rolled from Kyrien's back. As she plummeted toward the battlefield, her vision focused on one of the beings at the fore. It was bigger than the others, its weapon poised to strike. Tucking her knees as she flew, Catrin drove her heels into the creature's chest. The throng parted. The big one fell, and the black tide flowed back in as if the big one had never been.

Catrin wondered if she existed, and a familiar numbing feeling crept over her, soaking her slowly then accelerating. Dark hands grabbed her, and blades bit into her aura, yet she barely felt it. Once again the mass parted, and when Catrin forced her head up to see what had happened, her eyes landed on Prios. He looked horrible, his energy looking to have been sliced to bits, but the determination in his eyes drove the darkness back. He opened his mouth to roar, and though no noise came out, Catrin watched the demons retreat from his silent cry. Catrin drew on the energy around her, and painful tingling rushed in to drive away the numbness. Catrin told herself the pain was better even as she cried out.

Prios knelt down and brushed her hair away from her face. With extreme effort, she turned her eyes to meet his. He smiled back and winked.

In the next breath, he was spinning and roaring at the Gholgi. The dragons retreated and Kyrien helped drive off the last of the demons.

Zander stood holding Catrin's limp body, his legs trembling and his heart skipping. How had he found himself here, holding the Herald of Istra next to her dragon and watching other dragons drop from the sky? It was the most surreal and bizarre thing he had ever experienced, and he wasn't certain he could handle it. His back ached and his legs shook. "Help," he said far too low to be heard over the cries of the wounded and those trying to help them. "Um, I think I need some help here," he said a little louder.

He steeled himself when Morif turned. The old warrior was fearsome to look upon, and everything about him made Zander uncomfortable, his long hair and beard, metal rings braided into them, just highlighted the sunken place where his left eye had once been. Truly, Morif could look a man into the grave.

When he saw Catrin, the look on the grizzled face softened as much as Zander had ever witnessed. "We must get her back to the infirmary!"

"No!" Zander said involuntarily, and he nearly dropped Catrin as he choked.

"What is it?" Morif asked, his face no longer anything but hard. "Speak up, man."

"I . . . don't know . . . I don't know why, but I just know she needs to stay with Kyrien. She asked me to hold her, but I can't do it any longer."

Morif stepped forward to take Catrin from Zander's quivering arms, and Zander saw something he would never forget: Morif turned as pale as a whitefish, and his eye went wide. Zander saw it for only the briefest instant, as Catrin suddenly went rigid in his arms. Doing his best to hold on to her and not fall, Zander took two steps backward and bumped into Kyrien's side. As he looked up, a pair of massive eyes glared back at him, and it was more than he could stand. Zander fainted.

Holding his ribs, Chase took one step at a time. As he turned a corner, he found his way blocked by what had been the Upperton Apothecary, now a large pile of firewood partially obscured by the body of a dragon. Fear overcame Chase, even knowing the beast was dead. This was a super-predator, a killing machine. He would need to learn as much as he could about these feral dragons as fast as he could. Climbing over the dragon's tail was terrifying and painful. He didn't think anything was broken, but he was severely battered.

Beyond, he saw a very alive Kyrien supporting Catrin with his maw as another man fell to the ground. The bodies of dragons, men, and demons littered the valley floor. Amid the chaos, Morif brought order. Already the wounded were being loaded onto litters and carried up to the hold. Chase's second in command stepped in to support Catrin, who was now standing on her own. Chase moved faster despite the pain, tears gathering in his eyes.

"We need help over here," Morif shouted and Chase almost laughed; leave it to a one-eyed man to see him first. Morif always found a way to surprise him, and this day was no different. "Are you all right, sir?"

"Sort of," Chase said. "I think I'll live."

Morif grinned. "A little pain is a good thing. It reminds us not to be reckless."

Chase had often uttered the maxim himself, and he couldn't deny the truth of it.

"It took you long enough," he said when he reached Catrin.

She almost smiled.

"Prios is back!" came Millie's shout from above, and Catrin did smile briefly. The destruction around them defied optimism.

"You have that look on your face," Chase said to Catrin. "What is it?"

"Kyrien is injured," Catrin said. "We've got to figure out a way to protect him. If the ferals come back, he'll be defenseless."

"They will come back. There's a big one that has claimed this as his territory. We're not sure where he sleeps, but during the day, he keeps a constant watch on this valley. The people call him Reaver."

"All the more reason I need every able person down here now. We need to build fortifications around Kyrien to protect him."

"There are no fortifications we can build that will keep them out, Cat."

"Well, we have to do something!"

"The only things that've worked so far are spears and fire. I'll get people working weapons and training. In the meantime, we need to get you back in the hold. You look horrible."

"You're not looking your best either," Catrin replied. "And I'm staying here. Kyrien needs my protection." Chase looked Catrin in the eye and knew that arguing would do no good. Then he saw a look of pain and guilt flash across her face. "Sinjin?"

"He's fine," Chase said. He saw relief in Catrin's eyes, but the guilt was still there. "And Durin as well."

"That ornery rascal could survive just about anything, I do believe."

"Get back in here. I don't care who you are. You need rest!" Millie's shouts drifted down to those below.

"I believe that would be your husband coming now."

CHAPTER SEVEN

Followers are like leaves before a strong wind. Leaders are the wind.
— Morif, soldier

Nearly a fortnight passed, and the darkness pressed them no further, though the dragons kept constant daylight vigil. It seemed they were waiting for something, or someone. The thoughts haunted Catrin. Prios was busy running a hold in turmoil and under siege, though the times she saw him, there was tenderness in his eyes. As they passed in the hall, he would reach out to her, their hands caressing each other, ever so briefly. Sometimes she'd see Sinjin trailing her husband, watching everything he did. Catrin had seen less of Sinjin, and it pained her. There was guilt in his eyes, and she couldn't seem to convince him that she would forgive him for whatever it was. Something haunted his eyes, and that troubled her more than anything else. Knowing she needed to concentrate, Catrin quieted her mind.

Squinting, she winced at the pain of pushing her needle through the supple but thick leather once again. She could have given this task to the seamstresses, but it would have been impossible to convey to them the image in her mind. She often wished for Kyrien's skill at communicating in images and feelings. Catrin could see every detail from any angle, as if he had implanted the memory of this object directly into her head. A saddle! Catrin could hardly believe it. She was working on a saddle for Kyrien, and it was unlike any saddle Catrin had ever known. Certainly the seat, cantle, pommel, and horn were similar, but there were no stirrups. Instead there were multiple cups of leather and iron on the flaps that could be used in a similar fashion to stirrups.

So many details had flowed into Catrin's mind. A collection of girths made with thick strands of wound cotton waited in a corner, but none of Catrin's many straps were complete. First she needed metal rings with a flat edge on one side, which only Strom could provide. Her childhood friend was far too busy, yet he refused to take on an apprentice, saying he was still an apprentice himself, though none would argue his skill with metal and fire. He had mastered the art of bringing things to life from only a picture in his mind. Wielding his hammer like a paintbrush, he created works of art. Now, though, much of his time was spent making pot stands, candleholders, and anything else needed by the hundreds if not thousands of refugees now forced to live in the great hall.

After draping a roughspun sheet over the saddle, Catrin left her workshop, pulling the rawhide curtain to cover the doorway, not wanting rumors to spread. She also didn't want to worry Sinjin, unable to imagine how he would feel about his mother riding Kyrien with the ferals and demons guarding the valleys.

The cool air turned warm as Catrin walked toward the forge, and with every step, the heat became more oppressive. Sweat ran into Catrin's eyes well before she reached the smithy. Within stood Strom and a man Catrin knew she should recognize, but she could not recall a single detail about him. Hoping he would not engage her, she stepped into the smithy. She needn't have worried. Though people seemed to fear Catrin less these days, she rarely had to wait for anything. Those in her path leaped to get out of her way, and it sometimes frightened her. What had she become?

"If one more person asks me when their commission will be done, I'll throttle 'em," Strom said by way of greeting.

Catrin smiled. "I'm sorry you have to make everyone else wait so that my requests are fulfilled." She turned her head so he would see her grin. "I know that must be terribly difficult for you."

"What makes you think I've made anyone wait on your account?"

"Well," Catrin said, knowing she was risking not getting the parts she needed anytime soon. "I figured there must be some reason everyone was asking when their commissions would be ready. Something must be slowing you down. I figured it must be me."

Strom's dark skin glistened as he breathed heavily, and Catrin saw his face darken even more as he flushed. "You've no idea how much time it takes to do what I do! The next person who questions how long it takes to do things can forge their own cook pots! Ungrateful lot. To the fires with all of you!"

Catrin could no longer hold back her laughter, which only seemed to fuel Strom's anger.

"And you just stuff a melon in it. I've heard about enough out of you. Why, I ought to melt these down and put you to the back of the line!" He stuffed a heavy bag into her hands, and she could hear the sound of rings and buckle pieces clinking against one another.

"Thank you, Strom."

"Get out of here before I change my mind! If not for the fact that it would just make more work for me, I'd do it. Now git!"

"I still need a sword, Strom."

"Don't make swords."

"Strom."

"The only thing swords are good for is killin' people. Don't make swords," Strom said and turned his back to Catrin, returning to his anvil and a rod of metal glowing red and white in the forge.

"Swords can protect as well. You know I don't want to kill anyone. I just need to be able to defend myself."

"Why not retrieve that staff of yours? It seemed to serve you quite well."

"I can't," Catrin said. "It's . . . alive now. I can't just yank it up, cut away the growth, and walk off with it, now can I?"

"I'll make you a new staff, then."

Catrin sighed. They'd had this argument before, and never had she won. "Not even one as talented as you could re-create that staff. It lay dormant for thousands of years and then bloomed when I planted its heel in stone. No. Not even you can replace the Staff of Life." Part of her knew she was being unreasonable.

"I never said I'd create you another Staff of Life. You must have rocks in your ears, and perhaps between them as well. I said I'd make you a *new* staff."

"But a staff is not what I need. Now I need a sword."

"Did the voices in your head tell you that?" Strom asked, not looking at her.

"It's not like that. I just know I need a sword. That's all."

Strom waved a hand and grabbed his tongs. There would be no more words spoken about it today, and she left him to his work, knowing she'd been partly correct about her requests causing him grief from his other customers. If it weren't so important, she would have waited her turn, but this meant everything. She didn't know exactly why; she just knew. With Kyrien so close by, she'd begun to wonder which thoughts were her own and which belonged to her dragon. Though many of these strange, new thoughts surprised her, she always seemed to agree with the course of action Kyrien desired. It didn't seem to matter.

Strom's comment about her staff had been well aimed. Part of her wanted nothing more than to rest her hands in the grooves left by her own fingers. The memory of her grip biting into the flesh of the staff was one she'd rather not relive, but that event had linked her to the Staff of Life forever. By some magic, she'd planted the Staff of Life within the Grove of the Elders, at the center of the destruction she herself had wrought. The staff had given her the greatest gift of all. It had taken root and bloomed. Twenty-one acorns it had yielded, just enough to replant the mighty trees she had destroyed.

"I hope the day has greeted you well," Brother Vaughn said as he appeared from around the bend in the hall.

"It has, and for you as well."

"How are your hands today? They were so red yesterday, I wanted to make you stop sewing, or at least let someone help you."

Catrin almost didn't want to bring her hands out of the pockets of her robes. Her knuckles and thumbs were inflamed and swollen, her skin shiny and slick in places. Knowing Brother Vaughn as she did—his persistence was legendary—she pulled her hands out slowly.

He didn't say anything at first. He just sucked air in through his teeth. "Come with me, young lady. I have something for you."

Catrin wanted to say no, wanted to get back to her work, but she also knew the pain would hinder her progress. Experience told her it was best to let Brother Vaughn help when he offered. It was difficult to believe any single mind could contain so much knowledge, and he seemed to learn more each day.

"When I came across this, I didn't believe it would work, and there seemed no place where I could test it, but there is a shelf of rock just outside the viewing chambers where the air is always moving, always in the same direction. It's a puzzle I haven't yet worked out, but that is beside the point. What's important now is that it works."

"What works?" Catrin asked, knowing it would do no good. No one loved surprising people with his findings as much as Brother Vaughn. He enjoyed seeing the looks on people's faces as much as he enjoyed solving monumental problems.

"You'll see," he said.

When they reached the viewing chamber, Brother Vaughn shot her a look of concern.

"I'm not going anywhere," she said with a sigh. Perhaps if Kenward had returned with the metal-rich thrones, she might have ventured back onto the astral plane.

"Young man, come here," Brother Vaughn said, and a teenage boy wearing the livery of Dragonhold rushed to do as the elder statesmen asked. "You're more limber than I. Reach into that hole and stretch your arm as far as you can to the right. You'll feel a gourd bowl covered with sticks. Don't spill it! Just gently retrieve it for me. Keep it right side up! You hear me?"

"Yes, sir. I'll try, sir."

"Don't try. Just do."

"Yes, sir."

Catrin watched the boy reach out. She was worried that no matter how steady his arm was, his trembling knees would defy his efforts. It took some time for him to stretch far enough and find the bowl with his fingers. Brother Vaughn stood in tense anticipation. A look of extreme relief washed over the teen's face when he handed the bowl to Brother Vaughn, its covering of sticks intact. Catrin watched in silence, curious but trying to be patient.

"The constant breeze causes the water to evaporate," Brother Vaughn said. "And once I found the right level of airflow using different configurations of twigs, I was able to produce this." He removed the twigs from the top of the gourd bowl and extended it to Catrin. "Wrap this in cloth and rest it on top of your hands until it's melted."

In the gourd was a nearly solid block of ice. Ice in the warmer months was something they had all lived without since they no longer had the luxury of storing it in the cold caves. The loss of that resource was among the things Catrin most regretted. At times the thought of taking back the lands in the south had become almost appealing enough to warrant the violence, but Catrin abhorred war, and she had no wish to see her own people killed. That point chafed. Her people had divided themselves and taken what was rightfully hers. Only the luck of the gods had provided sufficient shelter for everyone. The discovery of Dragonhold remained one of the things Catrin was most thankful for. Another was Kyrien's recovery. His wounds had been many, and some had required the efforts of every healer within the hold, and Catrin was proud of what everyone had done.

The feral dragon attacks created fear of dragons, and Catrin had worried the people would turn on Kyrien, but instead they seemed to have hung their hopes on him. Not all dragons were evil killers, and many hoped Kyrien's kind would be their saviors. Catrin wondered the same, especially given her compulsion to create the saddle, riding clothes, and even the large, leather flaps whose purpose Catrin had yet to fathom. In truth, there were parts of the saddle and riding clothes she didn't understand, but she knew enough to create what she saw in her vision, a vision that showed little but her astride Kyrien. Only fog surrounded them, and Catrin could not glean a single hint as to what the future would hold.

"Keep them dry and that should help," Brother Vaughn said and Catrin came back to herself.

"Thank you, Brother Vaughn. You constantly amaze me."

The older man flushed. "I do what I can."

"I must get back to work on the saddle. Thank you again," Catrin said, and when she turned to pick up the bag from Strom, she knocked it over. Two rings and a buckle slid out. On top of them rested a thimble.

Brother Vaughn smiled. "I knew Strom would take good care of you."

"He always does," she agreed.

There was a thrumming of life within the hold now, far different than it had been before the ferals and demons came. Though the uniting of their purpose was something Catrin had always hoped for, it would have been far better had it happened before the need was so great; now they found themselves grossly unprepared. All the work Catrin and her followers had done for nearly a decade now seemed insignificant in the face of their current circumstances. Unless something changed, they would eventually starve and be forced out of the hold, which was the only thing protecting them from the darkness.

Going out of her way, Catrin made certain to pass by the main entrance, where she could momentarily catch a glimpse of Kyrien, who rested below, still mending from his wounds. Around him had sprung up a bristling compound. Men wielding spears surrounded him, and walls of sharpened spikes had been erected around a wide perimeter, leaving enough room for Kyrien to move. It had been a rude awakening after the first fortifications had been raised and Kyrien turning himself had brought it all crashing down. Within the new fortifications rested four massive ballistae, designed to resemble the ones the Zjhon had mounted on their ships. Catrin remembered the fear they had instilled in her, and she hoped it had the same effect on the ferals. Already the dragons knew the feel of their bite, and the bones of the unlucky littered the valley floor.

No one liked eating dragon, but almost every part of the dragon carcasses had been claimed for some purpose. Many of the men guarding Kyrien wore shields made from massive scales, and the teeth had become highly valued as spear tips—far more effective than their iron counterparts. Kyrien seemed ready to climb his way out of the valley. Catrin could feel his impatient desire as if it were her own; in many ways it was. The visions of her riding Kyrien had brought with them an intense desire to fly, to see the world from above. Part of her knew it was crazy and that flying meant facing the ferals. The monsters seemed to be multiplying, and every passing day, the danger they presented became greater.

With conscious effort, Catrin pulled herself back into the hold, back to her workshop. It seemed strange now to be working on the saddle when there was dragon ore once again within the hold. Guilt stabbed at her whenever she looked at it. Kyrien had given so much of himself to be here for her and to protect her, and as if that were not enough, he also managed to bring her more of the precious stone. Now Catrin had no desire to create herald globes, and no more trade would fill their coffers. The dragons and demons effectively prevented that, even if they didn't stop the steady stream of refugees who came from the south in the night. Though Catrin loved her people as a whole, those who had opposed her in good times and now sought her help in bad times angered her. She was tempted to turn them away, to send them back, but she simply could not.

Every new body that entered the hold presented new challenges and changed the rationing requirements. There were those who vehemently objected to allowing the refugees in, but Catrin had had the final word so far. She knew there would come a time when she would need to change her stance, but for the moment she put those thoughts aside. Again the desire to finish her saddle came to the fore. Though she considered returning straight to work, she took the time to make good use of Brother Vaughn's gift and iced her aching hands.

With sweat soaking his clothes, Sinjin followed Durin, who walked at a terribly slow pace. "Hurry up. The sooner we get this done, the sooner we can go do something else."

"That's just the problem," Durin said without turning. "As soon as we finish this, they'll have something else needin' done. You watch."

Sinjin didn't argue. Durin was right, yet Sinjin didn't mind as much. The work helped him feel as if he were contributing something. So often he felt helpless and useless, but at least he could achieve menial tasks. The hard work and sweat also helped him regain his strength and even grow stronger. He could feel the power in his newly toned muscles, and he liked it. The past moon had been the most difficult any of them could remember. In many ways, Sinjin and Durin were but spectators watching a most terrible drama play out.

Sinjin curled the mostly full water buckets he carried, switching between right and left. He found he could alternate along with his stride and establish a rhythm; that was if Durin would keep moving.

"No more draggin' your butts through these halls, now; especially not the *champion* runner," Miss Mariss said when they finally returned to the kitchens. "I needed that water long before now, and you've thrown off the entire kitchen. Now tell everyone you're sorry. Listen up, everyone! These two sluggards have something they want to say to you." With a steel eye, she turned to Durin. "Well, boy, what do you have to say for yourself?"

"I'm sorry," Durin blurted, his eyes cast to the side. If he'd been looking her in the eye, he might have seen it coming; instead, he was caught completely by surprise when she smacked him on the back of the head.

"And what about you?"

Sinjin looked up. "I'm sorry we took so long. It won't happen again."

"Your boilin' right it won't. Now empty the wastewater buckets and bring more clean water back with you."

"Yes, ma'am," the boys said in unison, neither with a great deal of enthusiasm. Bringing fresh water was difficult, but taking out the wastewater could be most unpleasant. Miss Mariss saved this task for those who irked her the most, which meant Durin was first in line with Sinjin running a close second.

"Why do I get lectured and smacked on the head and you just get lectured? I'm tellin' ya, you can get away with anything," Durin said in a nasally voice, trying not to breathe through his nose. Sinjin understood the wisdom of that decision since it was often better to never know how bad the water smelled; for some reason, the worse it smelled, the more likely it was to get spilled. Doing the laundry and scrubbing the passageway floors was worse than the carrying. Sinjin would prefer to just get the task done, but Durin slowed once again.

"There's gotta be a better way," Durin said, glaring at one of the many basins throughout the hold, all of which were dry. The one he glared at now held some dried flowers. Everyone speculated that the hold had once had water flowing through it. Durin couldn't imagine how such a thing could have been achieved, and he often wondered if everyone else weren't wrong. Perhaps the basins had served a completely different purpose altogether. He'd often been tempted to pour the wastewater down one of the basins, but the idea of trying to get rid of the smell if it didn't work stood in his way. Of course, sometimes that was the only thing that stood in his way, especially when his shoulders and his chest ached.

"I don't want to get yelled at again," Sinjin said. "Let's go."

Durin set down the buckets and turned. "I need to rest."

Sinjin was about to make a sarcastic remark, but he noticed how slowly Durin straightened after lowering the buckets to the stone.

He turned to Sinjin with eyes filled with tears. "I'm not as strong as I used to be. Sometimes I need to catch my breath."

Familiar guilt engulfed Sinjin. His friend was only weak because he'd been hit by a weapon intended for Sinjin. "I'm sorry."

"Don't be. It wasn't *all* your fault."

Sinjin started to protest, but Durin just laughed, which turned to a cough. After a couple more steadying breaths, he hoisted the buckets and started moving once again along the hall. Sinjin shuffled silently behind him, his mind consumed with problems for which he had no solutions.

It seemed to take all afternoon to reach the God's Eye. There, small barges waited to carry waste products across the subterranean lake where they could be taken into the Chinawpa Valley and buried or otherwise disposed of. It was a tedious process that took more time and resources than anyone would care to admit.

Simms and Bradley manned the poles of the nearest barge, and they grinned at the boys as they approached. "More wastewater, eh?" Simms said. "Don't ya ever git tired of carryin' wastewater? Ya always stink by the time ya git down here."

Sinjin just stepped onto the greasy timbers of the barge. Though small, the barges could carry an amazing amount of weight, far more than Sinjin and Durin ever came with. Simms detested putting out so much effort for such small loads, but Sinjin and Durin had no choice in the matter; their instructions were quite clear, as were Simms's, but that didn't stop the older boy from complaining loudly.

"Don't have nothin' t'say?"

"Mind your tongue," Bradley said. "You don't want the Herald coming down here and lecturing us again, do you?"

Sinjin flushed at the memory and wished, once again, that his mother would learn that sticking up for him was not in his best interest; it only made things worse. The rest of the trip passed in tense silence, and Sinjin watched the cavern walls slide by. Archways along the walls marked tunnels that had been blocked by the ancients. No one quite understood how it had been done. While some tunnels had been blocked with only loose stone and mortar, most of those leading away from the God's Eye were blocked by similar obstructions for a short distance before the tunnels dead-ended in solid granite. Once three tunnels had been excavated with the same results, all efforts to explore the remaining tunnels had been abandoned. Still, Sinjin tried to imagine what wonders could lie beyond and what magic the ancients used to conceal and secure them.

"Hurry up," Simms said. "I'm not waitin' all day."

Sinjin grunted when lifting his buckets, and Durin looked unsteady on his feet.

"I'll help you with that," Bradley said, earning a glare from Simms.

Late-afternoon light streamed in from outside, casting a ruddy glow over the pocked stone floor. Guards flanked the entranceway, ready to close multiple sets of gates should the hold come under attack again. Thus far, their fortifications had repelled the ferals and demons, but many feared the enemy had merely been testing their defenses in preparation for a major assault.

"Hold," came the guard's command.

"It's just us," Durin said, clearly annoyed.

"State your business."

"We brought you supper," Durin said.

"Wastewater," Sinjin said, glaring at Durin. "Was that so hard?"

"Every time it's the same thing. 'State your business.' We're carrying water buckets, for Kyrien's sake."

Bradley laughed and shook his head as he led them through the ancient hall, which opened onto the more recently built timber fortifications, stairs, and lift mechanism. Men worked nearby, all guarded by soldiers with spears, and all seemed ready to retreat at the first sign of trouble. Sinjin couldn't blame them.

"Wastewater to the right," the overseer barked.

"Wastewater to the right," Durin mimicked, causing Bradley to chuckle.

It felt good to be outside and breathing fresh air, and this brief moment was one of the reasons Sinjin didn't mind the task. The air near the freshly dug latrines was rarely pleasant, and the three dumped the buckets and retreated as quickly as they could.

A low murmur suddenly flowed across the valley floor followed by a dark shadow. Sinjin, Durin, and Bradley ducked down and stayed still. The dragon did not return, and people continued their work, anxious and on constant alert. It was exhausting and those who worked outside could do so for only short periods of time. Too many were overcome with fatigue and became careless; that was all it took these days to get dead.

Instinctively walking hunched over, as close to the ground as possible, the three did their best to get back to the cavern in silence. Sinjin looked over the beds of herald globes charging in the remaining sunlight, and he worried over their safety, but if they didn't charge in the sun, they wouldn't glow during the following nights. Sinjin had always found it amazing that one day of charging in the sun was enough to make a herald globe glow for nearly a fortnight. So many of the things his mother was said to have done seemed far away, as if they were but fairy tales, but these brought those stories closer to his heart. This was something only his mother could make, and they were among the world's greatest wonders.

Torches and candles were still used by most with only the most affluent able to afford the luxury of herald globes, and only those with jobs that could not be done otherwise were allowed to make use of the hold's inventory. Many globes were used to light the common halls and work areas, but there were still many parts of the hold left permanently in the dark. Sinjin had not expected such darkness when he returned to the cavern, but the torches on Simms's barge were almost lost in the distance.

"One of these days, I'm gonna leave that moron in the middle of this lake," Bradley said to Sinjin and Durin.

CHAPTER EIGHT

The might of kings soars on leathery wings.
— Fedicus Illiani, historian

Heavy wisps of black smoke curled from whale-oil lamps as Thorakis turned the herald globe in his hand. Such a small thing. The most powerful person in the world had been working for more than a decade, and this was the best she had come up with. It was sad, really. Thorakis had achieved so much more without using a lick of Istra's power. His might had come from foresight and wit. His power rested in water, wood, and stone. All this he did on his own, his intellect his most powerful tool. He wondered at times what he could accomplish if he ever tapped his other talents. A deep sensation of cold ran through him, leaving him nauseated and unsettled, a cold sweat forming on his brow.

No one could know, he reminded himself. His power and will must come from his natural abilities alone. He renewed his vow, all the while stroking Seethe's head. The mighty serpent had grown quickly and now curled around Thorakis's throne, his bulk spilling onto the dais, his head resting in Thorakis's lap.

"I beg of you, sire," Grimwell said, kneeling before Thorakis and Seethe. "Address the troops. It is you they follow, not I. Please. Lead them."

Thorakis nearly dismissed Grimwell again, having heard this plea before and not liking the idea any more than he had the last time. He did not wish to leave Seethe alone, and the troops were not ready to meet his dragon yet. The feral dragon was still young and needed Thorakis to protect him. The thoughts came readily; he'd been through this before. "Proceed with construction of the aqueducts as I have requested. Be certain my specifications are met exactly!"

"Will you not speak to them, sire?"

"You try my patience, wizard!" Thorakis began with a wild gleam in his eye. Seethe shifted in Thorakis's lap, and Grimwell's eyes grew wide. A vision overwhelmed Thorakis as he saw himself delivering an oration like none ever achieved before. He could feel the energy radiating from the crowd as they cheered his name, and with every breath, he was filled with it. When he looked back at Grimwell, the wizard shrank away. "Yes. I will speak to them, wizard. Gather them and prepare them. I am ready."

Grimwell retreated backward from the hall, his eyes locked with Seethe's, and it was everything he could do not to run. Had he seen those who stepped from the shadows after his departure, he would have.

Within the modest room he called home, Brother Vaughn sat facing Trinda. "Please tell me about the dragons. How did you call to them?"

Trinda shrugged. "I sang."

"Had you sung before?"

"Yes."

"When and how often?" Brother Vaughn asked, hoping she wouldn't make him pull every detail from her.

"Just sometimes."

"And what happens when you sing. Please, tell me."

"When I sing, I think about things, and they come to me."

Brother Vaughn let that statement sink in. "What things have come to you?"

"Butterflies once. And birds once. And one time fish. And now dragons, I guess."

"Fish," Brother Vaughn said and Trinda nodded. "Will you show me?" She nodded again.

From the three-pronged stand that Strom had made him, Brother Vaughn grabbed his herald globe and a ball of string. Trinda looked interested but said nothing more. As they walked, he noticed how much Trinda shied away from anyone they passed and, in more than a few cases, how the people they encountered reacted to Trinda. It was a small hold, and Brother Vaughn hoped he could find a way to keep the girl safe. Many associated Trinda with the death of Catrin's and Chase's mothers, and no matter how hard they tried, some simply could not accept her presence in the hold.

As they passed through the dark halls, only the glow of his herald globe lit the way, and Trinda huddled within its light. Those they passed had their own business and paid little mind. At the dock, no barges waited, the area eerily quiet. Trinda drew a deep breath when she beheld the God's Eye, and Brother Vaughn couldn't blame her. No one seemed prepared for the sight of a natural vaulted chamber of such size and capacity to hold what could only be called a lake. This end of the lake received the least light and had no algae growing in it, which meant that the fish usually stayed at the far end of the lake, where food was more plentiful.

Using his string, Brother Vaughn created a cradle for his herald globe and showed it to Trinda, who looked dubious. He lowered the herald globe into the water, not really knowing what to expect. To his surprise, the light became brighter and cast distorted beams through the water, but it also did an excellent job illuminating the steep slope that dropped away from the cavern entrance. No fish could be seen.

"Would you sing now for me? And think about fish? Just the ones in this lake, mind you," he added, suddenly envisioning fish leaving the sea to find her. Trinda hesitated and Brother Vaughn said nothing, not wanting to coerce her. She closed her eyes for a moment, and Brother Vaughn thought she might not be ready, but then she nodded and began to sing a soft, wordless tune that pulled at his heart. Brother Vaughn lost track of time while he listened, and he forgot the reason they had come, forgot what he had asked her to sing for. When he looked down and saw the glowing water filled with writhing bodies, all aligned and pointing at Trinda, he jumped and lost his grip on the string.

Trinda stopped singing and tried to grab the string as it slipped beneath the water. The globe looked as if it might come to rest on a shelf of rock, but the shifting water pulled it out and sent it tumbling into the depths. Brother Vaughn watched in morbid fascination; the light grew brighter as it moved deeper. He could see the smoothness of the slope; there was nothing to impede his herald globe, which had left the string behind. Both of them gasped when the shape of a shipwreck appeared from the darkness and was then lost again in shadow. Just as suddenly, the light stopped moving, apparently stuck on a rock formation of some sort.

"You dropped it," Trinda said.

Brother Vaughn couldn't contain his excitement. "Did you see that? That was amazing! You called the fish to you, and that was wonderful, and then, like the great oaf I am, I dropped the globe, but even that brought discovery. Did you see that ship? It must have been built *inside* this cavern. Can you imagine that?"

"By the gods!" came Simms's shout. His barge was over where the herald globe had come to rest. "Would you look at that!"

Bradley, on another barge, quickly poled his way to where Simms waited, seemingly too stunned to move. Bradley looked down and, cursing, poled his way back to the dock. Simms remained where he was as if paralyzed.

"What is it, man?" Brother Vaughn asked.

"Get on," Bradley said. "You just have to see it."

Brother Vaughn hesitated a moment, unsure how Trinda would do on the water, but she stepped behind Bradley and onto the barge so fast, all he could do was follow. Bradley poled them back to where Simms was now issuing a steady stream of curses with occasional prayers interjected.

Below them lay an unmistakable form, or at least part of it. What looked back from below was a gleaming feral dragon, its menacing maw clear in the light. The globe had landed quite close to the eye of the giant serpent, which seemed to be made of enormous crystalline structures, as if the gems had naturally formed into the shape of a mountain-sized dragon. The beast's body faded into the darkness, but Brother Vaughn imagined it stretching to the far shore. The dragon's glare inspired awe and fear, and seeing the fish now gathering around the dragon's eye, attracted by the light, was among the most vivid images Brother Vaughn had ever seen.

"Are there any divers within the hold?" Brother Vaughn wondered aloud.

"There's Logan the spear fisherman," Bradley said. "That guy can hold his breath for a really long time. I bet he could get it back."

"Could you go find him for me?"

Bradley seemed hesitant to leave his post. Though he was working as a bargeman, he was officially part of the guard, and abandoning one's post was a serious crime.

"This is important. Let's go see your commander. I have something to ask of him as well," Brother Vaughn said.

Bradley followed. Simms looked as if he didn't care, but Bradley wore his concern openly.

"Don't worry. I'll take care of this."

"Yes, sir," Bradley said, looking no less uneasy.

Brother Vaughn could understand his worry and uncertainty. So many things were new in Dragonhold, and so few people knew with absolute confidence what they should do and to whom they should listen without question.

It came as a bit of a shock when it was Morif Bradley sought out. It would appear that Bradley ranked higher than one might think, and Brother Vaughn suspected Morif was keeping a special eye on the hold's entrances.

"What's all this about?" Morif said as they entered his home.

"Sir, I'm sorry, sir," Bradley began, and Morif held him in a steady, one-eyed gaze.

"I pulled him away from his post," Brother Vaughn interjected, and Morif turned his imposing stare.

"I've made a discovery! Well, several, actually, and I need a diver to get my herald globe back from the bottom of the God's Eye. And you should see what's down there!"

"Why did he bring you up here?" Morif asked Bradley.

"He wanted me to find Logan so he could dive for the herald globe Brother Vaughn dropped in the water."

"Then go get him," Morif said.

Bradley left in a hurry.

Morif nodded. "That's a good man."

Brother Vaughn nodded his agreement. Trinda tried to remain unseen. Millie was one of the people who couldn't stand the thought of her being in the hold, and Morif was conditioned to look after her interests. Somehow Trinda must have sensed that she was not welcome.

"And I suppose there must be something else, or I suspect you'd already be gone." He didn't look at Trinda, but he didn't have to.

"I need to borrow your herald globe," Brother Vaughn said.

"Why?"

"I just need to borrow it for a little while, and then I'll bring it back. I promise."

Morif harrumphed and pulled his globe from its stand. "Let's go see what we've got here."

He led the way back toward the God's Eye, never actually giving Brother Vaughn the herald globe.

At the docks, they waited for Simms to return. He'd been floating over the sunken herald globe when they arrived, and seeing Morif on the shoreline had him moving in a hurry. Morif didn't say anything, and it was clear by the look on Simms's face that he didn't need to. "Get me out there so I can see what all this fuss is about."

"Yes, sir."

Brother Vaughn and Trinda followed Morif onto the barge, and he felt the same sense of fascination this time when the mighty serpent came into view. He found entirely new details that he had missed before. The herald globe continued to glow brightly, though only an occasional fish now played in the light.

Morif said nothing; he just stood, stroking his beard. Brass adornments braided into the beard made a soft noise that seemed to soothe the old warrior. Brother Vaughn knew better than to try to get something out of Morif. The man would speak when he was ready.

Bradley returned with a man Brother Vaughn assumed was Logan. He was thin as a sapling with skin still sun darkened, something that was becoming increasingly rare. Bradley poled his barge to a stop not far away, and Logan spared not a word. He simply slipped into the water and swam toward the light. He moved like a seal as he swam, and Brother Vaughn worried he would drown. Even once the man had grabbed the globe, he appeared to rise to the surface far too slowly, but Logan broke the surface and seemed only moderately winded. He swam to Brother Vaughn and handed him the glowing orb.

Turning the herald globe in his hand, he watched as it dimmed to a softer glow. "May I see your globe?" he asked Morif.

The wizened veteran grunted and handed it to him.

"Was that the deepest you could dive?" Brother Vaughn asked Logan.

"No, sir. I can go deeper than that."

"Don't even think about it," Morif said, but Brother Vaughn was already moving, and before Morif could stop him, he'd thrown both globes back into the water.

Brother Vaughn hoped Morif didn't lose patience with him, and he wore an apology on his face for only an instant. Then he watched in fascination as the two globes cast slightly overlapping rings of light, and the first sailed down close to where the ancient shipwreck lay. The second soared beyond the dragon's eye and gave only the slightest glimpse of something else resting on the coils of the dragon.

"Do you think you can dive for those?" Morif asked Logan.

"I think so, sir. I just need a bit of time to breathe."

"Simms, get your butt back to the docks. There're people waiting." He turned back to the monk. "With all due respect, *Vaughn,* don't do that again."

"Yes. Um. Yes, of course," Brother Vaughn said, secretly hoping someone else would annoy Morif and take the focus off him. The barge was feeling rather small and more than a little crowded. A moment later, though, Logan disappeared under the water and moved into the light. First he went to the globe near the sunken ship, and Brother Vaughn nearly fell in as he leaned over to watch. Logan had the globe in one hand yet didn't start back up immediately. Instead, he glided along the side of the sunken ship and spent what seemed an eternity sifting through the wreckage. Brother Vaughn suddenly remembered to breathe, only then realizing that he'd been holding his breath as though he were underwater with the diver.

Even Morif rushed to see what it was that Logan brought back up. He handed the globe back to Brother Vaughn, and he seemed less enthusiastic about handing the object in his other hand over, but then he seemed to have a change of heart. "Here," he said.

Morif and Brother Vaughn both reached out at the same time, and it nearly sent Morif into the water. Brother Vaughn tried not to think about how that would've turned out but was distracted by the sight of a small, gold-trimmed box made of jade and wood inlay. The perfectly preserved artifact rested easily in Morif's hands. There seemed no apparent way of opening the box, and he handed it to Brother Vaughn.

"If that thing happens to entitle the bearer to wine, whiskey, and women, you'll give it back, right?" Logan asked.

"Deal," Brother Vaughn said. "Even if it's just two out of three."

"Fair enough."

Logan's dive for the second globe was as excruciatingly slow as the first, and it seemed he was having trouble dislodging the globe from where it had come to rest. Morif cast Brother Vaughn an accusatory glance, which Brother Vaughn did his best to pretend he didn't notice. After a few tense moments, Logan freed the globe and made his way slowly back to the surface.

"I don't know how you do that," Brother Vaughn said, "but it makes me breathe heavy just watching you." Though Logan's ascent had provided no new detail of what else waited on the lake floor, Brother Vaughn was thrilled by what he had learned. "Thank you all for your help! This is wonderful!"

Morif snatched both herald globes out of Brother Vaughn's hands. "You'll get yours back when we get to shore."

Chase shook his head. Before him stood Catrin in the craziest outfit he'd ever seen. She'd taken supple leather and created a tight but flexible body suit covered with straps, rings, and zippers. Her ears were covered, and over her eyes she wore clear lenses mounted in leather-wrapped iron rings, which were attached to a second pair of rings with flaps that tapered into a strap and buckle. "You look like Strom attacked an otter."

Catrin grinned back at him and turned around. Then she climbed up onto the saddle. Chase continued to shake his head as he watched her draw the straps and buckle herself to the saddle. The largest straps secured her at the waist, and other smaller straps formed an interplay. Cinching tight on one strap gave slack to another, and because of the clever design, Catrin could move around on the massive saddle while still being firmly tethered. It was brilliant and insane.

Hunching down as if she were in mid flight, Catrin moved her feet to an upper set of toeholds and wedged herself under the two massive shield flaps, which were lightly armored and apparently padded inside.

"You see," came Catrin's muffled voice. "There's enough room for me and a few things."

"Even if we could make a thousand of these, we don't have a thousand dragons. We have one and we're not certain he'll fly again."

"Don't you say that," Catrin said, looking imposing despite her ridiculous garb. "Kyrien could fly now if he wanted to, but *we* are not ready. *We* are unprepared. And why are *we* unprepared? Because *we* did not listen to *me*."

Chase let out a brief sigh, which was cut off by another sharp look from Catrin. How anyone could expect to be taken seriously with those goggles on was beyond him, yet somehow she pulled it off. The pair of knives holstered on each leg did help, he supposed. "Yes. You're right. Let's not have that argument again. My point is that I don't think this saddle provides a solution to our immediate problems."

"What's your solution?"

Chase searched for words, but he could find none that hadn't already been said by Catrin herself years before.

"Then don't look down your nose on what might be part of the solution."

"Perhaps it will help to mollify the Arghast as well," Chase admitted. "They're quite unhappy that you've not taught them to fly yet."

"Don't start with that either. How am I supposed to teach someone how to do something I don't know how to do?" Catrin asked in futility. "At least not without a ship, that is," she admitted. "That doesn't change the fact that I haven't ridden a dragon . . . yet."

"The problem is this: If we take that saddle down there and put it on Kyrien, the people are going to expect you to fly. The Arghast will expect you to fly. And we both know it isn't even close to safe for Kyrien to fly with Reaver patrolling the skies and demons on the ground. What makes you think the ferals won't immediately gang up on Kyrien?"

"I don't intend to fly yet. There will come a time, yes, but not yet. For now we will just need to explain to everyone that it is simply a test to satisfy my curiosity and that we will not be flying."

"You know how much turmoil this will cause."

"I do and I cannot fix that. People are going to have to come to grips with the fact that the world has changed. We ourselves must either change or die. Deal with it."

It was clear to Chase that he would not win this argument. The truth was that he partially agreed with her. Still, he did not look forward to the uproar it would cause. "When?"

"Now."

With little besides hard breads coming out of the kitchens, Durin did his best to avoid them altogether. Since Miss Mariss now refused to let anyone take more than one portion of food, no one could bring him food, and hunger eventually won out. If Sinjin were around, it wouldn't be so bad, but Brother Vaughn had sequestered him away with only Trinda for company. Durin felt for his friend; carrying water buckets wasn't nearly as bad. Trinda was the least happy person Durin had ever met, and she always managed to dampen his mood. When he took the family history into account, he worried even more about Sinjin's safety.

Worrying made Durin hungry. With a sigh, he made his way deeper into the hold, where the heat was nearly unbearable. Durin wondered how people managed to breathe the hot air for so long. It suffocated him. Strom's hammer rang an angry tone, and Durin stepped quickly by the smithy entrance. Taking his place in line, Durin waited, trying to be invisible. A line of guards approached; far more than usual, Durin noted with dismay. The guards would get fed first, and that meant a long wait and the chance that there would be nothing left by the time he got there. It had been happening more and more lately. Even with many in the hold cooking their own meals, the kitchens simply could not keep up with the demand for food—cooked or rationed. The stress it placed on Miss Mariss was obvious, and Durin felt guilty for hiding.

Just as he was considering asking Miss Mariss what he could do to help, though, the man next to him decided he didn't have time to wait for the guards, and he suddenly turned and left. Never one to miss anything in her kitchen, Miss Mariss immediately spotted Durin.

"You see that wad of guards come in, and you hide in line? I ought to make you carry buckets until your lazy little legs fall off!"

Durin considered telling her he was about to ask what he could do, but even he would not have believed it. Instead, he just walked to where the buckets of dirty water waited and grabbed two. Miss Mariss simply glared at him. As he made his way toward the kitchen exit, a guard charged through the door and bumped Durin, which sent dirty water into the air, most of which landed on Durin.

"If you're gonna spill it, then clean it up," Miss Mariss said with the closest thing to a smile that Durin had seen on her face in weeks. At least his misery served some purpose, he thought.

"Sorry, mate," the guard said. "I'd help you clean it up, but they want all of us—uh . . . we have something important to do."

Durin just put down his buckets and caught the clean rags Miss Mariss threw at him. He'd been breathing through his mouth, hoping not to smell how bad the water was, but it became tedious and he breathed in through his nose. To his surprise, the water did not smell bad at all. After cleaning up the spill, he tucked one of the remaining dry rags into his belt; the rest went into the laundry pile, which he suspected he would have to carry next.

What he really wanted to do was go see why all the guards were needed. With Sinjin closeted away and double the guards on duty, there had to be something afoot. When he reached the alcove where he and Sinjin used to hide, he stopped. Too many guards cast him glances as they passed, making it clear he'd get nowhere near the excitement. Already his back ached, and a short rest was too difficult to resist. He would find out what was going on soon enough. Not wanting anyone to know, he brought the buckets back into the shadows. Within moments, he was asleep.

CHAPTER NINE

Forgotten are those who fail to achieve. Doomed are those afraid to fail.
— Brother Vaughn, Cathuran monk

Blue skies filled with nothing but towering cloud formations, white and fluffy, appeared nonthreatening, yet most watched the skies in tense anticipation. Reaver had yet to make an appearance, but his presence was almost palpable. Few other dragons ventured in close to Kyrien, or the Pinook Valley at all for that matter, but Reaver seemed determined to root out the humans and especially Kyrien. He exuded frustration every time he attacked despite the scars he bore from previous attempts.

Chase's people learned from every encounter, and between Morif and Martik, they found either tactical or mechanical solutions to their weaknesses. Crews were now adept at loading, aiming, and firing ballistae, and stacks of sharpened tree trunks waited near each of the six super weapons. Each one had its own personality, and crews had to learn the quirks of their specific weapon. Misfires and mistakes had been costly, and those who still lived were determined not to suffer the same fates as their lost brethren. The visions of Reaver flying off with friends and comrades burned in their memories.

Kyrien moved among them, his every step causing men to scramble, and many walked a thin line between protecting Kyrien and being unintentionally killed by him. The saddle was nearly down the stairs, and Kyrien looked more alive than he had in weeks. Stretching his wings, he reminded everyone in the valley of his true size. From the stair, Catrin beamed down at him, trying to contain her impatience. Bringing the massive saddle down the stairs was a slow and arduous process.

Swiveling his head on his long, slender neck, Kyrien watched their progress and let out an echoing call when finally they approached. Catrin wished he, too, could contain his enthusiasm. No doubt Reaver heard his call and would come to investigate. Those guarding Kyrien reached the same conclusion and scanned the skies for any sign of the massive feral dragon. The men carrying the saddle also quickened their pace beyond what might have been considered prudent. In times such as these, safety was a relative thing.

Kyrien met Catrin's eyes, and the world ceased to exist. His gaze captivated her, and excitement filled the air between them. *Hurry.*

Alongside the final landing, Kyrien positioned himself, extending one wing so his girth was fully exposed. It was an awkward position, and it left him vulnerable, but it made it much easier on those who were trying to get the saddle in place.

"You'll never be able to clear the gap!" Martik said as he pushed his way toward those handling the saddle. It was clear the men were already spent. "I need some fresh bodies up here! Fetch a block and tackle, and find me an anchor point on the east face. And rope! We need at least three coils of rope."

No one waited long to obey. Though Martik held no title or military power, his genius was undeniable, and the people had come to trust his judgment. Trust, it seemed, was a better motivator than political power as people obeyed him with confidence. After securing the pulleys and ropes, Martik positioned people around the saddle and orchestrated their movements like a symphony, constantly reacting as conditions changed. Even with his skills and the peoples' trust of him, it was a dangerous task. Swinging wildly at times, blown by gusts of wind, the saddle struck at random, sending one man over the railing. Kyrien managed to catch the man on his side, preventing what might have been a serious injury.

"Bring me slack!" Martik shouted at the two men closest to him. "Steady. Steady."

The saddle dropped into place more quickly than Martik had intended, and Kyrien let out a *woof* when it landed, but then he shifted and squirmed until the saddle fell into place, looking as if it had been designed exactly to fit him, which it had, but Catrin was still amazed by how good a fit it was since it had been based on mental imagery alone.

Raising his body up on his two powerful legs, Kyrien provided enough room for the girths to be run under his belly. Catrin watched a young man slide under Kyrien, risking his life for her, knowing that he would be crushed if Kyrien chose to lower himself at the wrong time. Kyrien watched the young man and made sure he was well clear before the mighty regent dragon raised himself up higher, bringing the seat near to where Catrin watched. Using a loop in the rope lift, Catrin stepped up and allowed Martik and his men to raise her up and maneuver her over the saddle.

"This time bring me slack *slowly* and *evenly!*" Martik demanded.

The men holding the ropes did the best they could, but Catrin still landed hard. She didn't care. She was on Kyrien's back, just as she'd seen in her visions, though perhaps the next time she mounted, she thought, she would simply climb up. After pulling the girths snug and securing the breast collar, Catrin strapped herself into the saddle. Stiff leather resisted going into the keepers, and hooks resisted sliding through awl-punched holes, but she was eventually satisfied that she had constructed the saddle correctly. When she raised her hands in victory, a small cheer went up from the crowd, which Catrin noticed contained more than a few Arghast. Halmsa watched her with unwavering attention, seemingly absorbing every detail so he could relay the information to his tribesman.

What Catrin had not expected to see was Strom descending the stairs carrying a blanket-wrapped bundle. Noting the storm cloud he had in place of his face, Catrin wondered what could be afoot. When he reached the landing, the crowd parted and let him pass though he'd said not a word. The look on his face made it clear he would part rock if he had to. "Here!" was all he said to Catrin before he unwrapped the package and thrust a weapon, shielded pommel first, across the gap to Catrin. Martik stepped in behind him to make sure he didn't fall into the valley below.

Catrin opened her mouth to speak, but Strom immediately withdrew and walked to where Kyrien could easily see him. Strom glared at the dragon, who regarded him with what looked like mild amusement.

"There! Are you happy now?" Strom shouted up at Kyrien, bringing a shocked roar that ran through those assembled. Kyrien simply closed his eyes for a moment and bowed his head to Strom. "Good. Now stay out of my head!" When Strom turned away, the crowd parted even more quickly, not wanting to impede a man with the courage to browbeat a dragon.

Even Catrin found herself speechless as she watched Strom climb the stairs, leaving without another word. In her hand she held a blade like none she'd ever seen or imagined, yet it fit her perfectly. The pommel was contained within a shielded sleeve that allowed her to swing it without keeping a tight grip, and she guessed it would protect her wrist should she strike something unforgiving. The blade forked at the end into two blades, each tip shaped like an indented triangle that tapered to a deadly point. Though not covered in scrollwork, there was a subtle design that seemed to hide under the glossy shine, and Catrin could not imagine how the delicate image could have been created. Truly Strom had become a master of the anvil and forge, quite possibly with help from Kyrien, whether Strom liked it or not. After his outburst, Catrin guessed not.

Even the sheath had been designed to work with the harness that secured Catrin. Kyrien had been accurate in every detail. Catrin moved from side to side, her feet jumping from toehold to toehold, and she felt secure at all times without feeling trapped in place. If ever it did come to a midair fight, Catrin felt she would be able to take evasive and perhaps even offensive action without fear of plummeting from the sky.

Looking up, she found the eyes of all the Arghast who remained at Dragonhold regarding her with wonder. "Fly!" one shouted, and the others took up the chant, despite those who tried to quiet them.

Almost instantly someone else shouted, "Reaver to the north!"

"Demons to the south!"

"Fly!" demanded the Arghast.

Catrin froze, certainty beyond her grasp. Indecision held her fast, and Kyrien turned to look at her. In his eyes she saw acceptance of death and something more, something indefinable and magical. This was his only communication to her as their enemies approached. A furor had erupted around them as people sought to arm themselves or flee. There was no time for Catrin to unstrap herself. Morif ran forward with his long knife bared. He had two straps cut before Catrin forced him back. "No!"

"Now is not the time to risk everything, Catrin. You must get inside to safety. Cut yourself free and I'll get you there. I promise you. Let the guards defend Kyrien as they've done before."

"Demons to the north! By the gods, they're everywhere!"

This attack was unlike those that had come before. This was no feint meant to harass them and test their strength. This was a full-on assault. Among the demons walked giants in chains. Catrin felt her courage flee.

These beasts were like something straight from a nightmare. Towering over the demons, they looked like the massive statues in the Valley of the Victors come to life. Every muscle in their upper torsos stood out, pronounced and defined, giving them a hard and angular look. Short, coarse hair covered their legs and whiplike tails. Thick fingers and toes made appendages look more like battering rams.

Reaver swooped low from the north and skimmed over what were obviously *his* troops. Even the giants cowered in the shadow of Reaver, whose size made his aerobatics seem impossible. The twang of a ballista split the air, and a tree trunk soared over Reaver's right wing. The dragon dipped below it with ease and picked up speed.

"Hold your bolts! Wait for it," Morif shouted as he left Catrin's side. "Wait for my command!"

Catrin looked down at the straps that had been cut away, knowing she could not cut her way out of the saddle in time to retreat, she tried to think of a way to repair them, but then the world turned upside down.

Durin woke to the sound of footsteps rushing through the halls of Dragonhold. Shouts echoed from a distance, and a cold feeling washed over him. His muscles were stiff, attesting to how long he'd slept.

"Catrin has saddled Kyrien," someone whispered as he and a companion passed the alcove.

Durin shuddered. There had been hints and rumors that the Herald had been building a saddle and that she would use it to teach the Arghast to fly dragons, but he'd never really believed it. Catrin had always been a part of his life, and though she occasionally did things he couldn't explain, she didn't seem as powerful as the tales would imply. Excitement charged in and he wondered if she really could be saddling Kyrien. In that moment, he wanted nothing more than to get to the front gate and see what was really going on. He was tired of hearing about the battles and excitement that had taken place while he was carrying water, and he wanted to finally witness something for himself.

The distant shouts took on an alarming note, and it became clear that something was wrong. Knowing Miss Mariss would have his hide if he took too long to return with fresh water, he came up with a plan. The only way he could save time would be to run to the God's Eye, which he couldn't do with full buckets. Turning his eyes on the glowing rune that waited in the darkness, Durin smiled.

Slowly he emptied the first bucket into the rune. The glowing chasm seemed bottomless, and Durin grinned, knowing he'd just come up with a brilliant solution to some of his problems. A bit of steam rose from the rune, but Durin didn't hesitate and poured the second bucket in as well. Now he could jog to the God's Eye with empty buckets after taking a quick peek at what was happening in the great hall. Before he left the alcove, though, more steam rose from the rune and a high-pitched whistle sounded.

Durin considered running, but he had to find out what would happen next. The stone beneath his feet trembled, and a deep, bone-chilling rumble gained intensity. An enormous gout of steam rose from the rune, driving Durin back. The whistling grew higher and higher in pitch until it and the steam suddenly stopped. For a moment, there was silence.

Then Dragonhold moved.

CHAPTER TEN

In a war with the mindless, there is no room for surrender or mercy.
— Enoch Giest

Straps pulled tight as Catrin fell back in the saddle, driven far into the seat by the force of Kyrien's launching himself into the air, colliding with Reaver, and ending up locked together with the massive feral dragon. Catrin found herself hanging, upside down, and flying over an army of demons that approached from the south, the air pressing her goggles back into her face. Spears flew at her, and she dodged them as best she could. Her left side remained firmly strapped in, but with every move, the right side of her harness loosened.

Reaver forced Kyrien low over the trees, and branches assaulted her. A stand of ancient pine rose above the canopy, and Reaver drove them toward it. Kyrien roared and Catrin felt his muscles bunching. Just before she struck the trees, Kyrien flexed and rolled, turning Reaver over and driving him into the trees. A terrible snapping resounded through the valley, and Catrin felt Reaver let go of Kyrien. Again she was driven into her seat as Kyrien climbed sharply. After cinching up the right side of the harness as best she could, she gripped the severed ends of the straps. It seemed a futile effort, but it was the only thing she could think of.

As Kyrien turned on a wingtip, Catrin caught sight of Reaver righting himself and slowly gaining altitude, as he did, he let out a terrifying roar that Catrin felt as much as heard. With little more than a quick mental warning, Kyrien tucked his wings and dived at Reaver, who roared again. Dropping like a stone, Catrin felt as if she would lose her stomach. Then she moved into the upper toeholds and gripped the horn with straining hands.

Brace!

Almost too late, Catrin prepared herself. With a terrible impact, Kyrien struck Reaver, who had rolled over and extended his claws just prior to the collision. The terrible sound of three sets of lungs being emptied of air echoed in the canyon. The world darkened as they plummeted from the sky, tangled together. In a haunting moment, Catrin wondered if she were dreaming. All around them flew dragons, which dived in close only to retreat. Just before she thought she would succumb to unconsciousness, Catrin lurched sideways, seeing another feral dragon reach in and pull Kyrien and Reaver apart. Immediately both dragons righted themselves, and still branches raked them before they could regain the air.

Kyrien stayed low and sped south of Lowerton. Edling's Wall marred the landscape, a brown and gray line that divided her homeland. The new gate was progress, but Catrin would prefer the Wall ceased to exist. Following the river as it broadened, Kyrien flew low over a waterfall that poured into a familiar lake. Catrin had no time to reminisce as Kyrien dived straight toward the lake surface, pulling up only when they were within the cloud of spray. One dark shape rose just above them and nearly clipped them; another climbed too late and struck the water at full speed, driving a wall of water before it. The backsplash sent water high enough to soak Catrin and Kyrien. Fortunately, Kyrien used his speed to get them clear.

In the reflection of the lake, Catrin saw dragons diving at them, and she looked up to see dozens ready to strike. Kyrien seemed to sense them, and just before the strikes came, he took sudden evasive action. Catrin thought she would be sick. His sudden moves unsettled her equilibrium. A loud crack sounded as another dragon struck the water, this one cartwheeling across the surface of the lake then landing flat and motionless in the shallows.

Dark columns of smoke choked the air, and Catrin cried out when she saw her old family farm burning to the ground. Everywhere was the same: smoke, fire, and nothing alive but demons. Kyrien suddenly climbed as the sound of ballistae firing rang out. Catrin tried to figure out how the demons could have so quickly replicated the weapons used against them, but as they moved toward Harborton, it became clear that the demons and dragons were not working alone. Greasy, black ships clogged the harbor, and men in equally dark armor laid siege to the Masterhouse. All of Harborton burned. This was not as much an invasion as it was extermination.

The taste of bile filled Catrin's mouth as Kyrien turned sharply again but not fast enough. A massive ballista bolt struck Catrin's saddle and smacked into her side before she knocked it away. The air pressure around her changed, and Catrin turned to see the jaws of a feral dragon about to close around her. She could feel the heat of its breath as it soared ever closer. Once again the sound of a ballista firing filled the air. Kyrien turned, dived, and pulled up sharply, using his head and neck to drive the other dragon into the path of the approaching bolt. It struck with a wet *thunk,* and Kyrien peeled away before the other could entangle him in its death fall.

Seeing the armada that choked the harbor, including ships armed with ballistae and other weapons Catrin didn't recognize, she urged Kyrien to go back north toward Dragonhold. It had all happened so fast that Catrin could hardly believe it. Even the return north was faster than she would have imagined as Kyrien used every trick he knew to gain speed. Always behind them came darkness on wings. Not far from Dragonhold, Kyrien climbed and gave Catrin a view of the Pinook and Chinawpa Valleys, her home contained within the range of mountains that divided the two. She almost cried when she saw Lowerton being utterly destroyed. The demons climbed the stair while their giants held a barrier of lashed tree trunks over their heads, protecting them.

In the Chinawpa Valley, hordes of demons built an assault ramp leading toward the back entrance of Dragonhold. Catrin let out a cheer when she saw those within the hold fighting back. With a tremendous noise, the mighty, wooden stair and framework pulled free from the mountainside, using the failsafe mechanism Martik had designed. It was terrifying to see something that had seemed so permanent suddenly come tumbling down, taking the demons and giants with it. Elation turned to horror when Kyrien climbed toward an unnatural-looking cloud that hung over Dragonhold. Below, gaping holes in the landscape looked as if a god had been trying to tear the mountain apart. Enormous holes plunged to unknowable depths where Catrin was certain there had been solid rock only a short while ago.

Light glinted from newly exposed fields of massive crystals that jutted up through rifts in the rock and soil. She caught only a brief glimpse before a huge shape burst from the dust cloud and slammed into them. Another dragon struck them from behind, and again Catrin experienced the terrifying feeling of falling.

Kyrien managed to break himself free of Death's grasp, and Catrin was whipped side to side then pressed deep into the creaking saddle as they climbed. Kyrien's flight wobbled and Catrin could see gashes on his neck and upper breast. From her vantage point, she could not see his belly or hindquarters, but she suspected he had injuries there as well.

Gaining altitude, Kyrien dived in and out of the clouds, more than a dozen ferals giving chase. Their serpentine movements belied flight, and they appeared to be swimming in the air rather than flying through it.

It became very apparent that ferals were not mindless creatures and that they were not acting independently. Something was orchestrating their movements, and Catrin shivered at the thought. Not since Archmaster Belegra had she faced the power of slavery and coercion, and that was what the dragons' actions seemed like: the result of coercion. She could feel their anger and hatred; it did not seem directed at her and Kyrien, but that did little to keep them from taking it out on them.

Dark shapes moved within the clouds, never really giving Catrin a clear view until an entire formation of ferals suddenly dropped through the clouds at the same time, creating what was effectively a giant net that forced Kyrien down and into the open once again. Tucking his wings, he dived, and Catrin watched the mountains disappear behind them. The Arghast Desert lay ahead. There, she knew, would be massive thermals rising from the desert sands, and Kyrien could use those to gain altitude once again, but he continued to dive.

Soon Catrin saw what he was aiming for; near the head of the Pinook Valley, a small fire blazed, and around it stood more than a dozen men in black robes. Hatred rolled from them like rippling waves of heat, and Catrin recoiled. Kyrien extended his wings just a little, causing a rushing sound as he pulled up and reached out for one of the robed figures. Amorphous gouts of darkness leaped from the hands of the assassins, as Catrin knew they were. These monsters were here to kill her and everyone she loved. Using her sword as a focal point, she cast a violent burst of energy into their midst, hoping it would incinerate them all, only a small and lightning-quick feral dived into the narrow space between Catrin and the assassins and took the brunt of the blow. With a sickening crack, the dragon fell, struck stone, and would rise no more.

It was but one of many, and malevolent force concussed the sky, like explosions of pure night.

Leaning heavily to one side, Catrin recovered from another thunderous concussion that erupted not far from her head. Kyrien tucked and dipped down to soar low over the sands, stirring a roiling dust cloud in his wake and pulling up only when Catrin saw riders approaching from deep in the desert. A sizable group of Arghast tribesmen approached, and their battle calls lifted Catrin's spirits if only for an instant.

The tribesman launched their spears into the air. Catrin turned in the saddle to see a few spears hit their marks, but the ferals shrugged them off as if they were little more than bug bites. It was then that the dragons turned their anger on the Arghast. Catrin cried out for them to retreat, but Kyrien left her no time to see what happened next. Pumping his powerful wings and riding on the overheated air, he thrust them back into the clouds.

Whether by luck or by Kyrien's design—Catrin wasn't certain—for a brief time, they dipped beneath the clouds. Below them, amid towering peaks, lay a lush, green oasis, the air above it alive with birds. When Catrin had struck the well, this was what she had hoped would happen, but actually seeing it exceeded her expectations. It was beautiful. That vision sustained her during what seemed an endless flight. Despite her urgings, Kyrien would not respond to her. His flight was direct, his path unerring, yet she had no idea where they were going or how long the journey would take. Her heart yearned for her husband and son, but they were lost to her. The pain was almost more than she could bear.

Catrin let the straps hold her in place as her mind wandered aimlessly without direction or reason. She was exhausted and allowed herself to doze off in the saddle. Some time later, Catrin woke, soaked and freezing. The gray mist that surrounded them was an ever-changing landscape. Where the air became thicker, Kyrien would suddenly rise higher, and where it thinned, he would drop. It was an uneasy feeling. Catrin had done what she could to shore up the weakness. When the air tossed Kyrien in a certain way, she was sure she would be torn from his back, but the straps held firm despite the two that had been cut. It was during those times that she came back to herself, drifting out of the half sleep long enough to try to communicate with Kyrien. His continued silence worried Catrin as much as anything else, though she had worry aplenty.

The fate of those within Dragonhold weighed heavily on her mind along with the fate of the Arghast and even that of those south of Edling's wall. Despite their disagreements, she wished them no ill, especially not the likes of which was now taking place. There was little doubt that Master Edling wanted Catrin dead, but she did not reciprocate. While she wanted to see him fall from power and be forced to live like those he oppressed, she did not wish him dead.

The sight of the assassins had raised her fury like nothing else. Those people had tried to kill Sinjin twice already, and they had nearly killed Durin in the process. Someone was behind this evil, and Catrin burned to know who and why. For most of her life, she'd been misunderstood, thought to be a mighty hero or the basest devil, but she was neither of those things. She was just a wife and mother who happened to have access to Istra's power. Certainly she had abilities that no other could claim, but those powers did not make her invincible, nor did they make her wise; they simply gave her the ability to do things that could not be undone, and with that came tremendous responsibility. Most of the time, it seemed the wisest thing to do with her power was nothing. For years she had concentrated on preparing Dragonhold, and she had failed; those within were doomed. She tried not to think about it. It was simply too painful to imagine.

Now when the greatest need she'd ever known had arisen, she was mostly powerless against the forces that sought to wipe her people out.

Even the attacks she could launch lacked real power and accuracy. The darkness the assassins controlled was devastating, and Catrin knew she would need to learn a great deal in a hurry. The problem was that she had tried before and had made absolutely no progress. Her dragon ore carving had given her access to more power, but Koe was back within Dragonhold. The Staff of Life rested in the Grove of the Elders, possibly already in the hands of the demons. She'd been such a fool.

Cupping her hands, she collected moisture from the surrounding air until she had enough to quench her thirst. It amazed her that she could be so wet and still be so thirsty. It didn't quite make sense, but her mind was addled. Bright sunlight assaulted her eyes as the clouds suddenly dissipated. Desperately Catrin searched the skies around her for ferals, but she saw nothing but clear skies and occasional fluffy white clouds. The comets, though hidden, flooded the air with energy, and Catrin reveled in being beneath the open sky. She didn't know how long she and Kyrien had been flying, but she had the hunger of days without food, and she thought she might pass out.

On the horizon rose a smudge of darkness. Catrin quailed at first, but then she recognized the shape of a volcano protruding from the sea. Clouds gathered around its peak, but no smoke or lava could be seen. Kyrien glided closer and, as if reading Catrin's mind, landed on the black beaches south of the volcano, where a string of tiny islands waited. From the air, Catrin had seen whales and other large marine creatures. There should be plenty of food to be found, she thought, though by the size of some of the shadowy forms in the water, she would need to be careful not to end up food for something else.

Desperation and grief made the sunny day seem disrespectful. The sudden shock of icy cold water brought her fully alert, and she panicked, afraid she would drown while still attached to Kyrien by harness and saddle. Kyrien, though he did not communicate with her, obviously knew this and moved to the black sands. After unbuckling straps that were now cinched tightly took longer than Catrin would have thought, but she eventually wriggled free.

Light surf caressed the shoreline with more of a murmur than the roar Catrin recalled from the coast of the Godfist. A warm wind blew from the far side of the island, and the smell of brine was heavy in the air, its saltiness somehow refreshing despite its tang. Orange crabs with white bellies skittered along the black sands, holding their one massive claw up high, their pointed legs leaving scroll marks in the sand.

Along the horizon nothing could be seen but occasional whitecaps, and Catrin had no idea where they were. When she looked inland, Catrin saw steam rising from what looked like a giant wound in the landscape. Like claw marks, a series of glowing gashes marred the otherwise seamless black stone. The air above them shimmered, and jets of steam issued forth at regular intervals. Catrin backed away, unable to bear the waves of heat that radiated from the massive claw marks. Memories of an erupting volcano and the nagging feeling the gashes had been created by a giant monster made Catrin look over her shoulder more than once.

She found Kyrien sunning himself in a field of stone that looked almost liquid with its ridges and swirls. Catrin feared it would sink under her boots, but it proved solid. With his wings extended, Kyrien's many wounds were exposed. Seeing his flesh rent repeatedly and places where scales were missing brought tears to Catrin's eyes. Many new gashes ran alongside old scars, and some crisscrossed, making his hide look like old leather with only patches of scales.

Ignoring her own needs, Catrin laid her hands on Kyrien, hoping to ease his pain. The energy here felt pure and uncluttered, and Catrin drew deeply. Her vision swam, her legs trembled, and her knees buckled. She would have struck the stone hard had it not been for Kyrien, whose muzzle supported her. Many would have been terrified to be so close to his daggerlike, curved teeth, but Catrin knew he would never hurt her. He had once carried her in those jaws and had been as gentle as if she were his child. She had no fear of him, despite his looking like a giant snake made of moss-covered stone. His membranous wings and stout legs capped with claws that looked like they had been carved of solid marble added to his formidable appearance. His green-flecked gold eyes seemed incapable of conveying warmth, yet she could feel how much he cared for her.

Eat.

Kyrien's communication was clearly a command, and for some reason, it infuriated Catrin. "You haven't spoken to me in hours, and now all you can say is *eat?* What is it? What are you hiding? What don't you want me to know?" Her voice carried with it all her frustration, anger, and worry, and she instantly regretted her tone.

They can hear us.

That thought drove all suspicion from Catrin's mind and left guilt in its place. Of course there had been a reason. Someday she would learn to trust those around her, she reminded herself. It was not an easy thing to do when there were those who really were trying to kill her, her family, and her countrymen. Kyrien, though, was above such suspicion, and Catrin vowed to trust him from now on, no matter how strange his actions might be.

To speak to you I must speak loudly. They are coming. Eat.

"Will we go back?" Catrin persisted. "Will we save the people of the Godfist? Can we save them?"

Though Catrin sensed impatience from Kyrien, he raised his eyes to meet hers, and visions flowed across her consciousness, making it feel as if she were being drowned in a river of thought. What she saw made her want to weep. Such darkness and loss was overwhelming. Catrin knew now that much more than the fate of the Godfist was at stake. Even if she didn't know how the future would unfold, those terrifying glimpses were enough.

Eat. Rest. Prepare.

His words and emotion drove her back to the beach. There were no trees or vegetation to speak of, and Catrin knew that creating a fire would be impossible. She considered using Istra's energy to cook, but the thought nearly made her retch. Doing so would require more energy than the food would provide, and Catrin was weak enough. Along a rough section of the shoreline, she found a piece of black rock that had broken away from the rest of the flow. A deep ridge ran down the center of the slab, and it held a bit of water.

After chasing a few of the crabs, Catrin decided they were not worth the effort since she had worn herself out and not caught a single one. Instead she concentrated on the shellfish that clung to the rocks in pools. These at least could not run from her, though dislodging them was not always easy, she soon had enough for a decent meal.

Piling the dark-shelled muscles onto the indented slab, she carried them to the glowing gashes. After placing them near the edge of the gaping orifice, she backed away from the heat and waited for the shells to open. When they did, she rushed in and tried to pull the slab away, but it had become too hot for her to touch, even with her leather gloves on. Instead she used one of her knives to slide the muscles from the steaming slab.

Not waiting for them to cool, Catrin pulled the fleshy meal from within the delicate shells and was surprised by how good the muscles tasted. Soon all that remained was a pile of discarded shells. Part of Catrin wanted to go get more, but her eyes became heavy, and before she could form another thought, she slept.

CHAPTER ELEVEN

Adversity is often accompanied by opportunity.
— Medlin Reese, healer

Sinjin kicked at the still dirty floors in the hall known as the "false hall" since it went nowhere and seemed to serve no purpose. A few paces away, Brother Vaughn explained the mystery of the hall to Trinda, who seemed intrigued. Sinjin had heard it all before and knew that the mystery had very little to do with why they were there. Brother Vaughn had become convinced that forming a bond of friendship between Sinjin and Trinda was the way to mend the animosity between their families. At least he had not proposed they marry, Sinjin thought—at least not yet. He knew how these things worked, and he had no desire to find himself bound to the least pleasant person he'd ever met.

It wasn't that Trinda was mean or spiteful; that would have been easier to deal with since Sinjin could at least strike back. Instead she was almost always sad, her deep-set eyes seeming to hold the pain of ages, and any enthusiasm in the face of such anguish seemed trite at best. Though he had tried on several occasions to hold a conversation with Trinda, the most he ever received in return was a single-word response and most times just a nod.

"Look here," Brother Vaughn insisted. "Look at this corner, and tell me what you see."

Sinjin continued to drag the toe of his boot in the dust, knowing what it was Brother Vaughn wanted her to see. At times he wondered about the aging monk's sanity, for the strangest things would hold his attention.

"A seam," came Trinda's hollow response.

"A seam, indeed!" Brother Vaughn said with a triumphant look at Sinjin. "You see, m'boy. I told you this girl has an eye and ear for mysteries!"

Sinjin kept his eyes downcast, not really caring. All he really wanted was to get this over with so he could return to his normal life, not that many things were normal these days. He'd heard the whispered rumors that his mother would saddle Kyrien, and he'd even sneaked a few peeks at the saddle. Normally his mother shared all of her projects with him, and he'd spent much of his life in her workshop, but she wanted to keep the saddle from Sinjin. It seemed too surreal to be true, yet he had seen it with his own eyes, despite his mother's efforts to keep it concealed. Brother Vaughn wasn't convinced that Kyrien would ever fly again, and the presence of Reaver and the other dragons also reduced the likelihood of his ever leaving the valley. Without the protection of the guards stationed around him, he would be easy prey for the ferals.

Sinjin tried not to think about them, yet the images came to his mind unbidden—images of ferals clouding the skies and ruling the world from above. He would never look at the skies the same way again, and he found himself grateful for the stone that hung above him. Even if it did press down on his spirit, threatening to crush it, at least it protected him from the death that waited under the skies. Never again would he be able to walk in the moonlight without wondering if something was about to swoop down and devour him.

"Tell me: How do you think the ancients did this? And what do you think their purpose was?" Brother Vaughn asked, and he grabbed Sinjin by the shoulder and pulled him closer, a not-so-subtle reminder of why they were there.

"Maybe they wanted to give you something to think about," Sinjin suggested, and Brother Vaughn gave him a disapproving look. When Sinjin looked over to Trinda with a grin forming on his lips, he saw disapproval on her face as well, and he resigned himself to the fact that they would never find anything to bring them closer. This girl was simply no fun at all.

"Magic," Trinda said with a firm nod.

Brother Vaughn was clearly taken aback by that answer. The word *magic* seemed to bother the Cathurans a great deal. Sinjin recalled his mother telling the tale of how Mother Gwendolin had reacted to her use of the word, and it seemed Brother Vaughn wanted to scoff as well, but he resisted. Sinjin respected his restraint but didn't possess its equal. "A magical riddle, then. Perhaps all you need to do is wave a wand and speak the magic words."

Trinda glared at him, and Sinjin thought Brother Vaughn might scold him, but Trinda caught them both by surprise when she turned back to the barely detectable seam in the corner. "Open," she said as she ran her finger along the seam.

Sinjin nearly laughed out loud, but then the stone beneath his feet trembled. Before anyone could say another word, movement at the other end of the hall drew their undivided attention. Slowly a wall of stone moved across the opening that was their only egress. Though ponderously slow, the stone would close off their exit long before they could reach it.

With only the glow of Brother Vaughn's herald globe to illuminate what now seemed more like a tomb than anything else, Sinjin turned to Trinda. "I don't know how you did that, but I think you had better undo it, and fast."

Trinda wore a shocked expression, and Sinjin could see the fear in her eyes. In a moment that forever changed him, he reached out and put a hand on her shoulder. "Just try."

Running her finger along what was now an almost identical seam, which had only recently been an open hallway, Trinda repeated her command, "Open."

Nothing happened.

The silence that followed was the kind that could only be experienced when encased in solid stone.

Monsters approached. With a scream of primal fury, Chase charged to Martik's side. "Fall back!"

"Help me!" Martik shouted as he cut at the massive sap- and tar-soaked ropes that bound the stair to anchors in the stone of the mountain itself.

"There's no time!" Chase shouted. Grabbing Martik by the shoulder, he pulled the engineer back away from the approaching hoard. What rushed toward them went beyond the natural order and had been somehow perverted, twisted, and manipulated. Slavering beasts climbed with no concern for their own safety, as if all sense of self-preservation had been stripped from them. Chase could see it in their eyes: no fear, only hatred and death. This was not an enemy that could be reasoned with. It was a river of gibbering madness intent on their destruction.

Morif and a handful of guards stood before the onslaught, about to be engulfed.

"Retreat!" Chase shouted, but either none heard or none obeyed.

Beneath a shield made of bound tree trunks came the giants, and the demons crowded around them, protecting the giants with their lives, throwing themselves in front of any attack intended to bring down the lumbering monstrosities. Still, some attacks pierced the defenses. One giant opened its mouth to issue a gargling bellow, revealing its haphazardly arranged teeth stained brown and furrowed by deep ridges. The giant next to it responded by shrugging off the tree shield, sending it crashing down the rock face, where it struck the lower stair, crushing dozens of demons and cutting off the rest of those waiting in the valley below.

This seemed a small victory as the giants slowly picked up speed, roaring as they came, striking fear into all who heard their terrifying calls. Chase watched in horror as Morif charged to meet them, somehow fighting through the attacks of encroaching demons as though they were nothing, though Chase knew some of those attacks had landed squarely. The old veteran somehow kept his legs under himself. One giant raised its boulderlike fist into the air and sent it crashing down toward Morif's head. With more speed than Chase knew he possessed, Morif leaped aside and narrowly avoided a blow that severed massive timbers and sent splinters of wood into the air.

Men gathered behind Chase, waiting for his command, but his mind went blank. All the years he'd trained could not have prepared him for anything like this. Only the claws of a swooping dragon drove him back to action. After diving out of the winged monster's path, Chase made up his mind: he would not let Morif and his men die alone. "Ready your weapons! Form up in ranks!"

Those around him moved without question. Martik leaped at the command too, though Chase could practically hear the wheels turning in the engineer's head. He now realized the flaw in his failsafe release mechanism: in order to be strong enough to hold the stair, he had made it too difficult to release. His mighty trigger more resembled a lock.

"To Morif!" Chase shouted, and those at his back raised a chilling cry that split the air.

Even the giants took notice as the small fighting force poured onto the now swaying stair. A strangled scream rang out, and Chase watched one of his men tumble over the railing. Another went down under a dark blade, but the demons took losses as well, and with those below forced to climb the sheer rock face, it seemed the battle might be one they could win. That was until Chase looked back up to the ridgeline, where hundreds more demons poured over the crest, half running, half falling toward them. Giant claws snatched the man closest to Chase, and before anyone could do anything, the beast tucked its wings and veered away. Before it moved out of Chase's vision, he saw the dragon turn and close its jaws on the flailing guard.

The dark tide washed over them, and Chase knew that he and Morif had both made a mistake. There was no way they could win this battle, and the loss of them would only weaken those within the hold. He could almost hear Catrin scolding him for letting his battle lust overwhelm his good sense. A cold feeling of guilt washed over him and filled him with the greatest need. Catrin was counting on him, and he couldn't let her down. Since the death of their mothers, that had been his role, and beyond anything else, that drove him to remain alive.

As he struck one demon down, another climbed atop the first and leaped directly into Chase's chest, driving him backward into the railing, which struck him in the low back. Pinned between the rough bark and the leathery skin of the demon, Chase struggled with every bit of energy he possessed. The cords in his neck stood taught, and sweat blinded him, leaving only a reddish haze, but the bright flashes made him avert his eyes. The demon was suddenly ripped from atop him, and Chase wiped a torn sleeve over his eyes to clear his vision. On the stair stood Prios, alternating between casting lightning into those that assaulted Morif and the few guards still surrounding him and using fire to incinerate the demons advancing on Chase and his dwindling force. For a brief instant, the distance between them was clear, and Chase let out a hoarse battle cry.

Morif, covered in blood, returned the cry, and the two groups became one, slowly fighting their way back into the hold. All thoughts of victory had long since fled, and those left alive now concentrated on staying that way. As the last guard, a woman who had fought as valiantly as any of the men around her, got her boots on solid stone, Prios unleashed his fury on the ropes that Martik had failed to cut. For a time the ropes continued to hold. Demons and a single giant forced their way inside Dragonhold. The stairs looked surreal as the landing moved away from the mountain, gaining momentum. Creaks and groans gave way to snaps and screams, and much of the wooden stairs crashed into the valley below.

"Retreat to the God's Eye!" Chase cried out, his voice now high pitched and strained.

"The way is blocked, sir."

"Fall back to the forge!"

"The forge is blocked as well, sir!"

Nearly howling in frustration, Chase knew they were in trouble. The great hall was filled with refugees unprepared to defend themselves, and the guards who still lived were barely hanging on. Prios was their only hope, and as a mass of black bodies sought to surround the man who now looked as if his entire body were afire, Chase used the last of his strength to raise his sword and charge.

Jets of dust, stone, and debris clogged the air around Durin as he retreated. Shouts and screams pounded against his hearing while the deep bass of grinding stone made his bones tremble. What little natural light that reached this area was soon extinguished. Seeking fresh air, Durin moved deeper and deeper into the hold, back toward the kitchens and forge. Little fresh air was to be found.

Within the kitchens, what was usually orderly chaos was now true chaos. Fire clogged the air with smoke. Normally the kitchens where completely isolated from the great fire; the stone of the ovens formed the outer wall of the great hearth and were thus heated. Durin watched as people tried to guide the wounded around burning sacks of flour, overturned tables, and slippery puddles marking where canisters had broken. Of course, they were unlikely to find safety in the halls. The cooler air of the halls drew the smoke and fed the flames.

"Stay low!" Miss Mariss shouted above the terrible clamor. "Don't breathe the smoke! Get Millie out of here, and get me more water!"

Despite the fact that the dust had chased him deeper into the keep, Durin turned to go back, knowing the best thing he could do was listen to Miss Mariss. Staying low, below the growing layer of smoke that rolled along the tunnel ceiling, he moved as quickly as he could. From the darkness came Bradley, covered in dirt and grime, only his eyes clear of debris. "Go back," he coughed.

"But Miss Mariss needs water."

"Can't get there anymore. The way's block and the air is clogged with dust."

Durin heeded Bradley's warning; the young guard had always looked after Durin's and Sinjin's best interests. Seeing Bradley's distress, Durin grabbed his arm and draped it over his shoulder. "Come on. I'll help you." The fact that Bradley did not protest told Durin much, and he didn't like it one bit.

"Smother the fire with your cloaks!" Bradley shouted into the kitchens.

"I'm trying, you derned fool! Now help me! And where is that water?"

"The halls are blocked, ma'am. We've no access to water."

Had the kitchens not been burning, his statement might have brought some reaction, but instead people simply worked harder at putting out the flames. Osbourne and Brother Milo appeared moments later with buckets of water from the glass smithy. Osbourne was bleeding from a dozen places, and Brother Milo looked as if he'd been on fire. Again. Durin often wondered if the man's robes were made of tinder.

A terrible howling came from above, breaking through all the other clatter and sending terror through the hold. There were monsters within Dragonhold.

As people moved the wounded to the smithy, where the smoke had dissipated, Durin found himself wanting to do something, anything to help. His heart yearned to relieve some of the pain he saw around him or chase away the fear that permeated the hold. Demonic howls still resounded within the halls, and the sounds of battle were but distorted echoes made more frightening by their ambiguity. No one here could know what horrors were taking place within the rest of the hold.

Once again, Durin drummed up the courage to speak. "Strom, I need to tell you something."

The well-muscled smith ignored him. "Bradley, come with me. The rest of you, stay here and guard the wounded." Hammers swinging from metal rings on his belt, the smith moved with purpose.

"But, Strom!" Durin did his best to interrupt.

"Durin, keep your mouth shut and follow me. We might need your help."

Swallowing hard, Durin just nodded and did as he was told. It was a strange feeling. He'd worked up the nerve to tell Strom what he'd done, but following the smith into battle against the demons was an entirely different thing. He envied Bradley, who, armed only with a short sword and a dragon scale shield, seemed to find confidence having Strom at his side, and the two looked like great heroes to Durin. The continued echoes of battle made his guts go watery, and he wanted nothing more than to hide.

Near the great hall, Strom pulled a herald globe from the pocket of his leather vest. Ahead lay a mass of stone and rubble that blocked the hall. The ceiling had collapsed.

"We need to get this cleared. Step back. I'm going to pull some of these large stones down."

"Won't this make those around the hearth more vulnerable?" Bradley asked.

Durin agreed with his assessment.

"I'm going up there, but neither of you have to. Just help me clear a hole so I can get through. Then you two can fill the hole back up once I'm through."

Durin suspected Bradley would have said something in response, but Strom didn't give him the chance. Instead he started digging his way through the shifting pile of stone. Bradley and Durin did what they could to keep the area behind Strom clear, so he had an open space to deposit the rocks he freed. Several times rocks tumbled into an open space he'd just cleared, and Bradley had to pull him out. With every stone that came free, the sounds of battle drew closer, and terror nearly paralyzed Durin, but something made him move, made him help Strom.

Though he'd expected some sort of speech or announcement, Strom simply disappeared through the hole as soon as it was large enough. The big man was gone. Bradley did not look back to Durin or hesitate in any way; he followed Strom through the hole without a sound. A new battle cry filled the air beyond, and Durin's legs trembled. In that moment, though, his life changed forever. For once, he would not let fear hold him back from his true potential. Still, as he climbed through the hole, he asked himself, "What am I doing? This is crazy! What in the name of all that's good and right am I doing?" The last part became a scream as he tumbled down the loose rocks and directly into battle.

Strom hadn't gotten far before two demons pushed him backward. Bradley charged forward and leveled a kick at one, but the heavily armored demon shrugged the blow aside, which sent Bradley stumbling toward more demons and a pair of giants. Durin could see that more were pouring into the hold, a small band of guards all that slowed their progress. From within that group came fire and lightning, and Durin hoped Catrin and Prios would save them all. With no more time for thought, he ran forward and did the only thing he could think of. He fell onto all fours and slid between Strom and his attackers. Strom continued to fall back, and the two demons' legs tangled when they tripped over Durin. It was all the break Strom needed, and he used his hammers to finish off the dark hulks.

He looked terrifying to Durin as he rose and charged toward where Bradley was going down under a rain of blows. Again his battle cry filled the air, and this time, it was answered not only by the guards but also by Durin. Grabbing a gnarled, black staff from one of the dead demons, he charged behind Strom and landed blows on anything that moved. None of his strikes brought demons down, but they did distract, and that helped keep them off Strom. The smith's strength became apparent as he landed devastating blows with his hammers. Even when demons tried to grapple with him, he used his might and the skills Chase had taught him to send them tumbling into their brethren.

There was a shift in the battle, as lightning crept closer and closer to where Strom, Bradley, and Durin fought. Blood ran down Bradley's face, but Strom pulled the young man behind him and took the brunt of the oncoming attacks. Bradley did not cower and hide, though. With another cry, he lashed out at any demons that came too close. Wielding his staff, Durin landed a solid blow on the kneecap of a nearby demon.

Movement brought Durin to full attention. For the first time, a demon looked him in the eye. It grinned at him, showing black gums and holes where teeth were missing. Nothing had ever frightened Durin more than that grin. The smell of the demon's breath alone was enough to send a man running.

Durin swung his staff, but the demon easily stepped aside. Raising its angular mace, it looked one direction but stepped the other, catching Durin by surprise. Were it not for Bradley's dragon scale shield raised in his defense, Durin would have been dead. As it was, Bradley's defense was off balance, and both shield and mace struck Durin in the head, knocking him to the ground.

Strom seemed to realize how futile this fight was, and he started to push Durin and Bradley back toward the great hearth, but then he stopped. The guards were now accompanied by a hoard of people wielding anything they could find. Young and old, as ineffectual as they may be, they charged at the dark beasts. The demons seemed stunned when the people attacked; such ferocity was not to be expected from mothers and grandmothers and children, which made it all the more effective. The fact that Arghast warriors were dispersed throughout the crowd did not hurt either. Durin let out a cheer when he saw his own mother smack a demon in the face with a skillet. The victory was short lived as more demons rushed in, and he almost cried out as he saw people he knew go down. Durin could not bear to see his mother overrun, and he ran faster than he ever had before. Strom and Bradley matched his stride, and they bowled over the enemy.

When the three met up with the mass of humanity, Durin went straight to his mother, who was bleeding from a cut on her brow.

"Don't fuss over me," she insisted. "Teach those beasts some manners!"

As if responding to her command, Prios let loose a series of thunderous blasts that shook the mighty pillars supporting the great hall.

"From where did you come?" Morif shouted.

"From the great hearth! The way is still mostly blocked, but we can get through given time."

Durin guessed that Morif would try to direct them back toward the partially blocked hall, but for the moment, he called for a full retreat.

With four demons holding the chains around each of their necks, a pair of giants lumbered to the fore, and no one could stand before them. Those who tried were tossed aside or crushed underfoot. Durin's mother had recovered enough to stand, and she launched her skillet at the nearest giant. It struck the hulking beast in the shin, and it let out a terrible bellow. It shook the hall, dancing on one foot for a moment. Then the giant looked down at the petite woman and charged. Defiant, the tiny woman shook her fist at him. Durin tried to get to her, but someone else grabbed her and pulled her back before the giant could retaliate.

Prios launched balls of shimmering air at the giants' heads, and they exploded with thunderous claps. The giants raised chained arms to cover their ears, dragging the demons holding the chains into the air. Again Prios attacked. Seemingly driven to madness by the massive thunderclaps, the giants turned on their captors. Using the chains that had bound them more in spirit than in body, they swept the demons aside in their attempt to escape Prios.

"Now! To the hearth!" Morif yelled.

Chase, Strom, Morif, and Bradley ushered the crowd toward the halls. Demons still attacked, but they were far less organized, and the group made progress across the giant mosaic that covered the floor of the great hall. Durin found his mother, supported her, and helped her through.

"One at a time!" he shouted after helping his mother. "I'll help you. Just don't push and shove!"

"Do as he says!" Morif barked, and Durin felt a rare moment of pride. It didn't last. The rocks beneath him shifted and moved, and he went tumbling, smacking his head as he fell. Determined, he climbed back up and did what he could to help people through. It was a time-consuming process, which left Prios, Chase, Strom, Morif, and a few others to hold off the demons. From the sounds of the fighting, the demons had regained their strength and were attacking once again in full force, though Durin did not see any giants.

When the last helpless person was through, Durin turned back to those who stood and fought. "They're all through! How are we going to get the rest of you through?"

"Go!" Morif ordered.

Durin hesitated. He could not leave these brave men to die, and he knew they would not be able to get through without someone protecting them. Then Prios turned, his face bloodied and bruised, and with a finger, he issued a single silent command: *Go!* Durin did as he said, though he lost his balance and slid through to the other side when the booming started. Like the beat of an enormous drum, the thunder rattled Dragonhold to its core. Scrambling, Durin did his best to get clear as more men followed him through.

With each new face, he looked for Chase or Morif or Prios, but only the faces of guards came through. When Kendra and her mother emerged, Durin took a step backward and lowered his eyes, not wanting a confrontation with Kendra. He stopped for a moment and looked again, his gut telling him something was not as it should be. He had no more time to think about it as Chase fell through the hole, and Durin joined the men who moved to pull him free. Morif came moments later, but Prios did not come. The thunder continued and grew more intense. Rocks slid as the vibration caused them to settle into gaps.

Morif would not let the guards pull him free. Instead he climbed back up and stuck his head through the hole. "Now, Prios! Make a run for it! I'll pull you through!"

In the next instant, the thunder stopped, and in its place came the most terrible battle cry Durin had ever heard. Morif jerked upright as he pulled, but then he was thrust forward and began to disappear back into the hole. Durin tried to get to him, but a mass of guards rushed in to grab Morif by the ankles. The guards suddenly flew backward, and Morif came sliding through, bouncing roughly across the stones. "Let go!" he cried. "Let me go!"

The guards released his legs and he climbed, but a single thunderclap, far louder than all that had come before it, sent everyone tumbling backward again. Morif immediately pulled himself up and charged back through the hole. Moments later he reappeared, dragging the still form of Prios. For a moment it seemed they were safe until dark forms filled the gap and the silence shattered.

CHAPTER TWELVE

The most dangerous mistakes are those you don't realize you've made.
— Enoch Giest

Hot stones. That was what it had finally taken to keep the demons from pulling down the barrier of rubble that stood between them and the only survivors in Dragonhold, at least as far as any of them knew. When Durin returned to the smithy for another shovel load of hot stones, he saw Strom standing to one side, silently watching those who worked in what was usually his smithy.

Seeing his opportunity, Durin approached and spoke before he lost his nerve. "I'm the reason the hold moved."

"What?" Strom asked, looking confused.

Durin saw a couple more adults stop and wait to hear his response. "I didn't want to carry a bucket of almost clean water all the way to the God's Eye, so I dumped it into the glowing rune behind one of the statues. It started steaming and whistling, and when it stopped, the hold moved."

Strom didn't say anything at first. He opened his mouth a few times as if he'd speak, but he still didn't say anything. When he finally did speak, his eyes were far away. "Something so powerful and no idea how to use it." Then his eyes returned to Durin. "Now tell me every detail. I want to know what you heard, what you felt. I want to know how it smelled. Everything. Sit. Talk."

Strom listened with so much interest that Durin's hands and voice trembled. When Martik entered the smithy, Strom called him over and made Durin repeat every word. Martik, an experienced engineer, sat back heavily and stared, open mouthed, at Durin.

"If only Brother Vaughn were here with us," Martik said. "He'd love to know those runes actually do something."

Both Strom and Durin looked away, knowing his absence did not bode well for his safety. Already, Prios had sworn to go back out after Sinjin and any other survivors, but it was uncertain if there was anyone at all still left alive in other parts of the hold. And many felt it better to spend their time reinforcing the barrier and not bringing it down to fight a losing battle.

"Keep building up the barrier," Strom told Martik, and he pulled Durin from the smithy. "Brother Vaughn may have saved us without even knowing it."

Strom wrinkled his nose as he poured a foul mixture into a glowing rune. "What *is* this?"

"Wine and pickle juice," Durin responded with a shrug. "It's all that was left." But then he fell back. Wisps of steam escaped the rune, then more steam came and the whistling sound grew. An instant later, the whistling abruptly stopped, and the floor trembled. When the trembling stopped, Durin watched the truth settle onto Strom's face by the light of a shaking torch. By pouring liquid into the rune, they had done something that would have wide-reaching consequences. For Durin, it was the second time he'd had one of these realizations, and the second was no better than the first.

"By the gods," Strom said, looking down at the steaming rune then at the now open hall leading into the darkness.

"You said Brother Vaughn called that one *respite*. That should mean safety, right?" Durin asked, wanting reassurance and knowing that had been Strom's argument for selecting the rune, but screams from above drove them both to move.

"What have I done?" Strom asked aloud as they ran. "What was I thinking?"

"You said it would've taken too long for everyone to agree on what to do, so you were making the decision for them."

The screaming and shouting continued, and Strom looked like he might be sick.

"Where in the depths have you been?" Miss Mariss barked when they arrived at the forge.

Strom couldn't find words, and Durin followed his example.

"Idiots. The keep has up and moved again, and by the sound of it, some of the demons are trapped as well. They certainly don't sound happy."

"I know now why the keep moved," Strom said at last, and Miss Mariss stopped. "Durin caused it the first time, and I caused it the second time." Miss Mariss looked as if she would shift from stunned to a full-blown rage, so Strom spoke more quickly. "I wasn't sure it would work. Durin's experience could have been a coincidence, and I knew it would take too long to come to a consensus, and we needed everyone to continue working on the barrier, so I . . ."

"You acted like an irresponsible fool and could have killed us all. You should be ashamed of yourselves, both of you. Now the demons are even more determined to break down our barrier."

"Respite," Durin said, looking up at Strom.

"A new corridor has opened," Strom said. "I think Durin and I should explore it and see what new resources we have available to us."

"Or what new dangers we face. You fools. Fine. Go. Just try not to make things worse."

Durin flushed and he could see Strom wasn't faring much better. It made him feel very good that even someone as strong and skilled as Strom could still feel guilt under Miss Mariss's stare. Perhaps there was hope for him yet, Durin thought. Then again, he knew Miss Mariss had not yet realized there were pickles and wine missing.

Strom grabbed more torches and his hammers. Durin looked around for something to arm himself with but found only a rasp. Strom gave him a disapproving look. "You're gonna have a hard time filing your way out of trouble." After what looked like a moment of pure conflict, Strom reached up and grabbed something from the back of the tallest shelf in the smithy. He shoved a cold, black handle into Durin's hand. "I want that back."

"I thought you didn't make weapons?" Durin asked after drawing a gleaming, curved blade from the sheath. The handle felt good in his palm, solid and smooth but with an unusual texture that provided a sure grip. Durin looked in amazement at the finely crosshatched lines that made up the grip. Never before had he seen such precision. The blade itself was black, but the edge gleamed silver and promised blood.

"Knives are not always weapons," Strom said without looking at Durin.

"You don't expect me to believe that you made this for cutting cheese, do you?"

Strom stopped and glared.

"Right. Uh, sorry."

Not far ahead, in a room that had once been a storeroom, despite the glowing runes in the floor, now waited respite—at least Durin hoped that was what awaited them.

The silence was often worse than the hunger or thirst; still it was generally preferable to the sound of Brother Vaughn trying to get information from Trinda. The sullen girl's responses drained the energy from Sinjin, and he wondered how anyone could be so unhappy.

"It needs more," Trinda said, pointing at the herald globe, whose light was fading. Sinjin turned away, not sure how to respond to such an inane statement. It seemed unlikely they could charge the herald globe in the sun without first finding their way out of where they were trapped.

"He doesn't like me," Sinjin heard Trinda say, and he turned toward where she and Brother Vaughn sat.

"I don't think that's true," Brother Vaughn said, and he waved for Sinjin to come closer. "Now that's not true at all, is it?"

"It's not that I dislike you," Sinjin began, but his tone changed under the weight of Brother Vaughn's gaze. "It's just that you are sad a lot, and that makes me feel sad."

"You feel sad because I feel sad?"

"Yeah, that's what I said," Sinjin snapped, earning another glare from Brother Vaughn.

"You should be nice to me."

"Why's that?"

"'Cause someday you're gonna need somethin'."

"And you'll be there to help me?"

Trinda just raised her eyebrows and looked doubtful.

"Perhaps you'll both need something, and wouldn't it be nice if you were there for each other?" Brother Vaughn said.

Sinjin and Trinda both rolled their eyes at him, and in rare moment, Sinjin saw Brother Vaughn's frustration show through the cloak of calmness he usually wore. He took a breath to say something, but then the world began to move. "Hold on to me!" he shouted.

Sinjin grabbed Trinda and pulled her with him, wrapping his arms around her. She didn't struggle and though she was older than he, she seemed but a child, slight and frail, counting on him to save her. It was an odd feeling that bloomed in Sinjin's chest. Dust seeped into the air as the deep grinding reverberated through the keep. Relief flooded through Sinjin as the walls moved, and once again the way they had come in was clear. Still the keep moaned and trembled. Brother Vaughn pulled Sinjin forward, and Sinjin half carried Trinda back toward the main hall, which led between the God's Eye and the great hall. As they neared the junction, Dragonhold returned to rest, and what had become a near-deafening roar suddenly stopped. What remained was far from silence, and it chilled Sinjin's blood. Howls and grunts echoed through the halls, sounding like the cries of tortured animals, and only occasionally did he hear the shouts of people. Sometimes those calls were more frightening than those of the demons, especially when they ended in shrill and strangled cries.

Brother Vaughn stood as still as stone and listened, his head turned one way then another. "May the gods have mercy," he whispered, and he pulled Sinjin and Trinda back the way they had come.

"We can't go back that way," Sinjin said louder than he had intended.

With a sharp look, Brother Vaughn pressed a finger to his lips and pulled them with him. When they reached the part of the hall where they had been trapped, Sinjin nearly shouted in relief. The hall was now clear in both directions, and unexplored darkness lay ahead. Not even slowing, Brother Vaughn kept the group moving at as brisk a pace as the light of his fading herald globe would allow. Soon it would go dark, and they would be lost. Brother Vaughn hadn't said that, but Sinjin knew it; he could read it in the old monk's posture. Still, moving into unexplored parts of the keep piqued his sense of adventure—if only their light would hold.

"So foolish of me not to bring a fully charged herald globe or some other source of light," Brother Vaughn said as their progress continually slowed while the unnatural sounds filling the keep grew louder. Then he drew a sharp breath. Sinjin followed the small circle of light that surrounded the herald globe as Brother Vaughn slowly moved it over bold runes that covered a tile floor.

"It needs more," Trinda complained.

Brother Vaughn ignored her, and Sinjin nearly clamped his hand down over her mouth to keep her quiet. The sound of demons continued to grow. Looking over each rune and mumbling to himself, Brother Vaughn cursed. Holding the herald globe out, he cast soft shadows over doorways cut into an elaborate, multifaceted room, shaped almost as if someone had cut a gemstone away and left this cavity. Stepping forward, he cast out the light to the far doorways, and he stopped suddenly when the tile beneath his boot sank down with a grinding sound followed by a sharp snap. Sinjin looked up as dust fell from above, and it sounded as if the ceiling were collapsing. Indeed the stone above them was moving, but before they could do anything, it stopped.

"This room is a trap," Brother Vaughn said.

"What kind of trap?" Sinjin asked, wondering if they would be crushed.

"I think it's a riddle, but I can't see all of the runes, and I'm not quite sure."

"It needs more," Trinda observed. Sinjin opened his mouth, but she didn't give him a chance to make his snide remark, instead, she snatched the herald globe from Brother Vaughn's hands. "Let me have it. I have some."

Trinda closed her eyes. To Sinjin's amazement, the globe began to glow more brightly through her fingers.

"That's enough," Brother Vaughn urged in a low voice.

Trinda's eyes opened. At first she appeared calm, but then her eyes slowly went wide, the light growing brighter all the while. Brother Vaughn reached for the globe, and power leaped across the open air with a crack. He jerked his hand back. Moments later, Trinda made a popping noise with her lips. She turned and handed Brother Vaughn the now glaring orb. Holding out his hand to shield the light, he accepted it.

Trinda turned to Sinjin, locked eyes with him, and shrugged. "I don't have any more." Then her eyes rolled up into her head, and she collapsed into his arms. Unprepared, he barely caught her and was trying to hoist her onto his shoulder when he heard a low growl—this one not distant. Brother Vaughn turned toward the sound, and the light drove the demon backward, but the growling continued from the shadows.

Brother Vaughn mumbled rapidly while scanning the now brightly illuminated runes. "What's lighter than a feather, worth more than gold, more precious than air, and cannot be seen?"

Silence hung between them for what seemed a long time. The riddle reminded Sinjin of how his mother had explained astral travel, how she said her spirit had flown free of her body and had moved as if it weighed nothing. "A soul," he said. After casting a surprised look, Brother Vaughn stepped onto a new tile in the floor. Nothing happened.

"Excellent," Brother Vaughn said, already scanning more tiles. "What never stops moving but is always in the same place?"

Brother Vaughn's movements had cast part of the room back into shadow, and the growling grew more intense. Turning to face the demon, Sinjin watched in horror as the beast stepped into the light, its eyes now adjusted. Its first step had no effect, but the second sent the ceiling tumbling another notch.

Brother Vaughn leaped to another tile with a wheel carved into it. Sinjin followed, Trinda still draped over his shoulder, and he nearly took a bad step onto the wrong tile, but Brother Vaughn steadied him.

"What's heavier than air and flies with no wings?"

Sinjin tried to think of an answer, but the demon leaped closer to them, stepping on two separate tiles, both of which sank down. Sinjin fell to his knees. Locking eyes with the demon, he saw panic in its eyes, but that fear turned to anger and hatred. "Just go," Sinjin said.

"I can't figure it out," Brother Vaughn said, but Sinjin pushed him, and off balance, he had to make a choice in mid step: water. The ceiling held, but Sinjin pushed again, seeing the demon preparing to attack. "But I don't even know what the riddle is," Brother Vaughn said in a high voice when Sinjin pushed again.

Neither was prepared when the demon lunged.

Flying sideways, Sinjin realized that he'd been hit by the demon. Clinging to Trinda, he waited for impact, knowing they would eventually hit something solid. What they slammed into was Brother Vaughn, who cried out and tried to guess which tiles to step on as he was thrust forward. The grinding sound of stone on stone resounded again, and clouds of dust fell from overhead. Screaming, Sinjin thrust Trinda ahead of him and jumped with all the power he could muster. Feeling the stone closing in on them, he landed roughly and had poor footing when he made his final push. The stone slammed down and caught the toe of his boot, which he struggled to pull free. It was then that he saw the other demons glaring at him over the rubble. The falling stone had only partly obstructed the hall, and the demons were already clearing the way.

Trinda climbed to her feet and cast him an accusing glare. "You hurt me."

"I was trying to keep you alive," Sinjin said, but it didn't look as if Trinda believed him. At that moment, he didn't care. Brother Vaughn helped him stand, and with the herald globe wrapped in his robes, they moved deeper into the unknown at a near run, the light still seeming overly bright, especially with the howls coming from behind. Nothing more was said about the incident. Trinda seemed embarrassed and retreated even further within herself. Sinjin watched her closely, not wanting her to suffer. Though she annoyed him at times, Sinjin realized that all he really wanted was for her to be happy, and the fact that he could not bring her that happiness was what really made him uncomfortable. After a while they slowed.

Once he caught his breath, Sinjin said, "My mom had trouble the first few times she accessed Istra's power, and I'm not sure if she has ever become truly comfortable with it, except for the things she says just come natural. I think maybe that's how your singing works."

Brother Vaughn raised an eyebrow when Sinjin met his eyes, but then he just smiled, nodded, and said nothing more. Trinda looked at him sideways and shrugged. Sinjin had no more time to speak before the light revealed a chasm whose jagged edge made it appear as if the earth waited to swallow them. Brother Vaughn unwrapped the herald globe. The light danced from dainty, crystalline structures that looked like flowers with glass daggers as petals. They dotted the walls of the ravine. The dark rock they clung to drank in the light rather than reflecting it, which made the brilliance of the crystals stand out in greater contrast. Before them lay a bridge of sorts that formed a pathway across the chasm, but the closer Sinjin looked, the less he liked what he saw. The drop down to the top of the span was farther than he was comfortable jumping, and he wasn't sure they would be able to climb back up—here or on the other side. No solid surface topped the span. It was just a pile of stones that sloped downward on either side and into the darkness.

Brother Vaughn held the herald globe over the ledge, and Sinjin stepped back from the dizzying height, but he was drawn back by the shadows on the distant cavern floor. A pattern emerged from the nothingness, random yet orderly. Right angles and plumb lines made what he instantly recognized as a city. Moving the herald globe to the other side, Brother Vaughn illuminated more architecture, yet on this side there were nearly no straight lines. All the buildings formed curves, arches, and other structures that seemed drawn from nature. Sinjin sucked in a breath when some of the shadows began to move. The others had seen it as well, and all three turned to run back the way they had come, driven by instinct to flee the things that creep in the darkness.

The noise of the demons grew more clear and distinct, and panic set a lump in Sinjin's throat.

"We're going across," Brother Vaughn said after a moment.

Trinda just looked at him, but Sinjin could see she was trembling. "I'll help you," he said. "It'll be fine. You'll see."

Watching Brother Vaughn climb down was little help, as it was more of a controlled fall, arms waving and body dancing as loose stone provided unsure footing.

"You're next," Sinjin said, but Trinda just shook her head, not meeting his eyes. "We need to go, Trinda. Don't worry; Brother Vaughn will be there to catch you if you fall."

Trinda raised her head and looked him in the eyes, tears falling from her own. "I can't. I'm scared. I want to go home now." The last statement was said with a quavering, high-pitched note, and the tears came more quickly.

Feeling helpless, Sinjin was torn by fear, empathy, annoyance, and helplessness. There was nothing he could do to help her, yet he could not leave her behind. With a sigh, Sinjin stood with his back to Trinda and held his arms slightly out to his sides. He didn't have to say any more. Trinda scrambled up, wrapped her arms around his neck, and clung to him. Sinjin hadn't been certain he could do it, but she was much lighter when she was conscious, and he stepped over the ledge onto the steep incline, which ended abruptly where the larger stones were piled. Brother Vaughn waited, looking concerned. For Sinjin there was no more time for thought. Once he put his weight on his forward leg, the loose stone broke free and sent him skidding downward. Trinda buried her face in his neck as they fell.

Trying to make sure he did not fall backward, Sinjin kept his weight forward, and for a moment they skidded gracefully, as if on sleigh rails moving over snow, but the smooth ride ended abruptly as one stone refused to move. Catching his toe, Sinjin pitched ahead. Tucking his legs and throwing his weight forward, they rotated in the air, and Sinjin landed slightly forward on his feet, which sent him sprinting straight into Brother Vaughn, who gave a great *woof* as the air rushed from his lungs. The three went down in a heap, and larger stones rolled away, clattering down the steep sides of the pile. It took a moment for them to determine that no one had been hurt, but the need for escape kept the inspection brief.

With the herald globe wrapped tightly, Brother Vaughn led them into a landscape that consisted of only a pile of rubble and darkness. Distorted echoes made it sound as if enemies approached from every direction, a mourning wail mixing with the grunts, barks, and growls. As the demons drew closer, one gave out a deep roar that sounded like thunder. Moments later came the clatter of stones down the slopes, and Sinjin knew the demons were on the pile of rock and gaining on them.

"We've got to move," Brother Vaughn said.

Sinjin stepped in front of Trinda and again raised his arms out to his sides. She wasted no time in climbing up onto his back once more. It looked as if Brother Vaughn would offer to carry her, but when he met Trinda's eyes, she just buried her face in Sinjin's neck. Half running and half falling, Brother Vaughn and Sinjin made their way across the loose and shifting stone, all of it the same deep black. Nothing new emerged from the scenery, just ubiquitous stone leading off into the darkness. Always expecting to see the other side suddenly materialize became exhausting. Outside of the stone on which they tread, they could see nothing above or ahead. It was as if they had left the real world behind. Perhaps they were already dead, Sinjin thought, but then a chill ran over his skin, and a rumbling boom echoed for what seemed an eternity. Brother Vaughn stumbled when lightning split the air and showed a frightening landscape. The pile of stone continued for what looked like a day's walk, and on the other end, above where the stone pile met with a towering wall of rock, waited a city that dwarfed those in the valleys below.

"What kind of place has lightning inside?" Trinda asked.

Sinjin wondered if they had not somehow come out of the mountain to open air, but it did not feel that way. He could feel the land pressing down on him, its weight always a reminder that the world could come crashing in at any moment. Trinda weighed on him in more than one way. Her whispered questions deserved answers, but he had none; all he could do was run. When the world lit up behind him, Sinjin spun around in time to see a giant demon, its treelike arm raised in the air, blazing like the sun, a thread of lightning throbbing and pulsing as it poured energy from the roiling clouds above into a single point. The shape of it stayed in Sinjin's vision long after the lightning vanished. The giant rolled to the side and took what sounded like a dozen smaller demons with it. The darkness closed back in and left him blind for a moment.

"Our bodies form the highest point," Brother Vaughn said. "Get down, Sinjin. Get down now!"

Feeling the hair rise on the back of his neck and Trinda choking him as she clung to him for dear life, Sinjin got low as fast as he could. Lightning struck the demons again, and when it did, they could see the rest still moving toward them. Sinjin prayed for the lightning to continue, but the darkness remained. Only a pattering rhythm filled the void. The first drops of rain struck with such surreal randomness that Sinjin could hardly believe it, but the patter became a roar, and a deluge rushed in.

"We've got to move," Brother Vaughn said, and Sinjin did not argue.

Now slick and glossy, the stone provided even worse footing, and they moved slowly. It seemed as if they weren't moving at all against the persistent, rain-filled wind. He blinked when he saw the stones ahead move in the deep shadows cast by the lightning. He couldn't believe it, but soon they found out why as the stones were crawling with crabs. Sinjin remained still as the crabs gathered closely around his feet; their powerful claws ready to tear through the leather of his boots. Taking a deep breath, he was about to ask Brother Vaughn what to do when Trinda began to sing.

Sinjin wasn't certain if it was just the rain that drew the crabs or Trinda's singing, but they came in such numbers that he could only assume they heard her call. Either way, they did hamper the demons, even if only for a brief time. Cries and howls had come as the demons walked along the writhing blanket of crabs, and Sinjin assumed that he'd been right about the claws being both strong and sharp. The crabs had drawn around them first but then had moved toward the demons. Still more were coming, and the way before them remained clear, making it certain these creatures were under Trinda's control. The rain, however, continued to pelt them.

Shouldering his way forward, Sinjin set his mind to taking one step at a time, each one difficult, but his runner's training kept him from faltering; he could work through the pain. Brother Vaughn struggled alongside him, not having a much easier time of it, despite the fact Sinjin carried Trinda. She remained quiet for a time after she stopped singing, and Sinjin suspected it had drained her, just like his mother's activities often did to her. There always was a price to be paid.

When the rain subsided, Sinjin almost wished it hadn't as it had at least given them a meager bit of cover. Now all that stood between them, the demons, and the giants was an open expanse of rock. The distance between them was difficult to gauge, but it was shrinking. The demons seemed tireless, and Sinjin felt as if he had jellyfish instead of legs. The light of the overcharged herald globe still shone brightly, and there was no hiding. The awaiting city still looked to be hours away.

"Never before has my will been so tested," Brother Vaughn said. "It would be so much easier to just give up."

Sinjin simply grunted in response, unable to form the words. Seeing someone he admired as much as Brother Vaughn falter was enough to shake Sinjin's confidence to the core.

"Please don't let the dark things get me," Trinda said, and her words spurred them both on. "Let me down. You need rest. I can walk as fast as you are carrying me."

Sinjin couldn't deny it; his pace had slowed, and not just because of how slowly Brother Vaughn was moving. He was exhausted, his will nearly spent. He lowered Trinda to the stones and put his arm around Brother Vaughn. Trinda, the better rested of the three, led the way, the gleaming herald globe in the palms of her tiny hands.

Brother Vaughn stumbled and Sinjin could not keep them both from falling. Neither was hurt, but neither attempted to rise. Each breathing rapidly, they took an involuntary moment to rest. Trinda watched with a worried eye and urged them to hurry, but it was too much to ask. Even when Sinjin did manage to regain his feet, he could not get Brother Vaughn from the stones. The older monk tried to stand but lacked the strength. The time was costly. By the time Brother Vaughn regained his feet, the demons were within bow range. Sinjin did not see any bowmen, but he was looking at the situation based on his training, and he knew they were perilously close.

Trinda was crying now, and with every step, she urged them to hurry. She knew as well as Sinjin that they would not make it to the city ahead. It was a goal beyond their grasp. Once, he'd tried to imagine what would happen if they did reach the city, but it had become a nightmare, and he tried to keep his mind within the confines of the current problem. To each side stood a possible route of escape, but Sinjin did not know what awaited them in the darkness below. All of them had seen movement down there, and he didn't think crabs were the only things living within the darkness. For a moment Sinjin wondered how anything could live in here at all. Then a fading rumble of thunder reminded them of the rain.

The sound of demons running, their crude armor creaking and their booted feet striking the stones, was the only warning they had that the attack had begun. Sinjin had somehow expected them to slowly catch up, but the demons had been keeping a burst of speed in reserve, and now they rushed forward. Acting on instinct, Sinjin reached out to the energy around him, energy that he knew existed and that his parents could access. He, too, should be able to access it, he presumed. Trying to remember to breathe, he reached out with his fingers and tried to grab on to it with his mind, as his mother had always said. It had been a long time since he had tried to access Istra's powers, but never had he tried when his life depended on it. That was how his mother had come into her powers, and perhaps that was what it would take for his abilities to manifest. Given his encounter with the assassins, it seemed unlikely, but there was nothing else he could do but try.

Crying out and thrusting his arms forward, Sinjin released the accumulated charge. A small spark leaped between his outstretched fingers, and there was a light crackling sound, but his efforts yielded no other effect.

Trinda just stared at him and said nothing.

His face flushed and his pride deeply bruised, Sinjin turned to her. "Is there anything you can do? I'm sorry. I failed."

"You tried," Trinda said with a shrug. "I have a little more now. I'll try too."

Before Sinjin or Brother Vaughn could say another word, Trinda cupped the herald globe, and it grew steadily brighter until it shone like a star, and she threw it as hard and as far as she could. The herald globe sailed high, higher than a girl of Trinda's size should have been able to throw, and Sinjin understood that Trinda's powers continued to manifest, even if his own did not.

Shielding his eyes, Sinjin supposed it would buy them a moment when the demons would be blinded, but without a light to guide them, he wasn't certain how much good it would do them. He didn't have to think about it long. The herald globe ended its flight, and even from a distance, it seemed as if the globe exploded before it ever struck the glossy black stone. A massive burst of energy radiated from it, leveling the demons and sending a wash of angry air over Sinjin, Trinda, and Brother Vaughn.

"By the gods," Brother Vaughn said. "What did you just do?" Then he seemed to recall himself. "Never you mind that question, dear. You saved us. That's what you did." Still, when Brother Vaughn found a still-slightly glowing and perfectly preserved herald globe at the center of an area where even much of the black rock had been blasted away, he retrieved it with cautious awe. "Come. We must leave this place. Quickly."

CHAPTER THIRTEEN

The true measure of a person can be seen in the way they treat those less powerful than themselves.

— The Pauper King

For Sinjin, reaching the end of the stone bridge was like waking from a bad dream only to find himself in a new nightmare. More howls came from behind, and he grunted with exertion as he did his best to give Brother Vaughn a boost. His strength was fading, and Brother Vaughn had to find what toeholds he could to complete the climb. Trinda was much easier to lift, and Brother Vaughn was there to reach down and grab her, but that left Sinjin standing alone at the bottom of a nearly shear face. Down low, the face was smoother and devoid of toeholds. Brother Vaughn took off his outer robe and held it down to Sinjin. With a running start, Sinjin jumped without a great deal of confidence, but fear and adrenaline brought him close to success. With his second jump, he got a grip on the robe. The sound of tearing cloth was nearly as frightening as the sight of Brother Vaughn nearly going over the edge, but the robe held and Brother Vaughn regained his balance.

Even with the robe to hold on to, it was a difficult climb. When Sinjin finally reached the top, he slid down into a heaving and quivering mass.

"I'd let you rest, m'boy, but we've got to go," Brother Vaughn said, and Trinda showed her agreement by pulling on Sinjin's shirt, her eyes pleading.

Sinjin knew they were right; he could hear more demons coming, and he knew they needed to move, but he could not get his body to respond. He felt Brother Vaughn grab his jacket between the shoulders, and he tried to stand, but he leaned heavily on the already abused monk. Trinda eyed them both with doubt, as if she expected them to collapse at any moment. Sinjin did his best to prove her wrong and, after a few minutes, was able to walk on his own, though he and Brother Vaughn stayed side by side in case either needed help. Trinda walked ahead of them without complaint. The herald globe glowed brightly, as if it had been charged in the sunlight, though not as brightly as it had been when Trinda had fed it her energy.

"Did you give it more?" Sinjin asked Trinda when his strength began to return.

"A little." She shrugged.

"And was it easy to give it just a little and not everything you had?" Sinjin asked, and Brother Vaughn looked up, awaiting her answer.

Trinda just gave him an annoyed look. "I didn't have very much." Her look made it clear she wanted no more questions about that.

Sinjin sighed and wondered if he would ever understand the ways of those with power. It seemed so foreign to him, even though he was part of the most powerful family on Godsland. He'd seen things no one else had, yet he could explain none of it, could feel none of it, and that terrified him. It was a fear he'd carried most of his life, and these days seemed no more likely to bring an answer or solace.

The sights around him would have been met with awe under any other circumstances, but Sinjin barely noticed the carvings and reliefs or the repeating scrollwork along the walls of the gracefully arching halls. Feeling like prey chased into someone else's territory, Sinjin forced himself to move faster, and he found himself offering support to Brother Vaughn, not knowing where he had found the strength.

Walking in a daze, he almost didn't notice the change. It had been gradual, but the light continued to grow until they no longer needed the herald globe to light their way. Brother Vaughn looked as if he wanted the globe back from Trinda, but she put it in the pocket of her dress, and the elder monk said nothing. Hues of amber cast a warm glow on the otherwise cold stone, and Sinjin felt a weight lift from his soul. Even though he could not access Istra's power, he missed the warm radiance of sunlight and, he supposed, the light of the comets as well. His mother always said that the comets were the most beautiful things she had ever seen and that they had not been in the sky when she was young, but for Sinjin, the comets had always been there. Even though there were more than when he was younger, he couldn't imagine a time without them. They were so commonplace to him, they did not seem so beautiful. Also detracting from their majesty in his eyes was that they seemed more like the force that divided him from his family and had caused most of the bad things that had happened to his mother. If not for Istra's powers, would the Zjhon have ever invaded his homeland?

The beauty of what lay ahead tore Sinjin from his melancholy thoughts. First came the sound of moving water over the rush of a distant fall, then the smell of lush grasses and apple blossoms. Before them waited an underground world that was full of life and wonder. White birds glided in the air over trees that were far wider than they were tall. Though the mighty cavern could have held greatoaks, it seemed most of the vegetation remained closer to the ground. Looking up, Sinjin's breath caught in his chest. A latticework of giant amber crystals formed a vaulted ceiling for the chamber, and these crystals acted as lenses, gathering and intensifying the light from above.

A herd of small deer gathered near a shallow pool for a drink. At first they looked like fauns to Sinjin, so slight were their forms, but several bore small but fully developed racks of antlers. Sinjin wondered what other strange creatures roamed the caverns and how they had come to be there. Then he looked at the waterfall, which cast rainbows about the cavern, and he knew that the river would bring life, though he still wondered about the deer and birds and whatever else might be alive in this place. The land and trees appeared almost manicured. Shadows occasionally moved within the trees. Sinjin did not know if it was merely his imagination, but as they moved closer to the water, his anxiety grew. Still the chance to get a drink of cool, clean water was too good to resist. Mostly ripe apples waited on a nearby tree, and Sinjin picked three, feeling like a thief. As he did, he noticed no apples on the ground nor stray leaves or sticks.

Trinda eyed the apple Sinjin handed her with suspicion and waited for Sinjin to take a few bites of his before she ate it. He couldn't blame her. There was something curious about trees growing inside of a mountain. He wasn't sure what apples grown in such conditions would be like, yet they tasted delicious. When they had finished the apples, Sinjin wondered what to do with the core. Brother Vaughn looked to be having a similar quandary, but Trinda just finished off her apple and threw the core on the grass. Sinjin and Brother Vaughn eyed it as if they might be punished for their disrespect of this place.

Trinda just put a hand on her hip. "Don't be silly. The deer will eat it."

Not knowing how long she'd slept, Catrin felt thick and groggy when she woke. The cries of gulls filled the air as they feasted in the shallows during low tide. Her skin felt coated in salt, and her hair lay in ropelike clumps. Black sand clung to her leathers and her exposed skin, and she wiped it away, trying to clear the fog from her sleep-addled mind. The sight of the endless horizon brought fear and anxiety, as if she were the only person left on Godsland. Looking around for Kyrien, she found nothing but empty beaches and bare fields of black stone. If not for the gulls, she would have been truly alone.

Tears gathered in her eyes as she felt the guilt of leaving her son and her husband and all of her people to their fates. Though she knew Prios would protect Sinjin and that Chase and Morif would do their best to protect them, she knew what was to come; she'd seen it in visions she prayed would never come to pass. Standing on a lump of rock in the middle of an ocean, she could not have felt more useless. Forcing her tears aside, she climbed to the highest point of the dormant volcano, the only sign of volcanic activity the still glowing gashes in the field of stone and an occasional burst of steam from the far shore. Standing at the edge of the crater, she scanned the horizon and still saw nothing. Within the crater itself, grasses grew, and Catrin was surprised to find berries and leafy greens growing among porous rock.

While she ate, Catrin began to sense the land pulsing with life beneath her feet, and in some ways, she felt closer to the land than she ever had before. Similar to the feeling she had when standing in the Grove of the Elders, it was as if she could reach into Godsland itself and draw upon its power. She let the land guide her to a place near the center of the crater, a place where moss carpeted rounded stones. Here she rested.

Composed and calmed, she moved with the pulse of the land, swaying and breathing deeply.

Using the technique Benjin had once taught her, Catrin focused on her center, which rested within the Grove of the Elders as it existed in her memory: a mighty field of black stone surrounded by twenty-one towering greatoaks. At the very center stood the Staff of Life, still blooming in the place where Catrin had planted it more than a decade before. At no time in history had the grove ever looked exactly as Catrin pictured it, at least not all at one time, but Catrin remembered this place the way she wanted it to be: a place of ancient power untouched by the mistakes of a young girl. Old guilt shrouded her heart despite the fact that she had done everything she could to rebuild the grove. Now only time would return it to its previous glory. The crater reminded her a bit of the grove in the way that the power of the land seemed more acute here. It also reminded her that the Staff of Life rested in lands now occupied by dark forces.

Anxiety poured unbidden from the depths of her soul, fears so dark and personal that she could not face them. In her most terrifying visions, she'd seen herself become the face of death, a wielder of such weapons that all would cower before her, and she had fought to become something else ever since. When making the herald globes, she'd been a creator, yet it seemed as if her true destiny was to be the destroyer. Perhaps in that the old prophecies had been right. Perhaps she had no choice but to become an avatar of death.

Is a sword only used to kill?

The thought echoed from Catrin's subconscious, distant and faint but nonetheless poignant. Catrin had used that very argument to convince Strom to make her a weapon: the sword that lay in her lap, gleaming in the preternatural light of Catrin's meditation. It was a tool—a deadly and dangerous tool. It terrified her. Always she had questioned her right to end the life of another, always she wondered what made her life more valuable than the other's, and always she felt unworthy of those who had died so she could live.

Your work is not yet done.

That thought came from a memory of the druid Barabas and his farewell to her. He'd given his life to save hers, and his parting words frightened her more than anything else. She had yet to earn that sacrifice. Her greatest challenges lay before her, which meant there was the chance she would fail, that she would dishonor those who had made the greatest sacrifice. Fear that she would fail all those who were counting on her came to the fore and threatened to smother her, but Catrin was no longer a little girl, and she would not let fear rule her. Something had happened to her when she became a mother; her own well-being had become somehow secondary to the needs of Sinjin, and as long as he lived, she would have everything she needed to overcome her fear.

Thoughts of Sinjin drew Catrin out of the grove, and her consciousness soared. In the past she had astrally traveled and had visions, but what happened next seemed more like a mixture of the two. Unlike past visions, she could exert control over where she was, but unlike astral travel, she felt uncertain of *when* she was. Something about what she saw made it seem unreal. It rippled and shifted as in dreams, and her thoughts influenced all that she saw. Her heart was drawn to the Godfist, and she soared over the seas faster than the swiftest bird. The Godfist rushed toward her, accompanied by a heavy feeling in Catrin's chest. Smoke rose over parts of the island—her home—and armies of demons and giants clogged the valleys, some even spilling out into the Arghast Desert. Black ships filled the harbors, and the entrances to Dragonhold were infected with darkness. To the south, everything burned; when she soared over the landscape, nothing moved. Then she saw them: feral dragons sunning themselves along a ridgeline, looking almost serene. Catrin knew better.

Desperate need pulled her back to Dragonhold, deep into the stone. There she felt a pulse of life, and it spoke to her, "Mother! Please help!"

Every ounce of Catrin's energy became focused on finding Sinjin and helping him. Nothing mattered more than being there when he needed her most, yet she could not prevent the present from pulling her back, from making her experience the now. When Catrin's eyes opened, she had no idea how long she'd been gone, but the sun was already dipping into the water.

A sudden, pounding thought from Kyrien forced all else aside.

Prepare yourself!

What Catrin saw on the horizon shocked her to her core, something she'd never thought to see, at least not from this vantage point: a flying ship! And it was not just any ship. Like a lover come home after far too long, Catrin recognized the *Slippery Eel,* her normally submerged battering ram now cutting the wind. This alone was enough to rock Catrin back on her heels, but the air around the *Eel* was filled with dragons, lightning, and fire. To add to her horror, the backs of the ferals bore riders who reeked of power. It was these men who cast lightning and fire at will.

Kyrien crashed into ferals, his saddle no longer on his back. He was not alone, though, and Catrin nearly shouted in triumph when she saw the other regent dragons coming to Kyrien's aid. She'd not seen another regent dragon since her flight from the Firstland many years before, but their beauty was unmistakable, even from afar. The ferals had their own fierce splendor, but the regents nearly glowed and shifted colors in the changing light.

Catrin drew a deep breath and prepared to face her destiny. Opening herself to Istra's power, she focused on becoming the sword Strom had made for her: sharp and dangerous but finely tuned to work for good. She found the sword in her hand and raised it high, issuing a battle cry from the core of her being. From the deepest part of her gut, she released all her frustration and channeled it into deadly intent. Energy crawled over her body as she waited, knowing Kyrien would guide them to her.

Soon Catrin could see the crew of the *Slippery Eel,* and she smiled at the thought of fighting alongside Kenward and his shipmates. Tempted to swim out to meet them, it was all Catrin could do to make herself wait.

"There!" came Kenward's shout across the water, and Catrin waved her arms. "I told you! None of you believed me, but I told you she'd be there, didn't I? Ha ha! I told you all her dragon spoke to me, and you didn't believe me! Now who's the crazy one?"

For a brief moment, Catrin grinned, knowing Kenward's crew would not hear the end of this anytime soon. Her grin vanished, though, when the ship slowed and lowered from the skies into the dark waters. Ferals dived at the ship, and only the maddened defense of the regents kept the ferals from tearing the *Slippery Eel* to pieces. Unable to contain her energy any longer, Catrin aimed her sword at the nearest feral and unleashed a torrent of energy that crackled with life. It struck the beast in the chest and knocked it from the sky. The seas around the *Slippery Eel* roiled as dragons continued to strike the surface, some dying, some fending off attacks. Only a few regained the skies and even fewer with riders still in place. Having seen her strike, the regents raised a call that stirred Catrin's blood. They recognized her!

A boat dropped from the side of the *Slippery Eel,* looking tiny and vulnerable in the frothing waves. Catrin feared it would capsize, but the men aboard knew their business and somehow managed to brave the dragons and the surf to make their way to shore. Catrin recognized Bryn and

Farsy. The former was as red faced and freckled as ever. Farsy looked as rugged as the sea, his leathery skin hatched with lines and his graying hair pulled back into a braid. Even his tattoos were faded, but his smile shone brightly.

Racing ahead, Catrin looked for the best place for them to land, a place with more sand than rock, and they made for the same place. As they approached, a rippling wave followed them, a monstrous head rearing from the water. Bryn smacked it with an oar and was knocked backward when Catrin's attack struck the beast under the chin, snapping shut its massive jaws. Moments later a regent struck the mostly submerged feral dragon from above, and Catrin had to concentrate on getting into the boat, hoping no more ferals waited beneath the frothing waves.

The ride back to the *Slippery Eel* would haunt her dreams.

CHAPTER FOURTEEN

We can reach our full potential only if we are willing to learn, which means we must occasionally admit we are wrong.

— Master Jarvis, teacher

Kenward grinned as he grabbed Catrin by the arm, pulling her onto deck. "Welcome back to the *Slippery Eel!* I told you all she was here, now didn't I? None of them believed me." In a quieter voice he said, "It's a good thing you're here; I was starting to wonder if I'd gone as mad as Nat Dersinger." Kenward's wink brought back mostly fond memories, but now was not the time for reminiscing, though seeing Bryn and Farsy brought joy to her heart in spite of the darkness that surrounded them.

"How did you do it?" Catrin asked as soon as her boots hit the deck. "How did you make her fly?"

"I thought you might ask that," Kenward said, his grin not fading. "I present you with my flight master."

From the prow approached a lithe man dressed in loose-fitting silks that shimmered as he moved, giving hints and glimpses of his taut form. It was his face that shocked Catrin, for she recognized him.

"Pelivor? Is that really you? By the gods, look at you!"

Stepping forward, he lifted Catrin into an embrace. "I knew we would find each other again. I've learned so much from you, though I've had to do it from afar. Now perhaps you will teach me in person."

"Right now the two of you need to get us out of here," Kenward said, and his words were reinforced by the thrumming of the ship. The *Slippery Eel* had come in perilously close to the rocks, and it would take only one strike from a feral to send them onto the jagged formations.

"Would you like the honor?" Pelivor asked. "I'd love to study your technique."

"Actually I've only done it a few times, and that was years ago. Please, show me what you've learned."

Pelivor nodded and Catrin noticed how much more confident he'd become. Not arrogant or vain, he was simply comfortable being who he was and secure in his knowledge and skills. He'd taught Catrin to speak Zjhonlander and how to read High Script, and there was no doubt he was among the most educated men she knew. Seeing him spread his arms and open himself to Istra's power made Catrin beam with pride. In that, too, he exerted calm control.

"You should have seen him the first time," Kenward said, seemingly reading her mind. "He nearly sunk us."

Pelivor turned his head and raised an eyebrow, and Kenward went silent, save a quiet chuckle.

The *Slippery Eel* gracefully left the water and turned on Pelivor's will, gliding just above the water's surface. Catrin watched him, wide eyed. When she'd first discovered the ability to make a ship fly, Catrin had been able to achieve little more than raising the ship up and riding the wind. What Pelivor did was much more impressive as he seemed to command the wind. Even as ferals continued to swoop and dive, he maneuvered the ship as easily as if he held the wheel but with more agility than any ship's captain could ever have hoped for. It did not seem that Pelivor had access to even a fraction of the amount of energy Catrin could pull from the air around her, yet he exerted such fine control that he did not need as much power to accomplish the task at hand. Catrin felt clumsy and inefficient after watching his precise control.

Standing beside Pelivor, she took his hand. There was no lurch, as Catrin remembered from when she'd been interrupted. Truly Pelivor had found mastery where she was inexpert and required the use of brute force. Slowly she opened her energy to him, and he turned to her, his eyes now wide. "You have so much!"

"And you need so little," Catrin said. "You amaze me."

Slowly Catrin began to see the intricacies of what he did, the way he created a latticework of energy that was equally strong yet required much less effort than Catrin's wing formations had. She considered lending him more energy, but he did not need it. Instead she concentrated on what she could do to make the ship go faster. Her efforts sent cargo shifting, and Kenward held on to the railing.

"Here we go again," Bryn said, and Kenward grinned.

Pelivor observed for a while. Then he interrupted her. "Everything you do is so . . . big. Let me show you something. I can't do it for long, but I think perhaps you could. He took her to the stern, where a strange apparatus had been erected. Resting on a pedestal of iron-reinforced timber, a hollow tube of wood looked to have been carved from a single tree trunk. There was nothing else, no moving parts and no ornamentation, just a strangely shaped tube of wood with a flare in the fore opening and a smaller opening in the aft.

Catrin watched closely as Pelivor took a long breath and drew as deeply as he could. Dividing his attention had a negative impact on the amount of lift his latticework structures provided, and the ship seemed more like it was bouncing across the waves, like a flat stone skipping over still water. When he applied his will to the air in front of the flare, things changed. Air clung to air, and as he forced it through the chamber, more came of its own volition, allowing him to compound the amount of force generated.

The effort came at a price, and Pelivor soon had to stop. The *Slippery Eel* slowed abruptly as the hull once again found the water, and Pelivor dropped to the deck. "Do you see?"

"I do," Catrin said. "I'm sorry I did not help you. Are you well?"

"I'll be fine in a moment. For some reason, I can't seem to do two things at once. Perhaps with more practice."

"You did very well. Already I'm learning from you."

Pelivor smiled.

Kenward watched the skies. "That burst of speed gave us a bit of time, but the dragons are gaining on us."

Catrin turned to see a writhing mass of darkness rolling in and out of the clouds, some attacking and others defending. It was aerial chaos, and the thought of being on dragonback during such a battle made her stomach hurt. Perhaps that was why Kyrien had brought the ship to her instead.

Grubb, the ship's cook, brought Catrin and Pelivor some of his restorative broth, which they accepted eagerly. It was always wise to take what Grubb offered; his skills in the galley were legendary, and Catrin was not disappointed. Though little more than a light soup, the meal warmed her belly and brought clarity to her thoughts.

In a short time, the broth was gone, and Pelivor turned to Catrin. "I suppose I should get us back in the air. If you want to try working the aft, just let me know, and I'll do my best to maintain control."

Seeing Kenward and the crew looking equal parts excited and terrified, Catrin grinned. "Let's do it!" Those words sent everyone into motion. Anything loose was secured, and the crew found places where they could hold on.

"I've waited a long time to say this." Kenward raised his voice and said, "Catrin, Pelivor, let's fly!"

Pelivor exerted his will with the same level of quiet confidence, and Catrin did what she could to emulate his control. Slowly she gathered air and forced it through the narrow chamber. A low howling sound grew in volume and pitch as the stream intensified. Soon it was accompanied by another sound that matched its intensity.

"Woo hoo!" Kenward bellowed as the ship moved forward faster than anyone could have imagined. The sails exceeded the speed of the wind and slowed the ship rather than speed it along, and Kenward shouted for the crew to trim them.

"You're doing it!" Pelivor shouted, sounding triumphant. "I knew it would work!"

Catrin looked back from the stern, watching as a spray of water rolled behind them, curling in on itself, racing into the space that had held the ship only a moment before. Dragons still filled the skies behind them, but the battle was breaking up; feral and regent dragons alike retreated to the clouds. The sun sank below the horizon, clouds obscured the moon and comets, and darkness enshrouded them. Knowing it would be foolish to fly blind, Catrin eased their speed, and soon Pelivor lowered them back into the water.

"The landings are the hardest part," he said as his shoulders heaved from the effort.

Though she knew she should rest, Catrin's body throbbed with excitement and anxiety. It was a heady mixture that she knew would prevent sleep.

"The seas only know how good it is to see you, Catrin," Kenward said as he wrapped her in a warm blanket. He and Bryn guided Catrin and Pelivor into the galley, and Grubb appeared with food more substantial than the broth they had earlier. Catrin was grateful since flying ships, or even propelling them, gave her a mighty hunger, and hearty fish steaks were just what she needed. From the wonderful taste, she knew Grubb had not gone light on the herbs and seasoning.

"How did you learn to fly the ship?" Catrin asked Pelivor when he'd finished his meal. For the first time since she'd arrived, Catrin saw him flush, and he seemed slightly embarrassed.

"It took quite a bit of time and many tries, but Kenward kept explaining to me what you had done, at least to the best of his ability. Finally I started building models of the ship and I played with them in the wind." This statement seemed to embarrass him, but Catrin admired his creativity. "One day I found something that worked, and after countless failures, I found some success. Kenward, of course, wanted more, and I began practicing every day. Each time, I got a little better. And now . . ." He shrugged.

"You've become a master," Catrin finished for him.

"He doesn't drop us from the sky as often as he used to," Kenward corrected. "I almost had to throw him overboard for trying to fly us into low-lying clouds. Who knows what flying through clouds would be like? We'd be blind and we might even drown!"

Pelivor flushed and would not meet Catrin's eyes.

"It's wet, true, and very difficult to see, but you can breathe just fine," Catrin said.

Kenward involuntarily spit out the wine he'd been drinking and broke into a fit of coughing. When he'd recovered, he said, "When will I ever learn not to try to match wits or questionable behavior with you, m'lady?"

Catrin shook her head. Coming from him, that was no compliment.

"Did you really fly through the clouds?" Pelivor asked.

Catrin told the tale of her and Kyrien's flight from the Godfist. It was difficult to get through without crying, but she managed—just.

"We nearly made it to the Godfist," Kenward said, "but Bryn spotted dragons—the nasty-looking black ones—and we turned back. The devils gave chase, and it took everything Pelivor had to keep us in one piece. The greenish ones like Kyrien came not a day too soon. That was when I started dreaming about you being stuck on an island."

"I'm glad you came," Catrin said.

"None of this lot believed me," Kenward said for what seemed the twelfth time, and Pelivor rolled his eyes. "So why are we going back to the Firstland?"

"What?" she said, standing up.

"Well, every time I dreamed about you being on that island—sometimes even when I was wide awake, mind you—I'd always see us sailing back to the Firstland. I figured you'd know why."

Catrin said nothing for a time, every part of her conflicted. Nothing mattered to her more than getting back to Sinjin and Prios, but she had no idea what had become of those within Dragonhold or even if the defenses had withstood the assault. If they still lived—Catrin's chest ached at that thought—her chances of getting inside were dismal. Letting their defenses down to admit her and Kyrien would open the doors for the hoard of demons, and Catrin did not want to put her loved ones in greater peril, yet staying away went against every instinct she possessed. She clenched the top rail of her chair and stared down at the table.

"Do you want to go back to the Godfist?" Kenward asked.

"Yes," Catrin said.

Kenward sucked in a deep breath. "I'm not sure we should do that."

"Then why did you ask?" Catrin snapped. "If you're just going to sail to the Firstland regardless, then don't bother asking me."

"I'm sorry, Catrin. I just wanted to know what you desired while still advising you on the dangers—"

"I know, Kenward. I'm sorry. It's just . . . Sinjin. How do I abandon my son? My husband? My people?"

"I don't know," he said, her pain reflected in his eyes.

Not able to look at her companions, Catrin gripped her chair and looked down at its seat.

"I'll take you home if that is your wish, Catrin," Kenward said.

Silence hung between them for a time. Catrin made no move to respond, and Kenward started to stand up from the table.

"I can't leave them behind," she said. "Even if it takes me to my death, I must go back."

Kenward swallowed. "I understand."

"I don't want you to take me, though. I'll call for Kyrien, and he can take me home."

"But how will you fly if you no longer have your saddle? You said that was the only thing that kept you on his back."

"I don't know. We'll just have to find a way."

"I don't know either, Cat, but I've seen dragons fight, and I don't think you want to be anywhere near when that happens. Maybe you should let me sail you home."

Again silence.

A feeling crept over Catrin, but she pushed it away, not wanting to let anything alter her course. She was a mother; nothing could stand in her way, but that feeling, which fostered doubt, would not be ignored.

Gripping the chair so hard that she thought she might snap it, a thought occurred to Catrin. "Kenward, what is your cargo?"

"Spices, seeds, a variety of things for homesick Greatlanders living on the Godfist, and a pair of boilin' heavy stone thrones for your highness."

"That's it. I can use one of the thrones to travel back to the Godfist."

"Oh, no," Kenward said. "I'm not going through that again. The last time you tried that, you nearly died. And how do you think I'd feel with your dead carcass on my deck? No, sir. Not me. Nope. Besides, you can't get to those thrones. They're acting as ballasts and are underneath the rest of the cargo."

"Surely we can manage to get one of them on deck," Catrin said.

"No. It took ten men and a hoist to get them where they are, and even if we could move one up here, I wouldn't. That would make us top heavy, and we'd likely capsize. I'm sorry. No."

"You owe me," Kenward said hours later, looking more agitated than Catrin had ever seen him.

Shifting, she tried to find a way to get comfortable on the cold, hard stone. She reminded herself that the throne was designed not for comfort but to act as an anchor to her physical form, which would guide her back to her body.

"I can't believe I let you talk me into this. What was I thinking?"

Looking out at clear, blue sky, Catrin knew better than to smile. The hastily cut hole in Kenward's deck provided just enough of a view for her purposes. Bales of herbs had been stacked as strategically as possible to provide the proper acoustics and the separation of the two individual chants. Many of Kenward's crew, including Kenward himself, knew both sides of the chant from their harrowing voyage to the Firstland in search of Archmaster Belegra. Those memories brought fear and mourning, and Catrin tried to put that out of her mind as she concentrated.

Before her, Pelivor knelt, looking up into her eyes. "I'll attend you. Just as I did all those years ago."

Catrin smiled. "I know I can count on you." She also nearly laughed when she heard Kenward complaining that he should just start keeping drums on his ships so he would not have to constantly make them from whatever was in his hold.

Voices rose slowly on either side, each with their own cadence and melody that uncannily merged into seamless harmony. When the drums did start, Catrin was impressed by the amount of vibration she felt. The crew had done well. Those vibrations allowed her to slip beyond her mortal shield, and Catrin flew free in a rush of exaltation. The open sky welcomed her, and she soared through it. Behind her, a silvery thread ran back to her waiting form. She, Prios, and Brother Vaughn had been right; it was indeed the mixture of metal and stone that created the anchor effect. Had the thrones ever reached the Godfist, everything could have been different. Catrin and Prios would have had the ability to safely travel astrally anywhere they wished; they could have been so much better prepared. Instead, she and Prios had nearly been killed just trying to travel a short distance to save their son. Catrin did not blame Kenward for the horrors they faced, but she did shiver at the memory of them and wished again that Kenward could have come sooner.

Instinct guided her as she sailed straight toward Sinjin, her course direct and unerring. The waves raced beneath her, a feeling of bliss nearly overcoming her as she flew. Such freedom! Twisting and spinning, she reveled in the glory of being naught but energy, free of burden and driven by pure purpose. Only the nature of that purpose brought Catrin out of her revelry. The thought of the demons that ravaged her homeland brought with it a dangerous odor, and the wind cried afoul. Those who stood against her overwhelmed Catrin's senses; single-minded hatred engulfed her, and it was that obsession that frightened her the most. It was not as if each of them hated her for his own reason. The hatred was homogeneous and felt as if it came from a single, dominating source. An oily and cloying feeling encroached on Catrin, and she felt insignificant and small. Every sense told her that she would be dead already if not for something surrounding her, protecting her.

No! her spirit cried as she sensed the falseness of the will that was trying to subvert her, and she recoiled, but it pursued her with relentless vigor. Only when another energy came close did the oppression wane, and Catrin could feel Kyrien as he reminded her what it felt like to be truly protected.

You should not go back . . . yet.

Catrin wanted to scream at him, to accuse and blame him. Lacking the form to utter the words, she cast angry energy at him, and still he remained unwavering.

We are not ready to face them . . . yet.

I cannot abandon them, Catrin wanted to scream.

The world spun as Kyrien overwhelmed Catrin's senses with a vision, a projection of his thoughts that felt as if they were her own. She experienced not some memory of Kyrien's past; she lived his fears as if they were her own. He bared his soul, showing her the things he knew were to come, as surely as if he were a prophet. The future horrified her, but it was not enough to dissuade her. No one and nothing could convince her to leave Sinjin to his fate. She had to see him. She could sense his fear. He needed her.

I must go, she thought with all her might.

Kyrien relented but stayed by her side. When the attack came, he thrust himself in front of her. Catrin screamed as his energy was torn apart.

Her spirit shouting a reverberating battle cry, Catrin gathered her energy and attacked. The silvery thread that trailed behind her blazed furiously, and energy raced along the thread to devastating effect. Dark forms gathered in the air around her, each twisted and deformed, as if nature itself had been subverted. Such single-minded rage and malevolence was difficult to face, but Catrin's web of lightning knifed through the air, seemingly random in its path, the tendrils were well-defined and tightly wound, which was a product of what Pelivor had taught her. Now she could create larger, more powerful, structures using less energy. When the beams of liquid light struck, they severed the bonds between the demons' spirits and their mortal forms. She could feel them as they were freed from compulsion, freed from a life of torture, and returned to the well from which they'd been sprung. More came, and Catrin attacked, again and again, relentlessly, feeling no pain and no weariness.

Voices called to her, but she ignored them. She was winning! She could defeat this enemy and find Sinjin and Prios. She was going to *win!* Kyrien's spirit overwhelmed her as his energy embraced her.

You must go back now.

No! I'm winning!

The cost is too great. You will die. The darkness is drawing you in and can strike at any time. You must turn back now!

Catrin didn't care if she died. It was not her life that mattered, but the thought of Sinjin growing up without his mother made her soul ache. A sparkling cloud of threatening energy gathered around the Godfist as she approached, and she could feel the pent-up charge waiting for release. What she'd seen so far had been but a feint; what awaited her now was a full assault. The enemy had tested her defenses and knew her weaknesses. Soon she realized that Kyrien had been right, but it was too late, the attack was swift, without further warning, and deadly. Catrin felt something akin to all the air being sucked out of a room, and the darkness reached out all at once, hurtling toward her with the most foul intent. The hatred battered her senses.

Catrin opened herself to all the energy she could pull across her lifeline, which now resembled a bolt of lightning racing toward her. When it struck, Catrin felt herself become the conductor. She felt as if she, too, were illuminated from the inside out and that she shone like the sun. The brightness fought the haggard darkness that reached out to her with lethal force. Without thought or reason, Catrin released the energy in a single pulse that sent a wave of light radiating out from her like a massive wall of water. The darkness was tossed before it, and lost in the wave, it dissipated and vanished. It was a small dent in the massive cloud of darkness, but it gave Catrin heart.

Kyrien soared around her, keeping her safe as she gathered energy for another attack, ready to give all she had left to annihilate this threat to all she loved. The air behind her began to sing, and Catrin turned to see what new threat she faced. A howling form flew straight toward her, and it took her a moment to recognize Pelivor. His speed was terrifying, and had she been in her physical form, Catrin would have taken a step backward. As it was, Pelivor's scream grew louder and louder, and Catrin realized it was not a battle cry, but a warning to get out of the way. Pelivor was out of control.

As he screamed past, Catrin felt a wash of energy douse her, and she could see the fire racing along a glowing cord attached to Pelivor's spirit. Just before he struck the cloud of darkness, he lit up from within and, flailing wildly, sent gouts of fire and something that looked like boiling air into the darkness before him.

Without another thought, Catrin followed him and, using what energy she could muster, blasted a trail before her. Still, the darkness clawed at her, its grip madness, its odor cloying and sweet. Issuing her own scream filled with horror and fear, Catrin felt the darkness close in behind her.

No feeling could compare to being cut off from the light, to lose touch with all that is sane, and to be immersed in chaos. Before her, only the vision of Pelivor gave her something to hold on to, and she tried to get to him.

His screams slashed the air, cutting into Catrin's soul, but she could not reach him. The same darkness surrounding Pelivor and falling on him like a pack of starving dogs on a fresh kill also assaulted her. She barely felt the attacks. Twice, bursts of light drove back the darkness, and Catrin ignored the demonic forces and the voices demanding she come back. The only thing that mattered in that moment was Pelivor. Each pulse of light he sent out gave Catrin a chance to get closer to him, and she felt as if she could stretch out and touch him, yet he was just beyond her spirit's fingertips. Screaming violently with effort, Pelivor reached out to Catrin wildly and savagely, lacking the control of experience. When he and Catrin did connect, there was a flash far brighter than any of those that had come before. In the next instant, Catrin opened her eyes, back in her body.

Standing above her was the most hideous visage she had ever seen. Gray and twisted, the face of the demon spoke of a slow and painful death. A curved blade gleamed in the light, and with a warrior's precision, the demon reversed its blade while raising it for a devastating strike. Something dark slammed into the side of Catrin and the demon. The demon's blade threw sparks into the air as it struck only stone, and Catrin realized it was Kenward who had saved her by tackling the demon.

Trying to regain control of her body after the astral travel, Catrin was dismayed to find that she could barely move. Her arms trembled with fatigue, and a glance to her left showed that Pelivor was not faring much better. The demon, though, was struggling to get Kenward off its back, and Kenward looked small and weak against the massive beast. Reaching over to Pelivor, Catrin grasped his hand in hers. He looked up at her, met her eyes, and nodded, knowing what was to come. The demon was overpowering Kenward, and Catrin released all caution. She drew as deeply as she could on her own energy and what she could get from Pelivor. His eyes went wide, and the air between them sang a high-pitched note before light arced between Catrin and the demon with a crack that sent Kenward stumbling backward. Nimsy arrived a moment later and finished the demon off while it was still stunned.

"Are you hurt?" Catrin asked, not knowing exactly whom she was asking.

Pelivor shook his head but could not or would not speak.

"I'm fine," Nimsy said, but he grew quiet as Kenward straightened suddenly.

"What was I *thinking?*" Kenward asked. "It would be great to sail with Catrin again!" he continued, mocking himself. "Nothing bad ever happens when Catrin's aboard."

For a moment the comment stung, but Catrin remained silent, letting her old friend vent his anger and frustration. When she looked up and saw two jagged holes in his deck and down to see a dead demon in the bilge, it occurred to her that he was probably right.

"We'll just cut a hole in the deck! How could I ever have gone along with that, I ask you? And now look. *Two holes in my deck!* And you darn near took Pelivor with you! And why is it that as soon as you two trip off to play in the skies, we get attacked by demons straight from the depths?"

"Black sails on the horizon, sir!" came a shout from above. Catrin recognized Farsy's voice, and he sounded shaken. "An' that black cloud is back on the horizon. 'Cept it's bigger. And the wind has died."

Kenward stood with his arms out to his sides and his mouth wide open, but no sound came out. Turning to Catrin and Pelivor, he raised his palms. "Can you make her fly?" The look in his eyes made it clear that he really hadn't wanted to ask the question.

"I don't know," Catrin said.

"By the gods, does it always hurt this much?" Pelivor asked, his hands over his ears.

"Should I take that as a no?" Kenward asked.

"I can try," Pelivor said and Catrin nodded.

Kenward softened then and blushed. "Are you certain? Nimsy, Farsy! Help these two up on deck."

He hadn't really waited for Catrin to answer, but she just clamped her jaw and got ready to climb to the deck. Unsteady on her feet and feeling only loosely attached to her body, she was grateful for Nimsy's help. Pelivor's head lolled from side to side, and Catrin doubted he was up to the task; he looked barely conscious.

As the sun melted into the sea, the largest and brightest comets showed themselves in a wash of color that ranged from gold to deep violet. It was strikingly beautiful, and that alone brought Catrin hope and refreshment.

"Where are we going?" Kenward asked.

Taking a deep breath, Catrin stood on trembling legs. She'd seen the darkness laying siege to the Godfist, and she knew that the odds of any of them surviving were terrifyingly slim. Then she felt a comforting presence and heard the crew shout out. She saw Kyrien circling low over the ship.

Everything before her faded away, and Kyrien sent her a vision of darkness and loss that made her soul tremble. Then he flashed a vision of Catrin and Kyrien standing as the last defense of man and dragon alike. The vision replayed, and each time they made different choices. Over and over again the vision played in her mind, but every time one or both species were lost. For one waited a hollow victory; for the other, extinction. Catrin reeled at the implications and tried to control her reaction to the horror they faced. This decision—her decision—would affect all that happened from here on out, and she could only hope that she chose wisely.

Despite the visions, Catrin was determined to save them all or die trying. "We go to the Firstland."

"I knew it," she heard Kenward say, and she received a rather shocked look from Pelivor, who was slowly recovering.

"Let's see if we can get this ship into the air," Kenward said.

Pelivor smiled then winced. "I'll give it my best."

Catrin remained by his side as they tried to get the ship out of the water, but the still air made it impossible.

"You're going to have to propel us," Pelivor said.

"Are you sure you'll be able to get us out of the water?" Catrin asked.

"Are you sure you can propel us?" Pelivor asked Catrin.

"Not really," she admitted.

"Then we're even."

Walking to the back of the ship under her own power was an accomplishment, but it seemed insignificant in comparison to what she was about to attempt. Standing beside the massive, wooden tube that was bolted to the deck of the *Slippery Eel,* Catrin knew that getting the boat moving would be her greatest challenge. Forcing air into the tube had been relatively easy with air already rushing toward them, but grabbing still air and forcing it through was a great deal more difficult. Progress was painfully slow, and Pelivor offered to come back and help her get them started, but Catrin did not want him to exhaust himself by helping her. He would be responsible for keeping them airborne, a task they could not afford to have unfulfilled. Catrin waved him off and applied her will, feeling as if her head might split into two. At first the wooden tube emitted a low moan, and the ship sank lower in the water, but the ship did move forward, albeit in painfully slow fashion; still every bit of speed forced more air into the tube and helped drive them faster.

"Ships approaching from all sides, sir!"

An instant later, Kyrien turned, rolled, and dived into the waves off their port side. Hushed cries from the crew pulled at Catrin's senses.

Kenward's every attention centered on Catrin. "You can do it," he whispered.

Nimsy had remained by Catrin's side, and she leaned on him for support, knowing her task was impossible. Even with her greatest effort, the ship had not gained enough speed to sustain the reaction, instead requiring more and more energy from her. An instant before she released the energy flow, the ship thrummed and surged forward, as if they had been struck from the stern. And in fact, they had. Kyrien proved his swimming prowess by driving the ship forward. His serpentine body and tail propelled him through the water, showing the efficiency of his form. With no time to revel in the marvels of dragons, Catrin redoubled her efforts, and the air came to her more easily, partly because of Kyrien's efforts and partly because the winds had picked up.

"Did you see that?" came a shout from on deck, and Catrin risked losing her concentration to look around. Black ships approached from every direction, dark clouds following those from the west. Lightning danced in the charged air amid the rigging of the dark ships. Catrin felt more than saw the presence of someone using Istra's powers. She could smell the discharge in the air, and she felt the hairs on her neck rise. Again she regained her focus and applied as much energy as she could to increasing their speed.

Pelivor gave no warning, and Catrin heard men hitting the deck as the ship suddenly left the water at a steep angle and just as suddenly slowed when it struck the next wave. Three more times they skipped across the waves, and the crew barely held on. After the third, Pelivor gave out a roar, and the ship gained the air, catching the growing tailwind.

Catrin worked to shape the air as it entered the tube, and in doing so realized that the design was flawed. If she could change the shape of the inner chamber, it would be far more efficient, but she had no time for that. As the ship's speed picked up, so did their altitude, and she could only hope that Pelivor did not drop them from the sky.

Catrin returned her attention to the approaching ships, which were now far too close. The *Slippery Eel* was airborne but was by no means high enough to clear the approaching ships with their spiring masts and inky black sails. Once again they would need to rely on speed and agility. With Catrin and Pelivor not at their best, she wasn't sure how nimble their movements would be, so she kept her focus on speed. The adverse side effect was that the ships ahead drew closer at an alarming rate. A moment later Catrin's heart fell into her stomach as the ships before them crested a large wave. Racing down the trailing edge of the wave, each left the water at the exact same moment. Lightning flared and created a web between the three flying ships.

Pelivor turned and looked back to Catrin, and the ship dropped sharply. Pelivor never got to see the panicked expression on Catrin's face, as he needed every ounce of concentration to get more altitude. A cold feeling washed over Catrin as the realization sank in: all their advantages were gone, and they no longer had any way to defend themselves from the darkness that approached. Perhaps they could take out one or two of the ships if they had enough speed. She looked over to Kenward, who seemed to have come to the same conclusions. He just nodded to her and gave the order. "Arm yourselves and prepare for ramming speed!"

CHAPTER FIFTEEN

Our greatest limitations are often self-imposed.
— Dirk Burunda, mountain climber

Durin had known Prios his entire life and knew he was a nice man with Durin's best interest at heart, but he couldn't stop the fear from stirring in his belly. A tongueless man with such power was in itself somehow frightening, but it was the need in Prios's battle-weary eyes that terrified Durin. It made him accept that his actions may have resulted in Sinjin's death. That thought haunted him, and he wanted nothing more than to believe that this tunnel would lead him to Sinjin, Brother Vaughn, and even Trinda, but so far this new section of Dragonhold had proven to be little more than empty rooms and halls. The deep rumbles that came from the heart of the mountain had been the most interesting part of their journey thus far, that was, until Prios had arrived.

Durin and Strom had been walking at a brisk pace while they explored the halls, but some three hours into the journey, Durin had turned around to find Prios stalking him. His shriek had given Strom a start, but then they had seen the look in Prios's eyes. He needed to know if this was the way to where Sinjin was. No words were required. And of those who had come with Prios, none spoke. When Durin spotted Kendra and Khenna, he looked away, still troubled by their presence. Prios, though, had pushed them on, his herald globe brightly charged and shining the way.

Since then, they had been searching through an area that must have once held more people than currently lived on the Godfist. Durin found it depressing. Why would anyone choose to live in darkness, in a place of cold stone that seemed to suck the joy from the air? At least that was how it felt to Durin. Perhaps it was only the product of his current mood, but the tense silence seemed to indicate that the others felt the same. The inherent sense of order in the place also bothered Durin. Here rested an abandoned city, yet the halls were clear, and not a bit of refuse could be found. The chambers they did explore were bare as well, adding to the mystery. It was as if the city had been built as a precaution and had never actually been occupied.

Rumbling echoes continued to break the silence at seemingly random intervals, and each time Prios listened intently. It seemed impossible to tell where the sounds were actually coming from, but Prios continued to lead them with what appeared to be confidence. Strom walked by his side, not questioning Prios's judgment. More meticulously carved entranceways lined rough-hewn corridors, but it came as a shock when they reached an imposing hall, the corridor turning left and right around the perimeter of the hall, and the most elaborate entrance yet stood directly before them, ready to welcome them or devour them—Durin couldn't tell which. Mighty creatures, from dragons to giant cats, had been carved around the entranceway, and their beauty was eclipsed by only the fear they generated. Prios gave them but a single glance. Only

Strom's sideways look and his subsequent checks over his shoulder made Durin feel any better.

Every footfall sent echoes cascading through the halls, and Durin knew that if there was anything alive in this place, it surely knew they were there. The place must have been designed to carry sound from the dais to the audience, and it did its job well. Prios's sharp hiss reverberated throughout the hall, and Durin fought the urge to hide.

Before them lay the remains of what had once been a finely dressed man. His clothing had been almost perfectly preserved, though his body was a desiccated hull that somehow still clung to his bones. Most shocking was the simple dagger wedged between two ribs and leaving no doubt that this man, whomever he was, had been murdered. The thought made Durin look over his shoulder, though it was obvious this crime had taken place in the distant past. After listening intently to the faraway thumps and rumbles, Prios led them from the amphitheater, and Durin couldn't help looking over his shoulder, wondering if the murderer were lurking in the shadows.

The sound of creaking timbers and a low buzz filled the air as the dark ships encroached. Catrin turned to Kenward. "Do you remember the drills we ran when we were lost trying to find the Firstland?"

"We weren't exactly lost; we just didn't know how to get where we were going," Kenward said, but he stumbled when he saw Catrin's exasperated look. "Yes, I remember."

"Can we do something like we did that time you turned to the side at the last moment?"

"I don't know that it would work," Kenward said. "Much of that technique relied on the water, and empty air would not provide the same effect. That would just put our weakest side forward."

"What do you plan to do, then?"

"We'll slip between two ships, turn, and ram one of them in the belly."

"Slip between the ships that have lightning flowing between them?" Pelivor asked, his voice high pitched and strained.

"I didn't say it was a perfect plan. What do you suggest?"

"I suggest we try to gain more altitude. That's the only thing that will give us room to move."

Catrin swallowed hard, knowing she'd already given her best effort, and she assumed that Pelivor had as well. This last effort might be in vain, but she had to try. Working at the wooden tube, turbulent air fought her, demanding its freedom and refusing to do her bidding. Still, she managed to gain a bit more speed, and Pelivor, his outstretched hands crawling with energy, lifted the ship higher. The dark ships stayed just above the water, and from the *Eel*'s current height, they would slam into the masts and rigging of the approaching ships. Pelivor cried out as his arms trembled, and the veins stood out on his neck as he tried, without success, to get them high enough to clear the other ships.

"Get ready to board the ship to port!" Kenward shouted, and Catrin nearly lost her concentration. She could not bear the thought of the *Slippery Eel*'s crew going to their deaths. She could see the demons on the other ships now and with them, men. Dressed in black armor and looking as if they bathed in ashes, men worked alongside demons. It was a terrifying sight. Some wore the mark of the hammer, which was Thorakis's sigil, but Catrin could still not figure out why Thorakis would do such things and align himself with evil. It made no sense.

"One more try," Pelivor shouted as the ships moved close enough for lightning to reach out to the *Slippery Eel*'s rigging. Catrin let out a cry of her own as she reached for the comets, begging for the energy she needed, pleading with the goddess for more power. If only she'd had Koe or her staff, but she had none of that. All she would wield would be the sword Strom had made for her against his own will. It was a beautiful blade with a magic of its own, but Catrin was uncertain how much use that magic would be under these circumstances. Nonetheless, the feeling of the pommel in her hand steadied her, and she held the blade high.

Just as impact was imminent, the hull thrummed, and the ship lurched upward. Knees bent, Catrin absorbed the upward thrust and did her best to take advantage of the gained height. Pelivor shouted with what sounded like a mixture of terror and relief as they soared above the towering masts.

A momentary slowing and the sound of snapping rigging gave everyone pause as it seemed they had not gotten away clean after all. Catrin moved to the rail and looked down to see wings—not structures of energy but real wings, Kyrien's wings. Even as he helped to lift them into the air, he was taking the opportunity to attack the rigging of the ships below. Once he let go, he and the *Slippery Eel* turned on the wind and soared back low over the water, now well clear of the ships. The dark cloud that had been approaching was nearly upon them. It overflowed with energy and malicious intent, and Catrin did not want to be anywhere near it. To the east, another bank of clouds threatened. It, too, reeked of energy, but its charge, at least, was that of a natural storm. What approached from the west wanted her dead; she could feel it.

The dive back to low altitude had gained them speed, and Catrin shaped the wind to give it the most efficient flow. The air sang and, as the rigging began to vibrate, Kyrien thrust them upward and into the approaching storm. Screaming gouts of fire clogged the air, leaving behind trails of oily black smoke. One struck the deck, and immediately fire spread. With most of the crew holding on for their lives, the fire got a chance to establish itself. By the time the crew had tied a rope around Farsy's waist so he could let go and fight the fire, the flames were spreading. With Kyrien's unpredictable movements, there was not much Farsy could do to protect himself, and Catrin hoped that slim line of rope would be enough to save him from going overboard.

Another flaming projectile struck the mainsail, which was soon awash with fire. Catrin had to remind herself to breathe as Bryn climbed the rigging without a rope to secure him. Kyrien banked a sharp turn as another screaming ball of flames arched over the bow. Bryn hung by his arms alone, and he nearly swung in a complete circle as the ship banked, creaking and groaning against Kyrien's back, but when the ship righted itself, he landed deftly.

Catrin's efforts continued to lend them speed, and Pelivor kept most of the weight off Kyrien. It was only when they needed to climb or change direction that Kyrien would take more of the weight onto his back. It must be painful, Catrin thought, but she could sense Kyrien laughing.

I am stronger than you might believe.

Catrin smiled.

"I'm not so sure about this," Kenward said as they neared the leading edge of the towering storm cloud, its structures larger and more imposing than any fortress ever built. The *Slippery Eel* was about to disappear into it, even as lightning continued to illuminate it from within. "I didn't agree to this!"

Still, Kyrien drove them upward and directly into the storm. Almost instantly it became clear that the air currents within the storm were more unpredictable than Kyrien's movements, and the ship along with Kyrien flew erratically, sometimes dropping through pockets of air as if they would crash to the sea. Light flashed around them, and Catrin felt the ship building up a charge. It reminded her of when she'd been struck by lightning in Pinook Harbor. Her skin crawled with energy, and a coppery taste filled her mouth. The structures Pelivor used to provide lift seemed to gather the charge as they sliced through the excited air around them, and balls of floating lightning danced along the deck and through the solid walls of the deckhouse. The curses that poured from the galley made it clear that the lightning continued to the other side of the walls.

"I should have listened to my mother," Kenward said after having to duck ball lightning and nearly being thrown overboard by turbulent air.

"Now there's a first," Catrin said, unable to resist.

"Really?" Kenward said in mock horror. "You're going to hold that over me now? While we're flying through a storm I wouldn't sail through and being chased by balls of light and fire, if we're not tossed into the open air first. I'm not certain which death I prefer, but I'm pretty sure I don't want one of those balls of light catching up to me."

"Get low and stay away from the mainmast!" Catrin said.

"Oh, I don't like the sound of that at all," Kenward said. "Why do I even let you on my ship?"

Catrin got no chance to respond as the storm chose that instant to relieve the ship of its charge. She had expected it to hit the masts, but she had not considered that they were inside the cloud instead of below it. In a surreal moment that would forever be burned into Catrin's memory, she saw a fine, silvery web of energy form, and in the space of a breath, it grew to blindingly bright light that crawled over every part of the ship and its crew. In the next moment, darkness engulfed them and rain whipped around them, but the most terrifying part was the feeling of falling. Even stunned and confused, the crew managed to hang on to the now plummeting ship. Pelivor remained where he'd been clinging to the railing, but he appeared to be having trouble hanging on. Catrin couldn't blame him; neither of them had been prepared for this, and she did not know how much more she'd be able to endure, but for the moment, she knew she needed to get control of the ship.

Standing up and supporting herself against the deckhouse, Catrin tied herself to the steerage, having flashbacks of nearly drowning as a result of the same idea, but she forced herself to do it as the prow dipped. The ship dived straight down into the clear skies below the storm clouds, and the seas rushed up at them with incredible speed. More turbulence caused the ship to twist, and Catrin drew a sharp breath when she caught sight of Kyrien below them, falling in a flat spin, as if he were already dead. Catrin cried out across the distance and tried to communicate with his spirit, but she got no response, and his body continued to spin out of control. Knowing everyone aboard would suffer Kyrien's fate if she did not do something, Catrin gathered her will. She created structures more like those Pelivor used than the ones she had created in the past, and she found them easier to maintain, except the speed of the air coming at them was so intense that it tried to tear the structures apart.

"I knew this was a bad idea!" Kenward shouted, even as the angle of their descent lessened.

The speed made the rigging sing, and Catrin wanted to look down and see what had become of Kyrien, but the ship was far from under control. Backlit by a flash of lightning, a giant shape filled the air near them. One could not confuse a regent dragon with a feral dragon, and this was definitely a feral. Its black scales glistened in the rain, and it matched their dive. Using all her might, Catrin changed the angle of her wings, scrubbed off some speed, and sent them back into as steep a climb as she could maintain.

"Hold on!" she shouted.

"Now you tell us to hold on? How can it get any worse?"

Catrin didn't bother to answer Kenward. She let the port-side wing dissolve into nothingness, just as the feral attacked, which sent the ship rolling aside. A mighty crash resounded and sent the ship careening as the dragon planted its claws on the hull and thrust itself away from the *Eel.* Catrin tried to reestablish the port wing, but the spinning of the ship made it difficult to do anything but hold on. After several tries, she managed to right the ship. Soon after, Pelivor joined her and did his best to secure himself in a similar fashion. With his help, the ship regained stable flight.

"Watch for the feral!" Catrin shouted.

It wasn't long until someone cried out, "Here it comes!"

The information wasn't all that helpful in the sense that Catrin had no idea from what direction the attack would come, only that it would come soon. With a sharp turn to starboard, Catrin hoped she'd guessed correctly.

A muffled roar that sounded like a snake moving over rawhide, only a thousand times louder, shook the *Slippery Eel,* but the ship maintained stable flight. Momentarily allowing her concentration to waver, Catrin looked around, trying to figure out what was going on in the air around them, but once again, clouds had engulfed them, and she could see almost nothing. Even sound was dampened by the wet air, and the cries that rang out seemed distant.

Grubb brought a thick soup that sat heavily in Catrin's stomach and made her eyelids feel as if they weighed as much as a pair of hams. Nimsy braced her and took more of her weight as she swayed on her feet. It was simply too much to ask of her exhausted body. She needed rest more than anything. Vaguely she thought she heard someone calling her name. Wanting to tell the person to go away and just give her a little more time to sleep, Catrin realized she was falling; everything was falling.

Trying desperately to clear the sleep from her mind, Catrin lent energy to Pelivor, who looked as if he, too, would drop at any moment.

"We need to get the ship back in the water," Catrin managed to say between gasps.

Pelivor just nodded without fully lifting his head.

Darkness crowded Catrin's vision, and she remained conscious only by the sheer force of her will. Nothing mattered in that instant except getting the *Eel* back in the water. If it killed her, then so be it. None of this seemed worth it anymore. How could anything be worth the pain and suffering she endured? How could anything make up for the anguish of loss or the frustration of failure? Catrin howled in spite of it and guided the ship lower.

"First we need to get clear of that!" Kenward shouted as the feral soared straight toward the prow of the ship at incredible speed. At the last instant, the dragon reached out and grabbed a crewman as it passed. The man's screams pounded against Catrin's resolve, trying to convince her that she could not win; they would not survive.

Buffeted by the wind, the ship angled toward the waves, and Catrin stood, trembling, ready to release the energy and collapse the instant they hit the waves. Farsy's support appeared to be the only thing keeping Pelivor upright, and she knew he felt the same.

"Get down!" someone shouted.

Catrin saw it then, approaching for another pass, its eyes gleaming with hatred and purpose. Like a giant snake, it undulated in the air, as if swimming through the clouds. Folding its wings, it raced toward the *Slippery Eel,* aiming for Kenward. Catrin could not allow it to take him from the deck—not Kenward or any other member of the crew.

"I'm sorry!" Catrin cried out, not having time to warn anyone or ask permission. Instead she did something she wished she didn't know how to do. Reaching out to all those aboard, she borrowed their energy. None could resist and had no chance to avoid her embrace. As quick as lightning, her power locked on to them all, and they were hers to do with as she pleased. With the flick of her wrist, she could drain them all. It was so beautiful, and Catrin wanted more. How could she not? It was the most glorious thing she'd ever experienced, yet she knew the consequences, and it took only an instant to regain her composure.

Pelivor stared at her with the widest eyes she'd ever seen, and Catrin loosed a single, white-hot bolt of energy that left the air crackling and smelling of charcoal. The crew, still locked in a frozen rictus, was illuminated in morbid detail as the bolt flashed over the deck. Then they were lost in a conflagration that burned into Catrin's soul. She felt the dragon reaching for her spirit even as it died, as if its energy stretched beyond its mortal shell and sought to burn Catrin alive with its last reserve. Releasing the crew as quickly as she could, Catrin threw her arms up before her. There was no time to use the energy to shield herself, and she was suddenly awash with flame and lightning. It lasted only an instant; then it was gone.

Singed and in some cases still smoking, the crew moved as if they were drunk, and Catrin hoped she hadn't taken too much from them. Aware that she could kill a person by drawing too much energy, she worried what would happen if she drew *almost* too much energy from them, and she feared permanent damage. The thought was yanked away as she was suddenly thrown forward against the ropes that bound her. Icy water surged over the bow, drenching her and everyone else on deck. Pelivor appeared dead as he floated toward the rail on the receding wave, his body limp and almost liquid in its movements.

Everyone aboard was silent, and Catrin watched in mute awe as crewman regained their feet and began checking the rigging. It was not long before shouts came from below. "We're taking on water, sir!"

Darkness once again crowded Catrin's vision, and she could no longer fight it. She felt like an empty and desiccated husk that would never be whole again. With a heavy sigh of resignation, she slumped toward the deck, only the ropes holding her upright. As the darkness claimed her, she heard Kenward shout, "Man the bilges and buckets!"

"It's too much, sir!" came the response from belowdecks. "We're sinking!"

Even complete exhaustion could not overcome the shouting of the crew and the complaints of the rigging. Her vision blurry at first, Catrin awoke barely able to make out the dark shapes that ambled past, seemingly standing at the wrong angle. It was then that she realized the ship was listing heavily to port and the water was creeping ever closer, ready to claim them in its cold embrace. Kenward's orders contained a note of panic she'd never heard from him before. Of all the trouble they'd been through, this was the worst. Kenward's voice and the efforts of the crew who were no less exhausted than she, especially after her abuse of them, motivated Catrin and drove her back to her feet.

Water streaked down her face after a wave broke over the deck. The surf was growing, and the sight of the endless crests and troughs, now white tipped and blowing in the wind, made Catrin's skin crawl. Hanging at her side, Catrin's left arm was numb and unresponsive. Her right arm trembled as she steadied herself against the rail, the angle of the deck making it difficult to stand.

"The bilge handles are submerged, Captain. We've got to get ahead of this or we're sunk!"

"More men to the bilges!" Kenward ordered in a shrill voice. "I'll bail the hold by myself if I have to. This ship *will not sink!*"

Catrin reached his side and used her right arm to take a full bucket from Kenward. Without a word, Kenward dipped back down for another. Pelivor appeared a moment later, holding his head and mumbling something too low for anyone to hear over the furor. As the waves grew, the work became more and more difficult, and Catrin was thrown to the deck when they crested a large wave. It was as if the deck had jumped out from underneath her only to come crashing back up with explosive force. The taste of blood filled her mouth, and when she put her weight on her left arm, it was too much. She collapsed back to the deck with a whimper.

Strong hands grabbed her by the buckles on her leather pants, pulled her upright, and left her standing there. The world moved in unexpected ways, even more than the high seas would account for, and Catrin took deep breaths while she searched for balance and calm. Death was close now. It would take only a little more time and all of them would be lost forever. Sinjin would be left without a mother, and Prios would be a widower. The thoughts made her weep, but still she helped bail, Pelivor now lending her strength. Where he had found his reserve, she did not know, but she loved him for it.

When Kenward met her eyes next, she could see the defeat in his visage. Even giving everything they had left would not be enough. The *Slippery Eel* had taken too much damage, and there was no way she could be mended on rough seas and nearly full of water. Catrin wasn't even sure what was keeping them afloat. To everyone's surprise, they began to make some progress, the water dropping back below the bilge arms. Catrin suspected a regent dragon was helping them, but her suspicion was based on feelings alone. Nonetheless, this sudden improvement gave Kenward pause.

"We're not going to be able to keep this up," Farsy shouted from belowdecks. "Even if we can get the bilge emptied, I'm not sure we can plug a hole that big. Not in the water at least, and we might as well be a lifetime from dry dock."

Kenward scowled. "Do you all want to face my mother in the afterlife when I tell her you gave up?" His words got them moving a little faster. "Would you prefer to face my sister? Or maybe you'd like to answer to Prios?" The words seemed aimed at himself, rather than the crew, but the effect was the same. "There, see? We can do this!"

The water level dropped enough that one could straddle the hole in the ship and still have his head above water.

"Bring me oakum and planks! Use the shelves if you have to! Farsy! You're a lanky sprite. Use your feet to get some oakum around the front of the hole and then get a board across it. Bryn, you can hold your breath a long time. Swim down there and secure the planks. Just make the hole smaller. That's all I'm askin'. Just make it smaller."

By some unknown force, the water continued to drop lower, and Bryn was able to work with his head above the water line. Still, water surged sporadically through the remainder of the hole, the high pressure making it even more difficult to patch. Then even that flow lessened. There came a strange thump on the hull, and the timbers creaked. The deck rolled back to being almost level.

"What's happening?" someone asked.

"I don't care what's happening!" Kenward answered. "Get that hole fixed! We might live yet!"

There was a sound of relief in Kenward's voice, but Catrin knew his hope had the potential to be false. The damage to the *Eel*'s hull was extensive. By her guess, the result of giant claws and the collision with a rough, scaled hide. Looking over the side of the ship, she could see nothing in the failing light.

A towering wave brought them high above the trough, and as they were about to race down the trailing edge, the timbers creaked again, only this time much louder. Shouts came from belowdecks as the ship took to the air. Catrin turned to Pelivor, who looked as shocked as she.

Both knew there was no time to waste if they were going to capitalize on their good fortune. With practiced precision, Pelivor built his structures of energy, and the ship remained in the air, just barely clearing the whitecaps.

"You've done it!" Kenward shouted. "You've given us a fighting chance. Keep us in the air for another couple hours, and we might just be seaworthy again."

A couple hours—it might as well have been an eternity. Catrin knew they had no more than a few minutes. The world shifted between full color and a dull gray haze. Faraway voices called to her, and strong hands held her steady. In her dreams they flew across the desert, nightmarish creatures attacking from every side, and nowhere was safe. Dust curled up behind them as they flew, and Catrin could feel that this dream was different. This was a dream, yet it was real, and all of her senses were engaged. The battlefield was a maelstrom of aggression and pent-up rage, and all she could do was fly.

CHAPTER SIXTEEN

Some of the most beautiful things in this world will kill you quick as death.
— Farsy, sailor

Black sands rose from the sea, and the Firstland looked much different to Catrin. The land had healed itself from the devastation of the tsunami, and now Catrin could see the lush forests in their true glory. Chillingly beautiful was this unforgiving land of her ancestors, with the blacks and browns of the shoreline opposite fertile greenery that blanketed the land like moss on a giant stone.

All on board kept their gazes skyward, watching for ferals, and in Catrin's case, for Kyrien. She knew he lived, knew he had helped get them airborne, yet she had not seen him, and until she saw him, the reality of his survival would not be assured to her.

The fact that the Firstland looked like a beatific and idyllic setting and all around them was still and peaceful only served to unnerve the crew further. All of them knew they had come here for a reason and they might never leave. The placid beauty seemed almost inappropriate and garish in the face of their impending doom.

It didn't help that Kenward was not speaking to Catrin. At first she'd thought him simply angry, but he had attempted to speak to her and had failed. Each time he had opened his mouth, nothing came out. Eventually he raised his arms in defeat and walked away, mumbling to himself about flying through Catrin's nightmares and holes in his deck. Catrin knew she couldn't control her dreams, especially when she was beyond exhaustion, but still she felt guilty for having traumatized Kenward and the crew. The thought of flying the ship while sleeping haunted her.

"I'm amazed you could do it at all," Pelivor had said. "How did you do it? No, wait. Don't answer that. I don't want to know."

Perhaps it was best that Catrin could not have explained it if she had tried. Somehow she had transitioned from waking to sleep without letting go of the power. She'd done it once before, in Pinook Harbor, but that was nothing as complex as keeping a ship in the air. And that seemed to be the rub. In her altered state, Catrin's mind had somehow overlaid reality with her dreams, and as she had been dodging monsters and attacks of power and fire, the *Slippery Eel* had been under her command. Kenward had insisted that Catrin and Pelivor sleep for at least two full nights before they attempted to fly the ship again, and even now they moved through the waves under the power of the wind alone.

Catrin knew she would need her strength for the battle ahead. Kyrien had brought her here for a reason. He'd shown her visions of pain and death, and she knew the calm would not remain. Not knowing when the darkness would come made Catrin want to climb out of her own skin, and not knowing Kyrien's true fate gnawed at her.

"You need to eat something," Pelivor insisted.

The acid in Catrin's stomach stole what appetite she had, and she shook her head. Even the smell of Grubb's fish stew did little to attract her. Kenward stood behind Pelivor, and though he still said nothing, she knew he was coming around. With his arms folded over his chest, he raised an eyebrow and tapped his foot.

Sighing, Catrin accepted the mug, thinking she would just sip it to satisfy Kenward. After a few tastes, though, her appetite returned enough to finish the mug.

"You know I love you," Kenward finally said. "But I have to admit that I'll be glad when you're off my ship. You're nothing but the worst kind of trouble, and you seem determined to kill me and sink my ship."

"It took you all this time to come up with that? You're no poet, Kenward, but I can understand you feeling that way. Still, I think you're just jealous because I've managed to endanger your crew more than you have."

Those words drove Kenward back into silence that was finally broken by Grubb's laughter. "I say we keep her on board just to shut him up!"

A look from Kenward silenced him, but his shoulders shook as he walked back to the galley.

Kenward just shook his head. "I suppose you'll want me to take you up the river toward Ri? You know, the place where the Gholgi nearly sank us the last time we were here?"

The memory was burned into Catrin's mind. She could recall every sight, smell, and sensation of that day. It was also the first time she'd been rescued by dragons.

"Yes. I suppose that is what I want. I had hoped for guidance from Kyrien, some sign as to what he needed from me, but no matter how I try, he will not respond. He's alive—I know it—but I think he is waiting for a reason, and until he's ready, we're on our own."

"It seems we face the same dilemma once again," Kenward said. "I don't have enough men to send with you and still be able to defend the ship."

"This time will be different," Catrin said. "This time I will go alone."

"But you could be facing dangers far worse than those in the past."

"True," Catrin said. "I am not as well prepared as I would have liked, but I have done everything within my power to get ready for this, and now I must simply let the bones fall where they may." Instantly Catrin regretted her choice of words. No one else seemed willing to speak in the silence that followed. "Please. Just take me to the place where you dropped me last time. I'll either be fine or I won't, but staying aboard this ship will not accomplish whatever it is I'm here to do. Now I just need to get on with it."

Members of the crew approached her one at a time, each in his or her own way and only when ready. Catrin had known them since she was a teenager; she loved them like family, and to many of them, she was an adopted daughter. To have their love and respect meant the world to Catrin, and their words bolstered her confidence. If these brave and talented men and women believed in her, then surely she could believe in herself, even if she did face an impossible task: win a battle that would take place at a time and place beyond her knowing. Her only choice was to surrender to fate and hope that her knowledge and power would sustain her. It must have shown in her eyes, given the respect she got from the crew. Even those who had nearly died for her cause in the past looked at her with new eyes, as if they only now saw her true potential and sacrifice.

It was good that these things propped up Catrin's confidence as the next moment brought pure chaos.

Like a flock of birds launched from a shaken tree, dragons appeared all at once and, within moments, filled the air around the ship. Battle centered on the *Slippery Eel*. Ferals dived in to attack, and regents flew in defense. It was impossible to believe the ferocity and power of their attacks; even one strike would likely kill the entire crew of the *Slippery*

Eel. If not for the regent dragons, their greenish scales glinting in the sunlight, the *Eel* would have been lost.

Kyrien was nowhere to be seen. Catrin would have been able to pick him out of the chaos with her eyes closed, and she longed to find him and communicate with him, but her calls remained unanswered.

Crouching and shying away from another monstrous collision, Catrin thought the sound of dragons fighting might be the most frightening part of all. Not only did their growls make the air tremble and their screams inflict physical pain, the sound of their armored bodies slamming together was something Catrin thought no creature should ever have to hear.

"Full sail!" Kenward shouted. "Get this ship out of the water! We need to get out of here."

No one hesitated or questioned Kenward's words. His command gave them purpose and something to distract them from the horror that was taking place around them.

"Look out!" was all the warning anyone got before a pair of twined dragons struck the ship. Locked in a battle to the death, the two flailed and rolled, taking part of the rigging into the sea with them before disappearing under the waves. Had it not been a glancing blow, they'd already be sunk. Kenward was right; they needed to move.

Raising her arms to the sky, Catrin reached for the comets, and to her absolute shock, they felt a thousand years away, as if they had suddenly been flung back into the darkness. One look at Pelivor showed that he was experiencing a similar horror. Looking up, Catrin saw an unnaturally dark cloud blocking their views of the heavens. Like a stain on the sky, it roiled above them, sometimes lit from within by webs of lightning. The hair on Catrin's neck stood as she realized there was a filament of energy extending from her head and the ship and reaching up to the clouds above. Time was running out.

Denied direct access to the comets, Catrin reached to the air around her. Pelivor did the same and was soon trying to generate enough lift to get them out of the water. Catrin did her best to focus on providing thrust. Farsy watched from nearby with a glint in his eye, and Catrin smiled at him despite their peril. Under her direction, he had modified the tube of wood, changing the shape of the inner surface so it opened more at the entrance and remained more constricted midway along its length. The changes reduced the strength and stability of the wood, and Catrin could now feel it trembling as she forced air through. A low whistle began, and as they moved faster, it grew in volume and pitch. Over a steeper wave, the hull left the water, lurching suddenly to one side as a feral came at them unblocked until the very last moment.

The whistling continued to grow louder, and Catrin applied as much energy as she thought was safe. Again the crew had to trim the sails as their speed increased. Before they were even finished, the rigging began to vibrate, and the wind tore at the crew. Staying low to the water, they skimmed along as fast as they were able. Above, the skies were far too dangerous, and the *Slippery Eel,* even with Catrin and Pelivor in control, was no match for a feral dragon in open air.

"At least the water makes it hurt really bad when they miss," Kenward said. "We need to get through the harbor and into the river valley. Then there won't be room for many of these beasts in the air above us."

"Sails ahead, sir— What the—? *Sir!*"

It didn't take long for Catrin to see what the lookout had seen or for Kenward to start cursing. Thorakis's sailors seemed to be learning new things at an alarming rate. Hovering above the water came a formation of ships linked together by blood red lightning. The ships appeared equidistant from one another and flew as a single unit. Standing at the prow of the lead ship was a tall man in long robes, his arms cast out to the sides, lightning flowing from his hands and into the deck itself. Dark paint made him look like the demons that wandered his decks. Again these Gholgi-like abominations would haunt Catrin, and she watched in horror as similarly dressed men emerged on the prow of every ship in the array. When they raised their hands, a new web of power sprang into the air, joining over the lead ship, focusing, and splitting the air toward the *Slippery Eel*.

Catrin banked the ship to the right, accelerated, then slowed. White heat seared the air but went wide.

"Higher!" Kenward ordered.

Catrin and Pelivor did as he said. No sooner had they gained open air than a feral locked on to them. A pair of regents gave chase, but this feral was bigger and faster than most of the others. Closing the gap to the *Slippery Eel* and leaving the regents behind, the feral made it clear it wasn't going to give up easily. Dividing her attention, Catrin reached back out to the comets, and as the *Eel* moved out from under the dread cloud, the comets answered, flooding her with energy. The ship whistled as she pushed for more speed, but she wasn't certain the *Eel* could take much more. Instead she focused part of her mind on building up a charge and sending a finger of lightning back at the charging feral. The lightning connected, and in that instant, she felt small and insignificant. The will of the feral washed over her. None of what was going on around her seemed to exist; all that mattered was avoiding the wrath of the lord of the night.

Lost in his rapidly approaching eyes, Catrin watched, entranced.

"Why are we slowing?"

The voices were distant and meaningless. Nothing could be more important than what she was doing, of that she was certain.

"Catrin! Wake up!" Kenward shouted as he shook her.

It took Catrin a moment to realize where she was and what was happening, but then it all rushed back at once and nearly caused her to swoon. In the meantime the feral had drawn closer, and the sight of him sent Catrin scrambling to get them moving fast again. What lead they had was now lost, and the dragon would almost certainly catch them. The regents in pursuit flew in what looked like desperation as they climbed higher and higher. Watching as they disappeared into the clouds, Catrin's hope faded.

At the fastest speed she felt the ship could handle, the feral continued to gain on them. Twice more she attacked, and twice more it seemed only to infuriate the beast. Standing near the stern became a liability as the dragon overtook them. It came all at once, as if it had been holding back and only making them think it had been at maximum speed. The sudden attack caught Catrin off her guard, and she scrambled to cast out energy in hopes of warding off certain death. Behind the feral Catrin noticed two dark shapes diving toward the surface at unbelievable speed. Then those shapes extended their wings and pulled up to skim over the waves, sending spray circling in the roiling wind behind them. They hit the feral hard and fast, knocking him off course and away from the ship. It was a costly victory, though, and Catrin cried out when the feral struck like a snake and sent one of the regents into a lifeless spin until it crashed into the water with a series of sickening pops and snaps. Afraid of going much higher, again in the shadow of the unnatural cloud, Catrin guided them closer to the harbor. Approaching the tall ring of stone that surrounded much of the harbor, Catrin looked up almost expecting to see a Zjhon warship still nestled among the peaks, but it was gone, lost to the ravages of time and weather, she guessed.

When she lowered her gaze, she let out a gasp, which was immediately followed by shouts from the crew. Another formation of ships was leaving the harbor, just clearing the massive semicircle of stone peaks. The base of the passage was far wider than the top, and Kenward cursed when Catrin took them higher and turned sharply so the ship entered the narrow opening at an angle. In trying to match the angle of the rock face that would likely snap off the mainmast, Catrin pitched the ship onto its side, nearly losing Farsy. The wind whispered over the rocks as they passed, and an instant later, they emerged into the massive harbor. Instead of the giant sea and land creatures she'd been expecting, Catrin saw a waiting navy. A mass of ships clogged the waters, and enough land had been cleared to build fortifications. Smoke billowed from stacks on ships and from buildings.

The air above was no safer than that above the open seas. In fact, the rock faces made it even more dangerous to navigate. Bringing the ship down low, Catrin saw dark shapes in the water and knew that the large sea creatures may not be fully visible, but they were still there.

"If we set down," Kenward said, "they'll attack from underneath, just as they did the last time we were here. If we stay here, the dragons'll get us, and who knows what's waiting in that river valley. I don't recall it being a pleasant trip. And we had to turn back at those boiling statues."

"Do you have a better idea?" Catrin asked.

"No," he admitted.

"Then hold on."

"Get ready!" Kenward shouted to the crew. "This is gonna be a bumpy ride."

The whistle of the ship echoed off the canyon walls, and Catrin brought them higher, even as approaching formations of ships readied themselves to attack. These groups were smaller, some consisting of only three ships, but they moved with nimble grace and seemed capable of greater speed.

"This is insane!" Kenward shouted as they whisked over the first formation of ships, which remained just above the surface of the water. The air around them shimmered, and the smell of smoke polluted the air. "They're setting us on fire! Put us down! Put us down!"

Not wanting to lose speed, Catrin tried to only bounce the ship along the surface of the narrowing and shallow waters at the mouth of the approaching river. She'd envisioned the ship skipping like a stone, but the drag was far greater than she had anticipated. Everyone and everything aboard was thrown toward the prow. A jet of oily fire spewing black smoke struck the waves before them and set the water itself afire.

"Up! Up!" Kenward shouted.

Catrin would have obeyed his orders if she could, but it was simply too much to ask, and the ship struck the flames, which left the *Eel* covered in burning pitch. The crew watched helplessly as smoke streamed up through the railing. Realizing that even the water would not extinguish this fire, Catrin concentrated on getting the ship back into the air. Though it seemed like the worst possible thing to do, Catrin had a plan. Pelivor cried out as he exerted himself, the cut of his muscles standing out as the wind plastered his silks against him.

Just before they reached the next cluster of approaching ships, they left the water and banked to port, this time greeted by a series of thumps that slammed into the hull. No one knew how much damage they had taken, but crewmen were shouting from below, and some had to evacuate the deckhouse due to smoke.

"She's gonna burn up!" Kenward shouted.

Left with no other options, Catrin pushed the ship for more speed, even as the valley walls closed in on them. This time the carved figures that adorned the hillsides were even more intimidating simply because they might slam into one of them at any moment. Catrin soon found herself soaring through a narrow and twisting canyon, mere inches above the waterline and with far too much speed, yet the fires still burned.

No ships pursued them up the river, but a shadow passed over them and raced along the valley just ahead of them, as if the dragon were just biding its time, waiting for the best moment to strike its prey—prey that had nowhere to go and no place to hide. Feeling naked and exposed, Catrin tried to resist the fear that ferals seemed designed to create, but it was difficult to do. Crewmen wept on deck, and Kenward looked more frightened than Catrin had ever seen, but that may have had more to do with the way she was flying his ship. When he looked at her, he wore a looked of unabashed horror, as if she might truly be a monster.

It was no use. Catrin knew that almost every path would lead to their deaths, and even if her actions left them stranded on the Firstland, then it would be better than all of them perishing in the sea or the air above it. Staying low had its own dangers, proven by a protruding rock face that had remained hidden until the last moment, protected by a natural illusion. It smacked into the hull and sent them flying sideways. The dragon picked that moment to attack, and Catrin tried to split her attention between guiding the ship, providing thrust, and sending a defensive strike against the approaching dragon. She never got the chance to release that strike as Kyrien soared in between them and sent the much larger dragon careening away from the ship.

"No!" Catrin cried out, knowing that Kyrien was no match for a dragon more than twice his size.

Fly.

It was the only response she got from him before he collided again with the feral. Catrin could not watch, not only because it was too painful to see, but because the valley continued to narrow and every instant was critically dangerous to the ship.

"The fires are out, but there are holes in the hull, sir! Big ones! We're not seaworthy."

Kenward looked stricken but Catrin was not surprised. Still, it didn't matter to her; all it did was reinforce her decision. Ahead lay the Eternal Guardians, watching over the Valley of the Victors. The name seemed ironic to Catrin since all the images were of men, yet they had not ruled here for thousands of years.

"Catrin!"

"Hold on, Kenward!"

"Catrin!"

The panic in his voice made Catrin regret what she was about to do, but he said he had no better ideas, and she did what she could to save all of them, even if it pained her to do so. Though she'd seen them before, the Eternal Guardians formed a daunting barrier. Both figures crouched over waters that swirled around the stone they had sprung from. The one closest to them was worn to the extent that its visage was lost to time, which made it look all the more imposing. The other had only half its face remaining, but even that cast them a baleful glare. The feral grew larger in the skies before them and would pass above the Guardians about the same time they would reach the massive monument. No going over the monuments, then. "Hold on and stay clear of the masts!"

Splinters of wood filled the air along with a series of gut-wrenching snaps. The mainmast tore up the foredecks and slammed into the deckhouse before launching into the air behind them.

"Catrin!"

The word was now a high-pitched scream, like the sound of a man losing a limb. It was not a sound Catrin ever wanted to hear again, but fate had other ideas. Just beyond the Eternal Guardians, she urged the ship higher, scanning the landscape, looking for something she knew would be there but not really believing she would find it. With the feral gaining on them and Kyrien nowhere to be seen, Catrin urged the ship for more speed, the tube of wood singing a howling tune, vibrating and flexing as the pressurized air rushed through. The speed would not be enough, and Catrin forced more air in, but it was too much. With a suddenness that sent Catrin sprawling, the cylinder cracked, split, and exploded. Splinters dug into Catrin's flesh, a large chunk flying by and barely missing her face.

She turned back with tears of frustration and loss in her eyes. But then she saw a field of deep, rich grass strewn with megalithic granite boulders, as if they'd been tossed like dice by the gods. A smile came to Catrin's face, and she hoped that once again she would find solace in this idyllic location, despite the pure chaos that surrounded them.

The tops of trees slammed against the hull as they made their approach, and only the sound of Kenward's screams rose above the cacophony.

"Brace!" Catrin shouted and an instant later, she was vaulted forward, the ropes that held her digging into her flesh. The pain and sensation of being crushed was overwhelming, and she could not believe how hard they hit when they landed. The initial blow had jarred Catrin and Pelivor enough to make them both lose control over the power they wielded.

In the moments that followed, dragons unfolded themselves and Kenward wept.

CHAPTER SEVENTEEN

The most courageous acts are often committed by those who believe themselves already dead.

— Merchill Valon, soldier

The *Slippery Eel* lay on her side, groaning as if in her death throes, filling the silence left by what her captain was not saying. He looked at Catrin with horror in his eyes, and she wondered if this would be the end of the friendship they had developed. The loss of the *Slippery Eel* was bad enough, but the thought of losing Kenward as a friend brought tears to Catrin's eyes. It was only a single moment in time, but it was burned into Catrin's consciousness. Immediately after, time rushed forward and there were wounded to tend.

Though there were many cuts, scrapes, and bruises, the worst wounds had been Catrin's to bear. She winced as Pelivor removed the splinters of wood from her right side. Large and small, they dug into her flesh and made every movement painful. No one left the ship, as if they feared they would drown in the lush grasses. More likely it was the dragons surrounding the ship they feared. They looked like Kyrien, only larger, older, and far less friendly. They waited, though not patiently. Their eyes urged her forward, and their hearts tugged at her. She could feel them calling to her, calling to all of them.

Eventually Pelivor had removed most of the larger splinters from Catrin's side, and both of them stepped onto the grasses and toward the largest of the dragons. He brought his head down low and swayed back and forth in a rhythmic movement. The beautiful dance captivated them. Soon the entire crew of the *Slippery Eel* joined them.

"I'm sorry we crashed into your lovely valley," Catrin said.

If a dragon could smile, this one did, and there was a glint in its eye. *You are ignorant, child, but that is among your strengths. This valley has been waiting for you. It was made . . . for you.*

Those gathered heard the words in their minds, felt the mirth and the warmth in the dragon's communication. It instantly put them all at ease, despite the fact that they had been, up until that moment, fighting for their lives. Here, in this valley, under the protection of these dragons, they were safe.

I must ask you once again to save him. You must save Kyrien.

The compelling energy, though leaving room for free will, nearly sent them all scrambling toward the sound of distant wailing. Catrin's breath caught in her throat when she heard it.

It has begun. It cannot be stopped. You must save him.

Kyrien's call was the same as when she had first heard it, all those years ago. Trapped in a cell of stone, fed and made to grow too large to get out of the entrance, he would have been left to die a horrible death had Catrin not defeated Archmaster Belegra and set Kyrien free. The memories brought physical pain, and that's when Catrin realized the large dragon was now looking her in the eye, its head hovering only a hand's width before her face. She felt the sensation of something pulling on her skin followed by wet clicks, and Catrin looked down to see splinters on her boot and the grasses around it. The pain in her body dissipated. Moving its head back and forth, the dragon captured Catrin in its gaze once again.

Be strong. You must not fail. The future of us all rests in your hands. Do not let fear stop you. Not your fear or that of another. Know that dragons and humans are not so different. We, too, are gifted and flawed. Not all of us agree about what the future holds, and Kyrien is suffering for that. Go. Save him.

Nodding, Catrin could formulate no thought beyond the need to save Kyrien, his wails once again punctuating the silence.

Go. Now.

Catrin turned and walked to the northern end of the valley with a determined stride, her purpose clear; all that was left was to find him. If his wailing continued, that would not be difficult. Only when she left the soft grasses and climbed onto the uneven granite did she realize she was alone. The rest of the crew of the *Slippery Eel* stood entranced, and Catrin wondered if they would ever forgive her. It was better this way, better that she go alone. At least that way she would not be responsible for their deaths. She couldn't save them, but perhaps the dragons could.

Climbing with a mixture of sadness and grim satisfaction, Catrin moved toward Kyrien. The ascent was not difficult, and for much of the way, she followed a natural ridgeline that cut through two peaks. It wasn't long until Catrin saw things she recognized, and soon the hollow mountain emerged from the fog, its zigzagging stairs clinging to it like mighty serpents, crawling out of the archways that decorated the massive rock face. It had been in one of those halls that Catrin had faced Archmaster Belegra and only barely won. Now that mountain seemed entirely abandoned, only spirits roaming the dark halls.

Kyrien's wails echoed from the valley walls, and Catrin could not pinpoint the direction from which they came. Just past the hollow mountain, she turned north, hoping she was right. She listened, straining, and in the distance, she thought she heard someone calling her name. It was faint but persistent, and as she listened closely for Kyrien, she couldn't help but hear them calling for her. The voice was Kenward's, she was almost certain. And he sounded no more calm than the last time she'd heard him. She'd hoped the dragons would keep them in the valley and guard them while she went off to help Kyrien, but it seemed fate had other plans.

Torn and wanting to go back for them, Catrin forced herself to continue, though she cried at having to choose. If she was abandoning them, it was only for their own good. She doubted any of them would see it that way, but she persevered nonetheless.

Cold wind drifted to her, and beyond the valley lay the sea. Rising out of the surf, a megalithic beast climbed into the skies. Dark shapes filled the air around it, and its surface seethed like a kicked anthill. Demons scaled the rock face in unbelievable numbers, making it look as if the mountain were breathing. Ships crowded the shoreline, and formations patrolled the waters beyond. This was a well-organized, massive, lethal attack.

Diving and attacking anything that reached the higher parts of the mountain, Kyrien fought as if he wished to die. Her heart breaking, Catrin cried out to him, but all she got back was a wash of panicked energy filled with despair.

This is not how it is supposed to be. This must not be. I cannot take you to her, or her visions will come true. I must stop this!

Catrin wanted to stop it for him, and she vowed to try, but she knew her power would be insignificant before such massive forces. The demons and giants outnumbered her by tens of thousands to one. How could she possibly hope to make any difference? She was worthless and small. Nothing she could do would stave off the inevitable. It would be far better to die in as quick a fashion as possible; that at least would end the pain, end the suffering.

The thoughts themselves were the only warning she had, but Catrin knew the thoughts were not hers, and she turned to find a small feral dragon stalking her. Low to the ground, it remained still for an instant, as if hoping Catrin wouldn't see it, but as soon as Catrin raised her hands, it lunged. Lightning crackled between them just before they collided, and both were sent sprawling. Catrin wasn't exactly certain she had attacked, and she wondered if the dragon had struck her with lightning. It seemed unlikely, since the dragon could just as easily have snapped her up in its jaws. Deep down, Catrin was relieved; feral dragons with the ability to wield Istra's power would be truly terrifying things.

Even without power, the beast hunting Catrin seemed made of fear. A single look from it caused Catrin to tremble, and its every movement forced Catrin to envision her own death. None could stand before such a dark and menacing visage and not quail. Catrin did the only thing she could think of, foolish or not: she ran.

The dragon moved in slow pursuit, seemingly unworried by Catrin's sudden flight. What looked like a tree branch swung out into the air before her, but it was no branch, and it moved to intercept her neck.

The pole arm cut the air with a sound that promised death. Only narrowly avoiding the strike, Catrin ducked low and let her momentum carry her forward, which proved to be a mistake. She'd have had a better chance facing the dragon. At least a dozen demons were clawing their way toward her, and behind them came the giants. Each one was a walking exaggeration; everything frightening about the demons only made larger. And now Catrin was tumbling into their midst. Without much thought, she compressed the air around her and released it all at once. The blast sent demons tumbling, and even the giants took a step back. The smell of ozone assaulted Catrin's nostrils, and a quickly evaporating mist hung in the air around her. The air was cool and moist, and for some reason, that meant something to Catrin, though she didn't know exactly what.

Lumbering past their fallen and disorganized comrades, the giants continued forward, single file, unable to move two abreast in the narrow valley. Taking two steps back, Catrin turned and froze. The feral dragon rose up to its full height. Even if it was a small feral dragon, it still managed to be terrifying, and Catrin considered trying her luck against the giants. When they saw the dragon, the hulking brutes stopped, seemingly ready to assault her if she tried to pass but nothing more.

Cocking its head to the side, the dragon approached, low to the ground, its head now level and weaving in a hypnotic motion. It took one more step forward then stopped, looking up. A moment later, it was backing up the ravine as quickly as it could before turning and launching back into the sky. Catrin did not want to raise her head to see, but instinct made her look, and she nearly fell down in fear. Staring back was the face of the largest feral she'd seen, one she recognized from when it chased the *Slippery Eel*. This massive beast radiated terror, and Catrin raised trembling hands. The dragon struck, quick as lightning, and again Kyrien intervened. Dropping from the sky and flying between Catrin and the feral, Kyrien intercepted the strike with his side, and the regent dragon cried out in pain when the feral bit down.

Unleashing all the energy she could muster, Catrin sent fire and lightning at the feral's eyes. It arched back and released Kyrien from its deadly grasp, and Kyrien rolled away. Sensing movement behind her, Catrin lashed out at the giants, again going for the eyes. One managed to block the attack with a massive wrist guard, but another was struck full in the face and went down, leaving the third stuck behind its corpse.

Raising her arms for another attack, Catrin felt the air leave her lungs as Kyrien snatched her from the ground in his powerful claws.

This should not be! What have I done!

Catrin could almost feel the tears in his words, and she wept for her friend and for the fact that she was somehow the cause of his anguish.

Moving through the darkened halls within Dragonhold, Halmsa of the Wind clan was determined to learn as much as he could from Catrin, even if he could not learn it in person. Nothing in the prophecies ever said that she had to be there to teach them how to fly dragons. It seemed strange that something that had seemed so far away when he was a child was now here before him. There had always been a silent disbelief in the back of his mind that the things foretold would come to be, and now he was humbled. He had ridden a dragon, and now he was ready to try flying one. *These ferals are feisty,* he thought. It seemed like a challenge worthy of the Arghast.

Feeling like a thief within the hold, Halmsa searched for a room that he knew existed, yet he had few clues to its whereabouts. He knew that holes in its walls faced open air and that it must be along the outer walls of the keep, but still it eluded him.

A deep growl sounded nearby, and even its echo challenged Halmsa's courage. He reminded himself that brave men felt fear, but they did not let it make their decisions. Keeping to the shadows, he waited until the demon passed, this one sniffing the air as it went. Halmsa moved back toward the God's Eye, a thing he would not believe existed had he not seen it himself. Moving deeper into the mountain was contrary to his mission, but there were also more places to hide. He'd found nothing leading from the great hall, and this seemed a logical next step. The fact that it moved him away from those growls reinforced the decision.

His eyes had nearly adjusted to the darkness when a dim light appeared at the end of a descending hall. Quickly he moved closer, and when he reached a junction, he found another descending hallway bathed in a ruddy glow. Halmsa nearly shouted for joy, but he wisely kept his mouth shut. Moving toward the light, he found a room with two head-sized holes in the wall and beyond, open sky. Halmsa smiled despite his fear. He could not fail at this. This was the foretold time; he was certain of it. One of them had to step forward; one of them had to prove himself worthy of the title dragonrider, and Halmsa was determined to be that person.

In spite of the inherent danger of leaving his body completely unprotected in a part of the hold occupied by demons, in one of the few rooms that gets any natural light, he prayed for release from his prison of flesh. It seemed an unwise thing to hope for, but Halmsa wished with all of his heart as he stared out into the open sky. Reviewing the tales in his head, trying to remember exactly how Catrin had described astral travel, he tried not to despair. He had no access to the Cathuran chant or drums, and he chose to take another wild risk and hum a tune. Catrin had said it was the vibration that helped her and not the melody. Perhaps, he thought, the melody was there only to entertain those who must chant for hours at a time.

Humming, Halmsa stared out at the sky and strained his eyes, trying to look himself into the open air. A trickle of fear ran down his spine when he wondered if he would ever be able to return to his body should he break free of this mortal shroud.

Still humming, he closed his eyes and envisioned himself soaring through the skies, a dragon beneath him. When he opened his eyes, nothing happened. Frustrated, he sighed and sat back. That was when he remembered that Catrin had done the same; only she had smacked her head on the stone chair. Halmsa wondered if it had to be by accident and come as a surprise and exactly how hard he would have to hit his head. He was not afraid of the pain or a coward, but no man would slam his head against stone any harder than he might have to.

With his eyes open, he moved his head backward until it struck the stone lightly. Nothing happened. Doubtful but determined, he threw his head back and it hit with a solid *thunk*. He had been concerned he would have given away his position, cursing from the pain, but he barely felt it as he soared through the skies. Halmsa of the Wind clan could fly.

Faint sounds melded with the rush of the waterfall and the calls of birds carried on the light breeze. This place seemed impossible, yet it remained very real. The aroma of grasses mixed with mosses near the falls. The smell of moist soil and supple grasses painted the air. Sinjin even found ripe strawberries scattered throughout the grasses where the light was the brightest. The afternoon was drawing on, and the light changed to a deeper hue, making the place seem even more surreal.

With the shadows growing long and the light playing tricks with their eyes, Brother Vaughn suddenly pulled Sinjin and Trinda back behind a squat tree. Holding a finger to his lips, he slid on his belly until he could see the rolling hills beyond. "By the gods! Come out quick!"

Hesitating for only a moment, Sinjin followed Brother Vaughn and helped Trinda back to her feet. Looking annoyed, she brushed herself off, and Sinjin didn't bother to tell her that there was nothing to be brushed off. All thoughts of sarcasm left him when he spotted movement back near where they had entered the cavern. In an instant he recognized his father and Strom and Durin! He wasn't quite as pleased to see Kendra, but it mattered little. A huge grin crossed Sinjin's face, but it instantly vanished.

Hissing balls of flame leaped from the shadows and exploded, casting flaming pitch over anything nearby. Waves of what looked like gelatinous air rushed forth from another portal, and Prios's company was quickly pushed into a full retreat.

"I'm here, Dad!" Sinjin cried out, and Brother Vaughn looked as if he would scold Sinjin, but they both saw Prios look up.

Issuing a wordless roar, Prios ran toward them.

Sinjin could not stop himself. He had to get to his father, had to have his forgiveness. All of this was his fault, and he could no longer stand the guilt. Tears stung his eyes as he did what he did best.

He ran.

Stunted trees flew by in a blur. Tiny chipmunks scurried to get out of his path. And for an instant, his eyes met those of a hunting cat, which crouched in the lush grass. Every moment in time became images burned into his memory. It was as if he were in a dream. Surely none of this could be real, he thought as the demons poured onto the field like a dark stain spreading across the precious landscape. Birds filled the air, driven from the trees by the malevolent forces charging into their midst with a cloud of angry energy raging around them. Sinjin could feel the contempt if not the energy itself.

Moving out of the darkness and into the fading light came demons holding weapons of wood and iron, smoking and glowing. It took two demons to carry the barrel-like portion and another two to carry a smoking pot attached via a length of articulated wood and steel hose. Truly this enemy was evolving quickly, and Sinjin had no idea how to defend against such things. Seeing the barrel belch fire and blackness made his courage flee. Already flames threatened to claim the trees and the grasses smoldered. This alone raised Sinjin's anger, and his fury was perhaps the only thing that could conquer his fear and guilt. That these abominations would destroy a thing of such beauty was what allowed him to know that he was right, that his rage could be righteous and holy.

Watching his father cast out his energy to shield those in the line of fire gave Sinjin great pride, and he wanted nothing more than to be by his father's side, but there was still distance between them, and as the light mingled with darkness, more demons came—these like a knife between father and son. Sinjin could almost hear Brother Vaughn shouting for him to come back, and he could barely hear Trinda crying out his name, but he could not simply turn around when at a full run. It took time for him to slow himself from his fastest sprint to a speed where he could execute his turn, and by the time he did, the flames had grown far too close. He could see the eyes of the demons that wanted him dead, yet when they had him in their firing line, the flames did not come. Sinjin had expected to be engulfed in a conflagration, and instead something large and black flew at his head. Ducking, he felt only the slightest bump as something heavy but soft whizzed past.

A flash of light and fire ripped through the line of demons, and Sinjin saw his father for a moment. The look on his face terrified Sinjin, and he never wanted to see such a look again. Such pain, anguish, and desperation should be inflicted on no one. There was no more time for thought as a melon-sized fist landed on Sinjin's jaw, tossing him backward. Trinda's voice took on a shrill note. The demon grabbed him by his ankle and started pulling him back to their lines.

"No," Sinjin heard a high-pitched but firm voice say. Part of him knew it was Trinda, but she sounded different. She didn't sound afraid; she sounded angry. Sinjin's head continued to bounce along on the soft grass. "I said *no!*"

Trinda's command froze the battle as quickly as if the entire cavern had suddenly been filled with ice. Sinjin willed his body to move, but it seemed to care more about what Trinda wanted than what he wanted.

When Trinda turned her gaze to him, he found he could move again and crawled free of the demon's grip. When he saw the demon, frozen in place, he landed a kick square on its rear and sent it toppling forward. Looking back to Trinda, he froze again. In her hands was Brother Vaughn's herald globe; it shone like the brightest comet, and Trinda's eyes were wide, her face locked in a look of shock. When she made a popping sound with her lips, Sinjin knew what was coming, and he stepped forward to catch her.

"I don't have any more," she said, and she handed Sinjin the blazing herald globe before collapsing into his arms. A moment later the demons stirred, and Sinjin took the chance to look for his father, but he couldn't find him. Then he saw Strom crouching over a body, and his heart leaped. In the next instant, he was running with Trinda over his shoulder.

CHAPTER EIGHTEEN

In the most critical of times, decisions made in an instant can affect the rest of history. To experience such power is my greatest hope and deepest fear. If it comes to pass, I pray I choose wisely.

— Archmaster Belegra

Even clutched in Kyrien's claw, Catrin could see the demons below on their inexorable climb toward the top of the hollow mountain. The holes in the side of this mountain were larger, and it was apparent that these were not man-made halls. There were no decorated arches, straight lines, or right angles. The way this mountain had been hollowed out spoke of claws and jaws doing the work, and Catrin shivered at the thought of jaws powerful enough to crush stone and claws sharp enough to part granite. Kyrien's firm but gentle grip on Catrin was a marvel. Surely he could crush her without even exerting himself. She knew she was safe in his grasp, but the fact made her feel small and powerless.

I cannot make the decision. I simply cannot. You saved my life!

Catrin was unsure what he meant, but he either did not hear her or chose not to respond to her questions. It seemed he was so overwhelmed by his inner conflict that Catrin had almost ceased to exist. This would have been all right if his anxiety were not causing him to tighten his grip on Catrin a little bit more with each passing moment. As Catrin's mental shouts became screams, he realized what was happening and relaxed his grip. In his effort to let her breathe, the startled dragon overcompensated and loosened his grip too much.

In a gust of wind and the blink of an eye, Catrin went from catching her breath in Kyrien's claws to free-falling. She'd have screamed if there had been enough air in her lungs, but it was all she could do to breathe. Kyrien caught her before she took her next breath, and the impact took what air she had. It was thus that she found herself suddenly thrust into the uppermost hall, barely able to breathe and completely unprepared to face an enormous and unfriendly dragon.

I'm sorry. I could not choose. Now you must. I'm so sorry.

Kyrien wept in her mind, and Catrin reeled at the possibilities, trying to understand what he meant.

Coward! came a new voice in Catrin's mind, and it pounded until she thought her head would crack open. *Traitor! Failure!*

The words came from what Catrin now knew was the queen of the regents—the *only* queen of the regents. How she knew this, Catrin was unsure, but she knew it like she knew the sun would shine. Still she had no idea what choice she had to make. She knew it was important, but she didn't know why, and she had no idea what to do about it. Standing in front of the largest regent dragon she'd ever seen, Catrin desperately tried to catch her breath. The dragon looked down on her with a clear lack of patience, but Catrin had no choice but to take time to compose herself.

Cowed by the queen's words to Kyrien, Catrin quavered and wondered what he had done to deserve such an indictment. He'd fought so hard to save Catrin. How could the queen talk to him in that way? The more she thought about it, the angrier Catrin became. Soon she snarled at the regent queen, power flowing through her.

Moving like a giant snake, the queen made an aggressive move that brought her closer to Catrin. The huge regent looked down her snout at Catrin, poised and ready to snatch her up in her jaws.

I should just kill you myself. I should do what Kyrien failed to do.

Given the greeting she'd received, Catrin was not surprised by the communication. "Then perhaps I should kill you now and finish off what the demons are taking so long to do."

Catrin could almost feel the dragon laughing, but there was no humor in that laughter, only derision and something Catrin sensed beneath it, something she was shocked to find: fear. This magnificent and powerful dragon, queen of her kind, was just as afraid of Catrin as the human was of the dragon. It was difficult to believe, but she reminded herself that she was perhaps the most powerful person in all of Godsland, and perhaps this queen of dragons had good reason for fear.

You should not be here. This should not be happening.

"I don't want to hurt you or the other regent dragons. I don't understand why you hate me and why I shouldn't be here. If you want my help, then you are going to have to tell me what is going on!"

You cannot help me unless you cease to exist.

Catrin gaped. "Surely you can't mean that."

The bones have been cast. The choice is not mine; never has it been. The choice, instead, lies upon you, and may you have more wisdom than any other of your kind. May you find the dragon's wisdom in this pivotal time. The rest of this age rests upon you.

Never had another creature held Catrin's attention so completely, and yet the effect faded and Catrin sensed things around her, powerful things—*very* powerful things.

I have seen the future where the humans survive, and I've seen the future where the dragons survive. It is one or the other, you see. There can be no coexistence. Kyrien knew this and still he brought you here. He left the choice to you. In doing so he betrayed and most likely doomed his kind, unless, of course, I can convince you to take a nice jump from this ledge?

Catrin did not move. The words made no sense.

Kyrien is every bit the traitor and fool I say he is. He could have let you die, could have killed you himself, yet he'd rather doom his entire species, and for what? Love?

"Then kill me."

I cannot.

"Why not?"

The dragon managed to look exasperated, as if speaking to a dense child, *I cannot kill you because I have seen that future as well, and the only thing worse than a future without dragons is a future without dragons* and *humans. Now there is no other way. You must choose. I have seen the future if you live, and mankind will not stop until the entire planet is consumed. Is that what you want? The future without you is far less creative, but the world will continue to flourish, and balance will be maintained. Don't you see why it must be you that dies and not the regent dragons? Do you not love Kyrien? Do you not wish to save his life and let his kind flourish? Are you so selfish that you could let him die, just so that you may live? Is there no charity in your heart? Did your mother not teach you what it is to be selfless?*

The questions pounded against Catrin's resolve, and she took a step back. The last question, however, raised her hackles and put her on the attack. "Don't you dare bring my mother into this or I'll turn you inside out, right here, right now. You got that? You might think you can threaten and intimidate me, but I'm not afraid of you. At least I'm not so afraid of you that I won't fight you if I have to. And who says both of us can't survive? Maybe if we worked together, we could defeat the demons and the ferals. Then what would that future look like?"

That is the same path that leads to the death of us all. The chances are too great. There is no room for uncertainty when the fate of the world is at stake.

"No," Catrin said. "When you are unwilling to face the risk, you take away the chance for hope. Let's fly away from here now—"

Before she could finish, the dragon queen shifted and her pupils narrowed.

You either have no eyes or you wish to mock me. Which is it?

Involuntarily taking a step backward, Catrin took a good look at the rest of the dragon queen. Long and thick, her body was bloated and her wings small. A cold feeling washed over Catrin. The queen couldn't fly. When the demons arrived, she would be mostly defenseless, forced to hold her ground against the massive horde. There was no way she would survive such an attack.

Looking over the interior of the cavern, Catrin saw it was lit by only small holes that dotted the walls and outer edges of the ceiling. Most of the lair was smooth floor and nothing else, but here and there were neatly organized piles of massive stones. Some were little more than vertical columns, but others seemed to form something like a sleeping platform. Besides barricading themselves in, there was not a great deal to work with. It was only a matter of time before the demons reached this level.

Fool! You waste time when it is the most precious thing we have. You must choose. Now!

The thought of condemning the dragons to extinction made Catrin physically ill, and she couldn't keep from thinking there was some way they could all survive. Still she remained silent, and still more time passed.

Kyrien was a wretched fool to bring you here.

Farsy and Bryn by his side, Kenward watched with grim determination as their deaths became increasingly likely. An insurmountable army of demons and dragons was slowly swallowing a mountain, the same mountain where he believed Catrin to be. There had been a battle; that he knew. He'd seen Catrin fight from afar before, and he recognized the light and the sound of it. The sensations were burned into his memory from one of the most dangerous times in his life. A sick feeling clung to him, and when he looked to Bryn and Farsy, he almost wished he hadn't brought them with him, so dour were their faces.

Only the presence of the regent dragons gave them any measure of safety, and Kenward wondered about that. Already the numbers had thinned as two dragons would leave, and only one would return. Of the last pair that had gone on patrol, based on Kenward's assumptions, neither had returned, and he knew they needed to face a future without the dragons' protection. But Catrin had put them in an impossible situation. She had been his friend for a very long time; she'd saved his life multiple times and put it in great danger just as many. He knew she did not leave him in this way out of malice, and he knew the world was at war and nowhere was safe, but none of that prevented him from being angry with Catrin. Seeing one's death rapidly approaching, it can be difficult to think it is all one's own fault. Far better to place blame on someone else, he thought, than to go to your grave feeling guilty.

"What are we gonna do?" Bryn asked. "How do we even survive this? They're gonna come up here in larger numbers sooner or later, and then what do we do?"

Farsy turned back to where he saw Pelivor pacing. "Maybe the boy can get us out of here on the *Eel*."

"No wind in that valley," Kenward said.

"I know but—" Farsy continued. Kenward cut him off with a look. Still, Farsy had sailed with Kenward most of his life, and he knew when not to keep his mouth shut. "We got dragons, sir. Surely one o' them could get us in the air."

"The dragons don't seem to care what I say," Kenward said. "They only seem to listen to Catrin, and I'm not sure they actually listen to her. Seems to me they're the ones doing the talking. The more I think about this whole situation, the less I like it. We can't get to Catrin, and it doesn't look like she's going to get back to us. For now, we need to proceed as if we're on our own."

Bryn nodded sadly and a tear streaked his face. "Blessings to my friend, Catrin," he said softly, not meant for anyone else's ears, but by some trick of the wind, Kenward heard him nonetheless. "Keep her safe."

Kenward bowed his head and echoed the prayer. Farsy sniffed and wiped his eye. Then they headed back toward the peaceful vale, to a place that seemed trapped in time, unaffected by the war that raged so very nearby. Six dragons watched over them.

Go!

Catrin felt the queen's compulsion acutely, and it shocked her how close to the ferals the regent queen would stoop.

Fight them. Protect me with your life. Die with honor. You will be martyred, and your name will live on forever.

"Even if human beings cease to exist? No. I don't care for your bargain. I will, however, stay here with you and protect you until my dying breath. No species will cease to exist because of a decision I make."

Fool! the queen boomed. *Even the choice to not make a decision is a decision, and that choice will have consequences beyond your worst fear.*

Screams echoed into the chamber as dragons and demons clashed around the openings that led to this vacuous hall. When the dragon queen faced Catrin again, there was real fear in her eyes and what looked like the recognition of one of her visions, as if she now saw the future and what she saw terrified her.

You've condemned us all! You think to protect us, but no one as daft as you could possibly save us now. If there were any other way, I'd not give this to you, but now I must leave the fate of the world in your hands, and though I despise you, I love this world more than life itself. Go, fool. Prove me wrong if you can. The bones have been tossed, and my fate is sealed, but I will do my best to buy you time.

A sound like leather on stone accompanied by rhythmic clicks announced demons in the hall, and Catrin knew time had indeed run out; now she could only act on instinct. The regent queen swung her massive body around to face the threat, and her tail smashed into a stack of stones against the outer wall of the cavern, which sent the rock flying into the demons. Bones snapped as the stone crushed rows of dark beasts. More rock collected near the entrance, constricting the demons to a narrow channel.

Catrin watched as the queen erected defenses on top of the bodies of demons, using the fallen monsters as building materials. She would have aided the queen, but the mighty serpent swung her head around to meet Catrin's eyes. *Go!*

This time Catrin allowed the compulsion since it only told her to turn and look. Her eyes found a huge, irregularly shaped hall that wound away from the main cavern. Glittering light danced on the floor and walls of the hall beyond, beckoning to Catrin with its beauty.

You will find what you need in there, Destroyer. Know that you have received gifts due to only the most noble, Dragon Slayer. Know that your actions will be remembered by all or by none based on your choices, World Render. May your fool of a dragon, the betrayer of his own kind, find solace in the emptiness that awaits him. You two are perfect together. Now, go!

Coerced as much by the darkness in her heart as the dragon queen's compulsion, Catrin retreated into the glittering hall. As she turned the corner, she saw things she would never have dreamed existed. There was a saddle, like the one she'd made, only hers was the crudest representation of this masterpiece. Every inch glittered in what Catrin knew was dragon ore; she could feel the energy radiating from it. Looking up, Catrin saw that enormous crystals made up the ceiling, and beyond lay open sky. Light poured in from the multifaceted crystals as they somehow gathered, focused, and amplified the light. The feeling of it was overwhelming for Catrin; never before had she felt so alive, so powerful. The sounds from the great hall kept her from falling into a trance, and she quickly turned to see what other wonders awaited. She could feel complex energies around her, energies more organized and structured than anything she'd experienced before.

From her left, she felt a pull that was elegant and poised, yet there was a potency to its touch that promised wondrous power. Catrin's eyes fell on something that looked like a herald globe, only a thousand times more evolved. It was beautiful. Reaching out her hand, Catrin moved toward the clear glass that housed what looked like a spider, its red and black body perfectly preserved in what had almost certainly once been molten glass. Catrin could not imagine how such a thing was created, and she hesitated before touching it, nervous caution temporarily stifling her desperate need to feel it. Another crash from the great hall and a bellow from the regent queen got Catrin moving again. Her hand closed around the globe, and pulses of power coursed over her body, enshrouding her in a latticework of power that undulated and moved like liquid.

Knowing the saddle would be of no use with the flightless queen, Catrin drew her sword and held the spider globe high as she charged back into the main hall, determined to save the queen of the regents.

Only one dragon remained to guard the vale, and Kenward knew that they would soon be completely unprotected. The regent dragons were losing; that much was clear. There was nothing he or anyone else could do about it. His ship was grounded high in the mountains, and even if they could get her into the air or water, she was neither sea- nor airworthy. It would take weeks to repair her. Kenward shook his head, cursing his own foolishness. Why worry about fixing a ship that would never sail again? He should be thinking of how to dismantle the ship and reassemble a smaller ship along the water. The thought nearly brought him to tears. Never before had he been faced with the prospect of dismantling his ship, and it was like thinking of taking his mother apart piece by piece and trying to reassemble her somewhere else. He knew he couldn't do it. If he were to build another ship, it would have to be built from what existed here on the Firstland.

In truth, there were plenty of raw materials on the Firstland; what Kenward lacked were the skilled hands of shipbuilders and the leisure to employ them. As it was, he had only the hands of sailors. There was not a safe place to be found except where they stood, and with only a single dragon remaining, he wondered how long this place would remain safe. Thunderclaps split the air, and the screams of demons followed. Everyone in the vale scrambled to high ground, peering into the war-torn valley beyond and trying to catch a glimpse of what was going on. Most already realized that what they heard was Catrin, and if she was still fighting, then there was still hope.

Lightning and fire coursed in and out of the top of the nearby mountain, as if the mountain itself were breathing fire. Dark bodies were tossed into the air and fell back down into the clogged valley below, their bodies acting as weapons as they tore through the rest of the demons trying to reach the top of the mountain. A gasp from behind made Kenward turn, and he saw what had frightened Farsy. Pelivor stood with his arms raised, and power pulsed around his hands like liquid light. A stream of it stretched across the empty air, reaching for Catrin, but what was even more amazing and terrifying was the white hot line that extended from the mountaintop toward Pelivor, as if Catrin were trying to connect with him.

When the two streams of energy were still some distance apart, the air between them filled with a humming line of plasma, and once the two flows were connected, a thundering crack split the air and knocked everyone except Pelivor back. He stood rooted in place, engulfed in a raging torrent of energy. There was no fear in his face, though, only a look of awe and sudden understanding. Then he started to move like a machine, his fists pumping in and out, and each movement released a swirling conflagration that he hurled at the demons and giants.

Kenward knew this could be the savior of them all, but it also meant that the demons would know exactly where they were and would surely send forces here to deal with them. The last remaining regent dragon looked down at Pelivor and gave a cry. Kenward tried to discern what the cry meant, but it soon did not matter as the dragon leaped from its perch of stone and disappeared into the air beyond.

"So much for the loyalty of dragons," Kenward said.

CHAPTER NINETEEN

Sanity is but a temporary state.
— Nat Dersinger, prophet

Feeling like the wind itself, Catrin attacked. Everywhere she turned, demons flew like leaves in the wind. Her sword high and the spider globe sending light streaming out through the gaps in her clenched fist, Catrin roared a primal battle cry. Twice she pumped her fist, and thunder shook the mountain. Wild energy reached out from her and licked the walls. Her hair rustled in a preternatural wind that gusted within the charged field around her.

The regent queen turned to look at her. *You should be gone. Call him to you. Use the saddle and lance. Become your destiny and leave me to my fate.*

"I don't want you to die." It was the most honest thing Catrin could say.

You are a credit to your race that you would still feel that way given my treatment of you. I'm afraid it is too late to save me, and in attempting to do so, you are endangering your kind's future. We are lost but I'll not allow you to be lost as well. Now go! *Kyrien! To me!*

The last might not have been intended for Catrin to hear, but the powerful call must have been heard on the other side of the world. Catrin reeled with the power of it, but she knew now the best thing she could do was get Kyrien saddled and fight the enemy from the air. She could save the regent queen yet.

But Kyrien did not come. No one could have resisted that call, and Catrin's heart climbed into her throat. The world moved unexpectedly as darkness crowded her vision. The thought of Kyrien lost, all of his kind dead or dying, nearly brought Catrin to her knees. Needing strength, she reached out for something familiar and comforting. Like the swiftest arrow, power extended from her outstretched hands toward Pelivor. The essence of him slammed into her an instant later, and lightning cleaved the air between them.

Catrin staggered back to her feet, feeling the texture of the energy Pelivor lent her and, in doing so, learning all he knew about controlling the power and building efficient structures with energy. His mind amazed her in its precision and logic, the way he moved through problems by breaking them into smaller pieces and tackling each piece individually. Another energy responded to her call, and Catrin was shocked to see Kyrien land within the great hall. Blood dripped from what seemed a thousand wounds, and his nostrils flared with his rapid breathing. Frothy foam gathered around his legs, which trembled as he stood, panting. Never before had Catrin seen a creature that had given so much of itself. Kyrien looked as if he would drop over dead at any instant, and Catrin ran to him, her energy already caressing him, bolstering him, healing him.

No! his voice rang in her mind. *Save your energy for the fight. I will survive.*

Catrin wanted to argue, wanted to take the time to tend his wounds and give him time to recover, but he pushed her before him, his muzzle driving her toward the saddle.

If this must be done, then let us do it. I can no longer take the guilt. Let this be at an end.

Catrin moved as if in a dream, her mind unable to cope with the consequences of this day. Never before had she seen a species wiped from existence, and she prayed she'd never witness it again. When she sat astride Kyrien, goggles on and strapped in, she could barely remember how she had come to be there, and she marveled at the beauty of the saddle. In her hand waited the greatest shock: a lance of gleaming filigree extending from the sword Strom had made for her, as if the two had been made to fit together. When Catrin's memories began to return, she realized that the sword had been made to Kyrien's specifications, yet she could not reconcile why Kyrien would have done that if this were not supposed to happen. Taking a deep breath, Catrin had no choice but to return her attention to the present. Atop the saddle, Catrin felt secure; the many buckles on her leather flight pants allowed her to strap in. Again she was amazed at the foresight of her dragon.

Kyrien, though seeming only slightly recovered from battle, tucked his wings and charged back into the great hall. An unbidden battle cry issued from Catrin's lips, and it turned to a scream as Kyrien leaped from the heights without ever opening his wings. Demons clogged the entrances and flew into the open air before Kyrien's maddened charge. With a trail of energy leading back to Pelivor and the wind trying to tear her apart, they fell like a stone. There were lurches and bumps in their descent that Catrin eventually realized were the times Kyrien attacked. They dived along the mountain face, Kyrien extending his wings in only small amounts to make adjustments to their flight path. Catrin would have launched attacks of her own, but she could not get her body to respond; the forces acting on it were simply too intense. Even her scream was choked away.

Then the saddle pressed into her hard, and Kyrien extended his wings. Catrin saw the army of demons, giants, and men in orderly formations, waiting to fill the void when their comrades fell. Finally Catrin was able to control herself, and she reached out for energy. She nearly swooned. The saddle responded with alacrity. The charge of millennia leaped to her call. The fiery link with Pelivor surged, and the energy of the comets resonated in a way she'd never felt before.

You're burning up!

Only then did Catrin realize that she rode amid a maelstrom of fire, her body a conflagration. Without hesitation, she launched a dozen attacks at once. Pelivor's control combined with the saddle's energy and Catrin's will caused the world to explode. Ranks of the enemy, formerly so orderly and geometric from above, now looked as if they had been tossed by a giant wave. Trails of smoke filled the air as balls of fire streamed into those who scaled the rock face. Lightning reached out to anything close to the great hall, but in the back of Catrin's consciousness, she knew that she needed to be careful not to hit the regent queen. Determination filled her as Kyrien brought them around for a pass along those closest to the queen, and Catrin almost smiled as a cloud of demons filled the air before them, thrown from the great hall by a very alive regent queen.

"We can save her!" Catrin shouted.

Kyrien made no response.

The air around them suddenly filled with teeth and claws, reaching for Catrin and tearing at Kyrien's already tender hide. Nothing could have prepared Catrin for the maneuvers Kyrien undertook to keep them both safe. It seemed impossible that they were still alive. A sizzling, crackling sound followed by a loud boom made her wonder how much longer that would remain true. Light exploded around her, and Catrin felt the shock of it, even though Kyrien took the brunt of the attack. His flight became erratic, and Catrin scanned the skies, ready to protect the stunned dragon from any new attacks. Kyrien regained stable flight, but Catrin knew he was not fully recovered. Ferals came in close, and Kyrien's reactions seemed delayed. For a brief instant, Catrin's mind registered the fact that the dragons were all riderless. She wasn't certain what it meant, but she was certain it meant something. It was not something she could ponder long.

When the buzzing, crackling sound filled the air around them again, Catrin searched the clouds and seas, trying to find its source. It was coming from the ships, which were now moving in formation once again.

Catrin opened her mouth to tell Kyrien, but he was already turning to dive for the attacking formation of ships. Just when Catrin thought the lightning would strike, the air exploded with fire, but she felt no pain, only the radiated heat. Alongside them, a feral dragon was engulfed in a web of charged air. It folded up like a swatted moth, dropping beside them. When Kyrien pulled up, the dragon continued falling and struck a warship on the prow, driving it underwater in a shower of exploding timber and sending its masts crashing into the ship adjacent to it.

Missed me.

Catrin almost laughed—almost.

No dragons had gotten close enough for Catrin to use her lance, but it felt good in her hand, far lighter than she would have believed from looking at it. Even as thin and delicate looking as the gold wire comprising it would seem, it felt solid and gave her confidence. When she pointed it at the next ship she could hone in on, she applied her will, and the lance responded. The delicate wires hummed and shone, light dancing across them in rolling waves with shape and texture. Like mist over the world at daybreak, it flitted along the surface and even over the empty areas between the wires. Erupting from the tip of the lance like liquid smoke, it roared through the air toward the ship. When the beam of energy struck amidships, the warship did something Catrin had never seen before: it imploded. It started slowly then accelerated, essentially folding the ship in half and sending it to rest at the bottom of the shallows.

Kyrien banked away from another feral attack, and Catrin could hear the cries of man and demon from below. There was panic in many of those cries, and as unlikely as it was, Catrin felt as if the battle were turning in her favor. The ships had no way of avoiding her attacks, and it was just a matter of time before she took all of them out, stranding them, just as she'd done to the Zjhon when they had invaded the Godfist. Sending waves of devastation into the midst of every formation of ships she could see, Catrin did her best to cripple them. Only the ferals were able to disrupt her attacks. Kyrien's evasive maneuvers made taking aim exceedingly difficult, and many of her attacks missed their marks. Those that landed, though, were equally as destructive as the first.

Doing their best to stay above or behind Catrin and Kyrien, the ferals made for elusive targets. They knew how dangerous she was, and they had no intention of giving her a clear shot. Instead, they tried to hide in Kyrien's blind spot and attack Catrin from above. It was an extremely uncomfortable feeling knowing she was being hunted from behind, let alone from above and behind. Somehow Kyrien seemed able to sense them and managed to keep Catrin outside the reach of their attacks. Twice he was able to cause ferals to collide with one another. The first pair had simply flown off in separate directions, but the second pair collided with a sickening crack. Though the impact had killed only one of the beasts, the two became hopelessly tangled, and both plunged into dark water. Neither rose again.

The problem was that all of this was but a distraction from their true purpose, which was to defend the regent queen. It seemed only an instant had passed, but when Catrin looked back to the top of the mountain, waves of demons were swarming into the great hall, and no more flew from the entrances. Panicked, Catrin shouted to Kyrien, but her voice could not be heard over the rush of the wind. Still, Kyrien made straight for the great hall, his own anxiety radiating from him. Both seemed to realize that their attacks on the ships and ferals may have come at the ultimate cost. Catrin's skin felt clammy, a prickly feeling making her shift in the saddle. Hurling vortices of air before them, Catrin knocked the demons clear, making a place for Kyrien to land. Even as he glided in, Catrin pumped her left fist, and from her right hand issued pulses of power that traveled down the lance, intensified, and pounded back the demon horde.

Quickly scanning the area, Catrin could not, at first, locate the regent queen. Then her eyes landed on a swarming, black mass roughly the shape of the dragon queen. The taste of bile filled Catrin's mouth, and she did not hesitate in blasting away the demons using nothing but air, trying to be careful even in her haste. The giant dragon's great maw turned to them, demons still clinging to her face, trying to blind her. Catrin used targeted blasts of air to dislodge them, Pelivor's precision aiding her greatly. The thought of Pelivor caused Catrin to panic anew. The gleaming trail of energy still extended back to the sailor, but she could no longer sense him. Immediately she released the link, and all she could do was pray that she had not inadvertently killed her dear friend.

So many consequences rendered Catrin numb. No matter what she did, people and dragons were going to die. This realization made her choices a great deal easier to make. *Just act,* she thought. With remarkable speed, Catrin removed the buckles that held her in the saddle and leaped to the cold stone floor of the great hall. Demons flew like kindling before her, and more of the regent queen was once again exposed to the light. The mighty dragon showed wounds, but none seemed mortal. A spark of hope shone in Catrin's consciousness. *The future is not written in stone,* Catrin said to herself, and she leaped into the air, engaging any demons she found still standing.

The regent queen turned and looked at Kyrien. For the first time, Catrin saw something other than anger and hurt in the queen's eyes.

You should not be here, Kyrien. I do not want you to see this. No one should have to see such a thing. Now take the human and go. Please, Kyrien—for your own good—go.

Catrin could feel the emotion, and tears came to her eyes. Kyrien's feelings mingled with her own, and such grief was more than anyone should ever have to bear. Desperate, Catrin continued to drive away the demons. Rearing back, the regent queen reached a towering and imposing height. The demons fell back of their own volition, and even Catrin felt fear in the face of such tremendous power.

You are worthy. Protect him.

The words reached Catrin with a wave of compassion, and she could feel the honesty and sincerity as the regent queen looked her in the eyes. The air was sucked from her lungs in shock when she saw a single demon charging through the masses. When it broke into the open, Catrin was terrified to see it wielded a lance similar to her own, save this one looked as if it were made of black glass instead of gold wire. Streaks of light danced over the glossy surface of the lance, and without slowing, the demon thrust the lance into the regent queen's exposed breast. There was a wet sound accompanied by a terrible sigh. Not satisfied with simply running her through, the demon twisted the blade then yanked. Only instead of pulling the blade back out, it yanked it sideways. The lance shattered into thousands of daggerlike shards. With a final wheezing grunt, the queen rolled to one side and collapsed.

In that moment, Catrin realized just how perilous her situation really was. With the regent queen dead, the demons could concentrate on killing her and Kyrien, and she wasn't even mounted. Running back to

Kyrien, she leaped onto his back. His pain was palpable and unbearable. It tore at Catrin's resolve, soaking her in guilt and remorse and regret.

"We must live!" Catrin shouted. "You and I are not done—not even close. If we die now, then she died for nothing."

The last words drove Kyrien to reckless action, his anger a force that polluted the air around them. Demons drew closer, their ranks thickening until they blocked the light, which seemed to be moving farther away. It was a maddening view.

Be ready.

Catrin didn't need to ask what for; instead, she drew deeply from the stones in the saddle and the spider globe. When Kyrien started moving, Catrin unloaded a barrage of attacks that turned the great hall into pure chaos. None were safe from her fury, and the air around the openings was once again filled with flailing demons. A rare few managed to remain in the hall, and only one of those managed to stand. Catrin decided to blast those farther ahead since Kyrien could easily handle a single demon, but the beast reached down and, from behind a fallen body, produced another of the glass lances. Catrin thought her heart might just burst.

Planting its feet, the demon was in a perfect position to strike. All it had to do was let Kyrien's momentum carry him forward and he would impale himself. The shock of it stunned Catrin and slowed her reaction. The demon smiled a dark, wet smile as Kyrien approached, even though it must know its own death came just as surely. As the lance was about to pierce Kyrien's breast, Catrin acted out of pure instinct; she cast a wave of vibrating air that sang a high-pitched note. Part of her brain registered that Pelivor knew how to break glass with sound. Glass struck dragon scale, and for a moment the lance held its form, but then it fractured in a thousand places, just as it had been designed to do, only it did so before entering Kyrien's flesh. The look of triumph on the demon's face turned to utter terror as Kyrien ran him down.

Again, Catrin had to concentrate on the demons that blocked their escape. Kyrien needed speed to get them clear of the rock face. His trembling form gave evidence to her concern. Catrin, in contrast, felt as if she could sunder the world, and she feared she would go too far. When she lashed out again, she did so with as much restraint and control as she could. Using a delicate web of energy whose vibration was extremely high and resonance packed a nasty sting, Catrin went for the enemy's eyes. Though she doubted it did any permanent damage, the result was nonetheless astonishing as every demon in the great hall reeled in agony and disorientation.

Pushing stunned demons out of their way, Kyrien gave a heroic effort, trying to take advantage of Catrin's attack, but the effort slowed them. Some demons recovered their vision and moved to block their path. Catrin lashed out with short, precise strikes that pierced the demons and dropped them, the sounds of their deaths lost in the screams of the still blinded.

Holding her breath, Catrin gripped the saddle horn and squeezed with her legs, some of her straps still not secured. When Kyrien launched himself into the air, Catrin bent her knees and braced herself. Though they dropped sharply, they did not quite clear the rocky crags below the entranceway. Based on the abrupt jolt that felt like it broke every bone in Catrin's body, she wondered how Kyrien could endure, but he extended his wings and caught a favorable wind that sent them soaring into the valley.

The air below them hummed with arrows and bolts, and Kyrien turned aside. Only a few shafts managed to strike him, and his scales deflected those. Both he and Catrin remembered the last time she had removed an arrow from a wing joint, and Kyrien still complained that it ached before the rain. Using their speed, Kyrien climbed higher and out of bow range. A pocket of less dense air sent them downward, and Kyrien used it to turn them back toward the mountain. The view that waited would haunt them both. Accompanied by a victorious roar that frightened Catrin more than anything she'd ever heard, the head of the dead regent queen reached the entranceway and was sent tumbling down the rock face. It was an exceedingly stupid manner of celebration, as the rock face was crowded with demons, and the huge dragon head took out scores of them.

For a long moment, Catrin held her breath without realizing it then inhaled sharply when the ferals filled the air around them. In an instant, Catrin readied herself, but the attack never came. Instead the ferals attacked the remains of the regent queen. Kyrien's outrage flowed through the bond, but Catrin convinced him that the queen was already gone and that this could give them time to escape.

Though she no longer maintained the link to Pelivor, she knew that he was still in the dragon's vale—her vale. Kyrien raced along the valley toward the vale unbidden, and Catrin could only hope that her friends were still alive. Guilt and remorse stabbed at her as she second-guessed her decision to leave them. Had she truly been protecting them, or had she simply placed them in even greater danger. The thoughts made her want to cry, but she waited to see what reality truly existed.

She saw Kenward first; he was pointing at her and shouting, but she couldn't hear his words. Blood pounded in her ears, and she could hear nothing over the roar of it; not even the rumble of the wind pierced it. As Kyrien dipped low, Catrin sensed a presence above and behind her, and it was then she turned and saw the giant feral bearing down on them, claws extended and jaws agape. It was a terrifying sight that made Catrin's nightmares seem warm and safe. Nothing can be compared to the feeling of knowing you're about to be torn apart, and Catrin's body trembled.

With unsteady hands, she unbuckled herself as quickly as she could. Kyrien dipped low, allowing her to roll unharmed from the saddle onto the rushing grasses. Tumbling, she hoped she could stop herself before she struck rock. A moment later she found herself lying faceup on the grass, watching a pair of claws only just miss grabbing her, Kyrien having done his best to keep her safe.

Kenward ran toward her. Then Pelivor was there, helping her stand. The rest were huddled within the remains of the *Slippery Eel.* Pelivor led her back to the ship, and she could barely meet the eyes of those who waited. She had brought them all here, endangered their lives, then abandoned them. And after all of that, after betraying her friends for the sake of the dragons, she had failed. Now they would all die—her friends, her son, her husband, her people—all would die because of her folly. It hurt so badly that she thought she might crumble under the weight of it. The thing that made her feel worst of all, though, was the fact that instead of wanting to protect her friends, all she wanted to do was abandon them again.

Familiar hands pulled her into the hold, and tears came to Catrin's downcast eyes.

"Thank the gods you're back!" Farsy said, and Catrin felt wholly unworthy of his enthusiasm.

"I'm sorry," was all Catrin could manage to say.

A long silence hung between them, but the cries of dragon and demon filled the space.

She turned to Pelivor. "I know I can ask no more of you, but I will. Pelivor, you must protect us," she said as she handed him the spider globe.

He looked intrigued at first when he saw the globe, but when it dropped into his palm, there was an audible click and a small spark. His eyes went wide, but a smile crossed his lips. The smile faded when she handed him the lance, his hand sliding into the guard and closing over the handle of her sword. "The rest of you, please get the drums."

"Oh, no," came Kenward's voice from behind. "You're not leaving us again."

"I can go with or without your help, Kenward, but I am far more likely to return if you help me."

Kenward stepped backward, as if Catrin had struck him, but he knew the stakes. This was no time for hurt feelings. He could get her back for those later, provided they survived. The captain looked critically at Pelivor. "Can you protect us?"

Pelivor responded by smiling and holding his hands out to his sides. Preternatural breezes stirred the silks he wore, and light danced around him. When he spoke, it was not to Kenward. "Death awaits those who would do us harm!" The words rang through the vale, the deep bass of his voice amplified by the power flowing through him. The spider globe sent beams of light from within his clenched fist as he held it high. In his other hand, he held Catrin's lance, and he leveled it at an oncoming feral. He did not wait for the dragon to get close. He used the lance to focus his attack into a narrow beam of boiling liquid fire that seared the air with a roar.

Catrin turned to Kenward. "Drums!"

CHAPTER TWENTY

Only a fool stands between mother and cub.

— Wendel Volker

The journey to the Godfist took only the span of a thought, but Catrin's spirit slowed before actually reaching her homeland. Had she been able to, she would have traveled directly to Sinjin's side, but the air grew thick with energy and malicious intent. Hatred washed over her, and it made her want to scream. It was like being covered in fire ants.

Dark with malevolence, an unnatural storm, seemingly ready to swallow the world, dominated the horizon. Vast networks of lightning jumped across its surface, and the thunder was nearly continuous. Smaller patches of darkness coalesced and gathered into formations—dragons of black fire with riders of pure night.

Never before had Catrin witnessed such utter wrongness, such warping of nature, and she felt naked against the storm. Twisted darkness, launched from the fingertips of the black dragon riders, streaked toward Catrin. She prepared for the assault, casting out defensive energy. As he had in the past, Kyrien took the brunt of the attack, having seemingly appeared from nowhere, his energetic form of lightning and fire pulsing with light. He was a jewel amid the horror.

More attacks came and Kyrien could not absorb them all. Doing so would likely kill him, and Catrin cried out for him to stop. There were simply too many attacks coming at once. Catrin and Kyrien were alone against thousands, and their numbers seemed to grow continually. Weariness overwhelmed her and a sense of resignation took hold. This was a battle she could not win. When she saw Thorakis, the feeling of utter defeat solidified.

Shining like a black sun, he rode atop a gleaming feral dragon. Even at a distance, recognition caught in Catrin's throat. In one hand, Thorakis held a staff; in the other, a carving. A cry escaped Catrin when she realized he held the Staff of Life and Koe. Both were precious to her and held great power. Each had been shaped by her hand, in their own way, and she could not imagine standing against their combined might. Ever since she had carved Koe, she had not wanted to know what it would feel like to be faced with his aggressive stance, and now she knew; it was terrifying. There was only one consolation, and that was Thorakis did not rest his fingers in the grooves left by Catrin's grip. For some reason that made her feel better; the thought if his touching those places made her feel ill.

Thorakis gave her little time to contemplate his presence before he lashed out. Torrents of power slammed into Catrin, and it felt like being caught in the surf before a storm. Energy pounded against her with relentless force, and she felt as if she were being torn apart. In the next instant, she could almost hear Kenward shouting. His words had no meaning, though they did serve as the slightest warning before power surged through her. It was a source she recognized: the queen's saddle. The instant she felt one of the straps hit her physical hand, she sensed the saddle and Kyrien. Looking down, she saw his fiery form now under her, and together they felt more powerful. Their energies mingled and where she was weak, he was strong, and she felt she brought something to him as well. He was not incomplete without her, but together they were stronger. That thought comforted her, as did the momentary clarity with which she heard Kenward say, "Go get 'em, Cat!"

Emotion threatened to overwhelm her, but she kept it in check, using it instead to fuel her rage and fury against the darkness that sought to despoil all she loved. From Kyrien she sensed the burning desire for revenge, not so much out of spite, but out of the need to absolve his guilt. He had let the regent queen die. He had betrayed his own kind, and no knowledge could be so damning. Catrin could not completely understand his inner struggle; she could not grasp his relationship with the queen nor truly understand how he had betrayed his kind. It was very clear, however, that Kyrien believed he had done just that. Though Catrin had shown love to the regent queen, she hated her for that last bit of spite with which she inflicted this guilt on Kyrien. But the regent queen was dead.

Emitting a roar that would make a lion quail, Catrin unleashed a wave of furious attacks, the line of energy extending back to her physical form now blazing like a new star. Deep troughs tore through the darkness, but like the deepest ocean, more flooded into the void, making it look as if her attack had done no damage at all. Twice more she cast out weblike attacks, trying to break the darkness into smaller chunks, but again it flowed back together. Then there was no more time for attacks.

From every direction came a massive assault that dwarfed all those before it. It felt to Catrin as if her universe was collapsing in on itself, and she was at the very center of that crushing weight. Despite her power, despite her will, and even in the face of her closest ally, Kyrien, this attack made them seem insignificant. Nothing could withstand so much hatred. None could endure so many wishing they had never existed. It was the most terrible thing Catrin had ever experienced, being made to think that she was worse than useless; her very existence was harmful to everything else around her.

Seethe. Kyrien uttered a single word in Catrin's mind, and instantly she knew that Thorakis was not the true threat. The real threat was Seethe, the dragon Thorakis rode. Seethe was not Thorakis's dragon; Thorakis was one of Seethe's many humans. This realization struck Catrin like a thunderbolt, and she looked into the feral dragon's eyes, trying to understand the true threat.

You are worthless. Give yourself to me, and you will be part of something much stronger. How can you hope to stand against this?

The thunderous voice in her mind was accompanied by a wave of compulsion that made what Archmaster Belegra had done look like friendly persuasion. This voice sought to obliterate all thought but its own, and it hammered at her as the collective will of tens of thousands joined in. Then something occurred to Catrin: If the feral dragons were so powerful, why did they need humans?

This thought must have been betrayed to Seethe as Catrin heard pounding laughter in her head. *You are but tools to me, implements designed to achieve my will. I wouldn't bother keeping you around at all, but you do have such delicate fingers. But if you prove too troublesome, you are something we can certainly do without.* Seethe then flooded Catrin's mind with the vision of the death of mankind. Perhaps he'd meant to frighten her, but she'd seen it before.

You underestimate the power of a single will, Catrin thought with all her might, and despite the singularity of her statement, she felt the wills of others backing her. The world around her was suddenly filled with light; flaming dragons surrounded her and reinforced her will. One in particular caught Catrin's attention as it bore a rider, and Catrin nearly shouted in glee when she recognized Halmsa of the Wind clan, who looked as if he would burst with pride, but moreover he looked ready to die for Catrin. Somehow he thought that Catrin had fulfilled her promise to him and taught him to fly dragons, though she knew not how she had done any such thing. Still, she could feel his gratitude as he sent it toward her; it bolstered her soul.

It was a proud and brief moment. Then the world exploded. Both sides released the full extent of their might and fury, holding nothing back. The heavens shook and the pillars of Godsland trembled. Catrin felt the energy of the planet surging through mighty keystones—six of them. One of which was within the Grove of the Elders, another at the great shallows. Catrin did not know exactly where the others were, only that they existed. Anyone who controlled them would control the world. Catrin tried to bury that thought lest the dragons find out—that is, if they did not already know.

The vision of the Grove of the Elders persisted in Catrin's consciousness, like spots left by the sun. There she saw the mighty greatoaks as they had once been, and at the center of the grove stood the Staff of Life, blooming. It was an anachronistic vision, true, but it felt real to Catrin, who had planted the staff there. She'd been a fool to leave it there. Chase must have been right when he'd said the staff had given her acorns to replenish the grove and no more; it must have fulfilled its purpose. He'd begged her to bring the staff back to Dragonhold rather than leaving it in lands controlled by Master Edling. Now the staff rested in the hands of Thorakis, a once great man now subverted by Seethe. Thus, it rested within the feral's grasp—all that power, his to command. It was a frightening thought, and it was painful to feel its bite.

Koe reached out to her and left claw marks through her psyche. A creature of her own creation, she was defenseless against it, and Catrin cried out to Kyrien to retreat. Instead, the regents responded, throwing themselves onto Thorakis's attacks, and by their sheer numbers, they broke through and sent Thorakis tumbling into the darkness. Seethe bellowed and exacted a costly price for the victory, and Catrin felt the light dimming around her. Despite their heroic efforts, the darkness was still winning.

Though despair threatened, Catrin looked around her and found that she was far closer to the Godfist than she had been at the start of the battle. They had taken great losses, but their progress was more than the ferals would have them believe. Much of their power was in deception, and Catrin was now fully aware of this.

Seethe's voice was now quieter in her mind. *Your son is about to die.*

Doing what he did best, Sinjin ran. Slowly the demons recovered themselves, and Sinjin dodged their sluggish movements as he wove his way toward where he'd last seen Strom. The scene ahead was a blur, and when he broke free of the demons and into the open, he saw them: his father, Strom, and Durin, all laid out on the grass. Sinjin's knees went weak, and he thought he might fall; only the need to keep Trinda safe kept him from giving in. Kendra and Khenna were among the few still standing, and Sinjin realized how hopeless his situation was. He had left Brother Vaughn behind, something he now regretted deeply. The demons outnumbered them hundreds to one, and they were quickly thawing. Trinda clung to him. He knew she was already overexerted, and he didn't expect much help from her.

Seeing Brother Vaughn standing alone, between them a mass of angry demons, Sinjin abandoned fear. "Dad!" he shouted as he ran, and his thoughts turned momentarily to his mother. "Mother! Please help!"

Kendra came into view, and Sinjin angled away from her. Khenna stood nearby, looking ready to defend Strom, Prios, and Durin, all of whom remained unconscious. Sinjin had no time to check on their conditions as the demons resumed their attack. He wanted to drag his father and friends to safety, but he was left with no choice but to defend their unmoving bodies. After quickly putting Trinda down next to his father, Sinjin turned to face the demons with fury and desperation in his eyes. With the herald globe gleaming before him, Sinjin thought he saw another bright light. Not knowing its source, he threw the herald globe into the midst of the demons. Before the globe struck, he saw Brother Vaughn trapped on the shoreline of the turbulent river waters. A flash of light drove the demons back, and Brother Vaughn dived into the depths. Sinjin would have cried out, but an instant before the herald globe erupted, something slammed into the back of his skull, and the world went dark.

Breaking free from Thorakis, Catrin's spirit raced toward where she sensed her son and husband; their life forces dim yet calling to her. Below her, fields of amber crystal beckoned, and she burst through like rays of sunlight, only a thousand times brighter. Immediately she was faced with an amazing yet terrifying sight. The underground cavern was beyond images from even her wildest fantasy. Never before had she considered that an entire ecosystem might have survived underground for ages undisturbed. The stain of darkness and evil despoiled the view.

Catrin first saw Brother Vaughn alone, trapped by demons on one side and dangerous-looking waters on the other. Not knowing what else to do, Catrin cast her light into the demons. Somehow amplified by the crystals and with an amber tint, her beams sent demons tumbling backward. Others moved in to replace those, but Brother Vaughn took control of his own destiny and slipped into the churning water. Catrin could only pray that he would survive. After losing sight of him, she knew she could no longer protect him, and she began looking for Sinjin and Prios.

Her soul cried out when she found them, both laid out on the lush grasses along with Strom, Durin, and others. Khenna and Kendra alone remained standing, and they appeared to be fighting. Catrin did not understand what could possibly be happening. Confusion and anxiety overwhelmed her as she moved closer. Kendra looked angrier than Catrin had ever seen her, and she moved in to swipe her own mother's knees. Khenna, though older and not as nimble, had a great deal more experience and anticipated the move. With a simple sidestep, she gained the advantage on her now off-balance daughter. A single punch sent Kendra to the turf.

"Get her out of here," Khenna shouted, and a demon lifted Kendra's limp form in its arms. Catrin nearly retched. Then the woman turned back to Catrin's husband and son. "That boy comes with us. Kill the rest."

Roaring, Catrin attacked. Fire, smoke, and lightning raced toward Khenna but were deflected at the last instant and sent racing back toward Catrin. It was something she had once done to Archmaster Belegra, and she quailed, knowing she was about to feel the bite of her own power. Over the roar of the fire and the crackling of energy, Catrin could hear Thorakis laughing, a high-pitched and maniacal sound that turned into the roar of a mighty feral dragon now bearing down on her. Pain erupted all over Catrin as her very essence was scoured and eroded. Every instant, she lost something of herself, and she could hear the dragon calling to her, its voice assuring her that it could make the pain stop; all she had to do was surrender. Then her son, husband, and all those she loved would be spared. All she had to do was join them. The future was already written, and she could not change that which was recorded in stone. The thoughts battered her senses, and it was so tempting to simply give in, but the sight of her son in the arms of a demon shook her from the feral's delusion, and she launched another attack, aiming for the legs of the demon carrying Sinjin's limp form.

Again, pain erupted. Thorakis and Seethe attacked with overwhelming force and ferocity that exceeded anything Catrin had ever seen in nature. She knew the role of predators, but nothing she'd ever seen compared to the overwhelming desire to destroy—not to kill and eat, but to abolish from existence. This kind of evil would consume the world, and Catrin knew she was among the few things stopping that gruesome future from coming to pass.

"The future is not already written!" her spirit screamed as she blocked an attack and launched another of her own. Demons now stood over Prios, Strom, Durin, and Trinda—only the wisp of a girl alert and able to fight. Again Catrin thought it strange that she thought of Trinda as a child when the girl was actually her elder. And that frailty gave Catrin no confidence that she would be any use at all in a fight.

In that instant, Catrin had to make a choice: prevent the demons from escaping into the darkness with her son or save the lives of her husband and friends. Trinda's eyes looked up to her, pleading for mercy, and though Catrin had never really liked her, she rushed in to save them all, flames searing the air before her. Demons flew from her path, even as others carried her baby boy back into the depths of the hold.

Turning to race after them before it was too late, Catrin felt fiery claws rake her soul, and they bit deep. Thorakis used Koe to flay her, and the familiarity of the attacking energy made it all the more difficult to defend against. Even as Catrin was reeling from Koe's attack, feeling as if she were gulping for air even if not in her physical form, there was no way she could defend herself from the Staff of Life. Its ancient power slammed into her with unrelenting force; it knew her weaknesses and exploited every one. In the next instant, Catrin was back in her body, trying to suck in enough air to scream, then wanting nothing more than to cry as she looked out at what she knew was the last of the regent dragons.

Kyrien wept.

EPILOGUE

Crying as he ran, Durin couldn't believe how things had turned out. His best friend was gone, and there was nothing he could do about it. Brother Vaughn had either escaped or drowned, and there was no way for him to know which. His entire family's fate was unknown to him, and he doubted he would ever see any of them again. It seemed the end of the world had come, and he could see no possible future that included happiness or family. It was the kind of realization that could drive the weak to their knees, but through all of this, Durin had learned one thing: he was not as weak as he had once believed. Now he realized that he had not been lazy as much as he had been afraid to apply himself since that left him open to failure. Now he realized that failure was necessary for success, something that seemed far too philosophical for his usual thoughts. Durin, though, had left childhood behind in recent days, and there was no time for such thoughts.

Running alongside him was Strom, who carried a still unconscious Prios over his shoulder. Trinda ran with them, having difficulty keeping up. Durin thought she might want him to carry her, but he was not Sinjin, and even if he had grown up quickly, some of his childhood prejudices remained. Trinda would have to stand on her own two legs if she wished to survive. Even as he had the thought, he knew he would not leave her to die, but that didn't mean he had to like saving her. What was even more difficult was for him to admit that she had saved him. Strom had been the only thing defending them when Durin had come to, and Durin had been little help, even armed with Strom's wicked blade. Only when Trinda had stepped up and chastised the demons did the battle turn in their favor. It still seemed unreal to Durin that Trinda could do such a thing.

"Bad demons!" was all she had said, and it was as if she had struck them all with just her words. No matter what Durin believed, that moment had been the key to their escape, and only by moving deeper into darkened halls did they manage to gain any measure of safety. Again, Durin had to admit that Trinda had saved them since she had retrieved the herald globe, and to Durin's amazement, she had somehow recharged it. This girl was really starting to irritate him.

"We're completely lost," Strom whispered. "But maybe that's a good thing." Groaning as he shifted Prios on his shoulder, he looked as if he might not make it much farther, and Prios gave no indication of stirring.

"I want to go outside," Trinda said.

"I'd like to fly too," Durin said, not expecting a response.

"It's this way."

Given no other direction, Strom followed Trinda, the light of the herald globe drifting away as Durin remained where he was. The darkness closed in all too quickly, and Durin raced to catch up.

"Are you sure you know where you're going?" Durin asked after a number of turns down seemingly random halls. They passed halls that were still filled with items, but Trinda did not waver in her course, and Durin's imagination was left to run wild as he caught only glimpses of the treasures that waited within. He'd heard the stories about the artifacts Catrin had found at Ohmahold, and he imagined them stumbling on a similar cache of wondrous things. The thoughts helped to keep him from thinking about the fate of everyone else.

When Trinda walked into a circular hall and stopped, it took Durin and Strom by complete surprise. Without a word, she just stared at the markings on the floor of the chamber. Immediately Durin knew this room was special and the carved tiles were more than mere decoration.

"Step on the one that looks like mountains," Trinda said, looking at Durin.

Examining the tiles, Durin spotted one in the third row of tiles away from him, farther away than he guessed Trinda could jump. Even for Durin, he had to take a running leap to make it, and in mid air he heard Trinda suck in a breath. Perhaps she had not expected him to do as she asked; Durin wasn't quite sure why he had. When he landed, the stone sank beneath his weight, and he had a sick feeling in his gut.

"Not that one, silly," Trinda said.

Durin's sick feeling intensified as a low grinding noise filled the halls and the stone beneath their feet trembled.

www.ingramcontent.com/pod-product-compliance
Lightning Source LLC
Chambersburg PA
CBHW021950170626
46808CB00001B/89

9780981871486